On Cate Mortensen's seventeenth birthday, her family is scattered in a fight for survival, and she and her sister Melody are catapulted headfirst into a world where their phones are just hunks of plastic, they must scavenge for every bite, and they sleep with weapons in their hands. Traveling alone, and then not so alone, they follow the route their family planned to Alcatraz Island where the hope of safety and a real life awaits.

After more than a year on the road, Cate has found three things to be true. One: Zombies are a thing now. Two: Not all zombies are just zombies. Three (the game changer): Cate is immune to the infection.

THE END

M. Rose Flores

A NineStar Press Publication

Published by NineStar Press
P.O. Box 91792,
Albuquerque, New Mexico, 87199 USA.
www.ninestarpress.com

The End

Printed in the USA
First Edition
April, 2018

Print ISBN: 978-1-948608-48-0

Also available in eBook, ISBN: 978-1-948608-44-2

Warning: This book contains depictions of emetophobia, discussion of self-harm, suicide ideation, domestic violence, pregnancy, childbirth, and gore.

For Stephen

Everything I could say, you already know.

One: Pay attention.

Where did these zombies come from, and how did I not notice them until now? This isn't the worst we've faced, true, but zombies in general are dangerous and six at a time is not a number anybody should be comfortable with.

"Mel!" I call to my sister, keeping my eyes on the approaching zombies. "How's it coming?"

Melody is a little way up the road from me, elbow-deep in the engine of a rusty old pickup that she said would be an easy fix. She was so confident, in fact, that we packed all our stuff and the dog into the truck. That was two hours ago.

"Fine," she mumbles. "Getting there."

"Soon?"

"I don't know—yeah, soon." *Clang!* "Why?"

"Like, in the next thirty seconds?"

"Cate, why?"

"We've got company."

Mel growls and kicks the tire of the truck.

I yank the axe out of my belt loop just as three, four, eight, nine more come wandering out of the evergreens that surround the road.

"You've got to be kidding me," Mel mutters. She whispers through the open window to the dog, "Chaz, down."

Chaz settles on the front seat. A few of them may notice him if they get close enough, but they'll always pick people given the option. He'll be safe for now.

Safer than we are.

I swing my axe at the first one to approach, a clean hit to the back of the neck. The jaws continue to gnash after the body falls to the ground, but since that's all that's still moving, it's not a threat anymore. The three fast approaching on my right and the one foot-dragger on the left, those are threats. I shove back the closest one, sending it sprawling, bury my axe into the second's head, and work it free just in time to dodge the foot-dragger's claws. The miss throws it off-balance and it falls to its exposed kneecaps. I split its skull before it has a chance to stand.

That's one universally reliable factoid from zombie lore: head shot equals kill. The rest of it is a mixed bag of facts and fabrications.

By the time I dislodge my axe again, the one I shoved is in my face. I don't even see another coming at me until it knocks the axe out of my hand.

"Damn it!" I fish my knife out of my jacket pocket and dispatch both of them. When I'm done, I bend down and pick up the axe.

I hear the thick *squish* of Mel's little pocketknife penetrating rotten flesh and the subsequent dropping of one body, quickly followed by another, and the dull *thud* of her hammer and an exuberant *ha!* I turn to find her unscathed with three corpses at her feet. Go, Mel.

Before I can turn back around to assess my end, an especially rotten zombie takes my arm and pulls it toward its gaping maw. It bites down on the sleeve of my green canvas jacket, which I was wearing specifically for this reason. I let it think it has me while I split its skull. As the jaws go slack and the corpse collapses, I rub my forearm gingerly. *Ouch.* That'll be a nasty bruise. But it serves me right for not paying attention. Again.

I turn to check on Mel just as a gigantic zombie in a leather jacket—and is that a motorcycle helmet?—lunges at her from behind, bowling her over like a house of cards. Her glasses go flying, and she hits the ground with an *oomph*, dropping her blade as the zombie chomps at her face uselessly through its helmet. Her knife skitters across the pavement and out of reach.

"Cate!"

I run toward them, vaulting myself over the hood of a car, losing my axe for the second time as I do. She's pinned, and although the teeth are no threat inside that helmet, it's only a matter of time before the claws rip through her hoodie. She's trying to push it off, but it's one of the biggest bodies I've ever seen, alive or dead. Just massive. I shove my hand into my pocket but find it empty. Where the hell is my knife? No time. I grab the first tool my hand lands on, a big-ass wrench, rip the giant's helmet off, and swing for all I'm worth until its head is obliterated.

Mel retrieves her glasses and sits up, panting. That would have been a horrible way to go. She wipes her forehead with the back of her hand, shaking her head in relief. But her face changes and she points over my shoulder.

"Cate, behind you!"

Two more are right in front of me, so close they could reach out and touch me, which of course they do. One grabs my upper arm while the other closes in for a bite on the other side. I yank backward, shed my jacket, and stumble away from the two man-eaters but trip over the giant. Mel steps over me like an action heroine with her miniature .22 handgun drawn and ready. She puts them both down and helps me up. Four left.

We run around them in opposite directions, positioning ourselves behind them. I manage to kill one before the next has time to turn around. As soon as it does, I cave its face in with the wrench. When I turn to check on Mel, she's already wiping her knife clean and stepping—somewhat delicately—over the last two corpses.

"Dude, what happened?" she asks.

I know she's pissed; I had it coming. I don't apologize, though. The words sit stubbornly in my throat.

"Sun was in my eyes," I mumble. The excuse sounds even more flimsy out loud. "You said the truck would be an easy fix." I don't know why I resort to blame-shifting instead of just fessing up.

"Okay, how about next time *you* fix the car and *I'll* try to get us killed?" she snaps. "And you'd better clean the brains off my wrench!"

I silently retrieve my axe from where it fell and my knife from the eye I left it in, and wipe the brainy blade, then the wrench, then my axe, on the clothes of various fallen zombies.

That's something I didn't expect: there's very little blood in zombie killing if you're doing it right. The movies would have you believe that there are buckets of the stuff just flying around every time you whack one. But the thing is—and it makes sense once you think about it—their hearts aren't actually beating, and no beating heart means no pumping blood and therefore no bleeding. What ends up on the weapon and sometimes your clothing after you put a zombie down is a thick sludge made of gray matter and coagulated blood. It's still disgusting, especially the odor, but at least it doesn't splatter.

"I'm sorry, okay?" I slide my axe back into my belt loop.

Mel holds on to her last shred of anger, aggressively polishing her glasses with the hem of her shirt. Suddenly she's on me, squeezing the life out of me with her skinny arms. "Just keep an eye out, okay?" She strokes my hair the way my mom used to. "I don't know what I'd do if I lost you too."

"Deal," I say, breaking the hug gently. I scan the area while Mel tosses her tools into the bed of the truck. "Those shots will bring more in. We'd better get a move on."

Mel nods and pockets her gun. When she says his name, Chaz sits back up, tail wagging. She slams the hood of the truck. "Let's go. I think I just barely managed to fix this heap before they got here. Moment of truth..." She twists a couple of wires together and pumps her fist into the air as the truck rumbles to life. "Yes! Life!"

It's the best sound I've heard in a week. Mel and I have been traveling on our bikes since we had to ditch our last ride. The engine overheated, and while we were waiting for it to cool, a massive horde of zombies came wandering out of the forest by the highway. It was either fight and possibly die to save the car or get out quietly, take what we could, and run. We ran.

We did find a car the next day; drove it about five miles before we came upon a fallen tree that blocked the whole road. That didn't even count as having a ride.

But thankfully, Mel is handy with cars. Very handy. So when we find a working or workable car, we keep it as long as it's advantageous, and for the rest of the time, we have our bikes. It does limit what kind of vehicle we can use, since it has to have room for us, a seventy-pound dog, two bikes, and two packs, but it's well worth it to keep the bikes.

Mel hops into the driver's side and squeezes the wheel.

"I'll drive first."

I nod and slide into the passenger seat.

Chaz curls up between us with his torn-up tennis ball.

We pull away from the two cars that the truck was parked between, and we're about to drive off when I jump in panic.

"Wait!" I fumble with my seat belt and throw open the door.

"Cate!" Mel slams on the brakes as I jump out. "Catherine! What are you doing?"

I run toward the zombies we just killed and jerk my jacket out from under two bodies, ignoring the zombie I didn't fully kill that snaps at my hand as I do.

Mel glances at me sideways as we begin to pull away again, but she doesn't say anything about my outburst. Instead, she just sighs and asks, "Back to the coast?"

Our trip through Medford was a bust. I glance at the map, staring at the lines I've long since memorized. If we're lucky, we can be back on the marked route in a couple of hours. But luck is not abundant these days.

We both get discouraged and even a little irritable when a detour turns out to be fruitless. But I have to admit that we've had some really successful ones. We found better weapons and a fishing pole plus tackle in Hood River, and in mid-December, we found a house outside Newport in which to ride out a truly hellish winter. The previous owner was just another walking corpse when we found him, but he must have been a conspiracy nut or something because the entire basement was filled floor to ceiling with shelves of canned food and survival gear that we're still using today. There were also boots that happened to fit Mel's giant feet, thick jeans for me, those silvery space blankets, and loads of extra socks, which believe me, we needed. We even scored a bike trailer for the dog. So although the detours seem like unnecessary distractions from our ultimate destination, they are necessary. Every one.

We drive west, leaving a pile of twice-dead bodies behind.

Two: If you haven't prepared for the end of the world, you may want to start.

The world ended just before I turned seventeen. Not in the abstract sense of some personal tragedy that brings your life to a jarring halt (although there was plenty of that) but in the real and immediate sense where a chunk of the population dies of a mysterious illness and then comes back from the dead to consume the flesh of the living.

But I'm getting ahead of myself.

First, there were only a few vague news reports: an aggressive new strain of an old virus had reared its head in Arkansas. They gave it an abbreviation, P13, which didn't mean anything to any of us. Just another media-hyped sickness scare. The rumor was that Patient Zero was a kid my age from Little Rock who'd been hospitalized after an unfortunate encounter with a seagull and subsequently developed other, unrelated symptoms while hospitalized. But aside from that one sliver of information—or possibly misinformation—the reports were staggeringly vague. Vaccines were being cooked up "as we speak," the news anchors said, though again there were no details given.

When a case of P13 was confirmed in Manhattan, we got a little more: symptoms to watch for. The reporter rattled them off like she was listing game scores: "Severe flu-like symptoms accompanied by high fever, disorientation, and possible necrotic wounds. Anyone exhibiting these symptoms should be taken to the nearest emergency room for treatment. The elderly and children under four should stay indoors until the vaccine has been made available to the public."

"What d'you think that means?" my stepdad, Andrew, asked as we ate our dinner around the TV. "Is that us, the peons, the *little people*?"

"Probably," said Mel between fist-sized mouthfuls.

"I bet all the political elite were vaccinated eons ago. Figures."

I air-fived Andrew. "That."

"They probably planted the virus in that bird to begin with," he continued.

"Oh dear God," said Mel. "You two with the conspiracy theories!"

"Shh!" Mom swatted me on the leg. "Listen!"

"School citywide will be canceled until further notice—"

"School is canceled? Guess I don't have to study for that final after all," Mel quipped.

"Wait. Does that mean Homecoming is canceled?!" I wailed. "But my dress is perfect. It matches Sam's hair!" I buried my face in my hands. At the time, I was more concerned about getting to Homecoming than about the possibility of contracting P13 (don't judge me).

"Isn't that like weeks away?" Mel asked. "It'll probably be fine by that time."

Even when the virus was officially upgraded to a pandemic and air travel was suspended indefinitely, I allowed myself to remain in my carefully constructed bubble of ignorance: I loitered downtown with my friends, went to the movies with my girlfriend, Samantha, and regarded the closure of our school as more of a vacation than a source of concern.

Two weeks after the initial report aired, the president declared a state of emergency. The next day he flew away on *Air Force One* and never came back. My mom and half the news channels insisted he must have died in some accident, because why else would our leader abandon us? Andrew and the other half said he was probably running away "because that's what cowards do."

I think that was when my bubble began to wear thin. With regular television programming suspended and school still closed, the days bled together. But when my friends' parents and mine stopped allowing us to go out or to have each other over, time seemed to stretch and crawl. All my family did was watch the countless live reports from around the world: vigils that became protests that became riots; fires that swallowed whole neighborhoods. Police in SWAT gear advancing on civilians. Children crying in the streets. Our whole world had become a war zone, and the virus was winning.

But still I only thought of what *I* was losing, the sacrifices *I* was being forced to make. It wasn't until Samantha got sick and I wasn't even allowed to visit her in the hospital that I began to understand the severity of it all. We kept in touch via text message until she was discharged. But I couldn't see her.

Sure you're okay? I asked when she told me she was home again.

Surely sure.

Wasn't THE sickness?

Nope. Just a flu. Hospital was a madhouse tho. Cops all over.

Think they'll get it under control soon?

Hope so.

My parents kept saying that if Seattle went down, Spokane would be next. It wouldn't be on national news; cities that size rarely are. Spokane would simply consume itself in riots and sickness, unnoticed by the rest of the country. So when Seattle's riots bloomed rapidly outward, we made a run to the grocery store for essentials: batteries, food, candles, water, basic first-aid stuff. It felt surreal buying those things, like we were going camping or something. Because the truth was, with the exception of staying in most of the time, nothing major had changed for us yet.

A few days after the president disappeared, Manhattan was lost to riots and subsequently quarantined. They blew up the bridges and the tunnels. DC went down the same day, followed by Paris, London, Berlin, Mumbai, Tehran. Major cities around the world fell like dominoes into chaos and destruction.

I was glued to my phone, incessantly texting and scrolling social media, which was now my sole means of connection to the outside world. Between the kitten videos and selfies and memes, there was a video claiming to show aspects of the virus that mainstream media wouldn't cover. It was shared and reshared by most of my friends, a montage of different scenes, each more unbelievable than the last. Dark, pixilated phone footage appeared to show someone being shot in the chest and standing back up. Next was a close-up image of a man on a couch, his irises totally drained of color. He chewed the air, his head turning back and forth. In the last and most chilling scene, a child, maybe three years old, lay in a hospital bed with what looked like a scratch on her forearm. She was showing the wound to the camera and pouting, typical kid stuff. Out of nowhere two people in hazmat suits came in. They grabbed the girl and carted her off, no explanation whatsoever. Her mother cried and screamed as the video ended. The words "WAKE UP" flashed across the screen.

What the hell had I just seen? I hit Share and went to find my mom.

"Mom." I tapped her on the shoulder. "Mom."

She was watching the news. She shushed and waved her hand to shoo me away.

"Mom. Mom. Mom?" *Tap-tap.* "Moooom."

"*What*, Catherine?" she finally snapped.

"Watch." I shoved my phone in her face and pressed Play.

When it was over, she handed my phone back to me with a mumbled "interesting," and unmuted the TV.

I sighed, watched it again, and shook my head. How could that not bug her, that the news we had all been binge-watching had not once mentioned this? I sought out Mel, who I found in her room surfing her phone. She'd get it.

"Mel."

"Mm?"

"Watch this."

She didn't look up.

I snatched her phone—"*Cate!*"—and handed her mine, all queued up.

"Watch."

She did, stone-faced, and handed me my phone when it was over, holding out her hand for her confiscated device.

"Seriously?" I asked, reluctantly handing it back.

But she was already back in Twitterland, scrolling away.

"That one guy, his eyes!" I persisted. "And the little girl? And there's nothing on the news about it!"

"Wow, you're right," she said, studying the wall behind me. Then she shrugged. "Probably staged." Right back to scrolling.

The video stayed with me for a while, the way powerfully disturbing things do, forcing its way into my thoughts constantly and without warning, making me shudder. I watched it at least ten more times over the next few days, trying and failing to make any sense of it. I figured it was drugs or something, not a virus, that was making these people so aggressive, so uninhibited, and so damn resilient. Had to be. Didn't it? But what about the kid?

By October 29, the Spokane Police Department had tripled patrols. It wasn't abnormal to see SPD squad cars driving slowly up our street each night. Always with the lights on. The sirens remained off except for a *bwoop-woop* every thirty seconds or so. We figured it was mostly a deterrent to would-be troublemakers. In hindsight, I think it was likely more of an attractant to would-be people-eaters. We understood that things had gotten bad; with twenty-four-hour news coverage and cop cars all over the place, how could we not? We just didn't understand the nature of the problem.

We found out on Halloween.

There were only a few cases in town at first. We heard about friends-of-friends being taken to Sacred Heart Hospital and not coming out. On Halloween, the city went dark. The riots started that night.

My aunt and uncle were visiting with their son, Gary, and their foster son, Marco, for our annual Family Scare-a-Thon, during which we would watch the Halloween musts and eat candy that was meant for trick-or-treaters. We'd thought of not doing the Scare-a-Thon that year, with this mystery sickness so prevalent, but as I said, we did not understand the extent of it until that night. Apparently, not many people did. Trick-or-treaters walked about the neighborhood in packs.

Once we were all in our respective spots with several jumbo bowls of candy distributed, Andrew brought out the movies.

"What'll it be, gang? *Hocus Pocus*, *Friday the 13th*, or *Halloweeeeen*?"

"*Hocus Pocus*!" Mel and I shouted in unison. "Jinx!"

"Okay, so that's two for Bette and the gang… And?"

"*Halloween*," Uncle Bill said.

"*Hocus Pocus*!" Mom squealed.

"Not *Halloween*?" Andrew asked.

"*Friday the 13th*." Aunt Tess's mouth twisted into an evil little smile. "I wanna see Jason Voorhees hacking up some kids. Good wholesome fun."

"Jesus, Aunt Tess."

"Catherine, language," Mom scolded, whacking me on the arm with a Red Vine.

"How about *Scary Movie*?"

Mel threw a mini-pack of Skittles at Gary's head.

"Gary, shut up. You know we don't have that one, and it's a stupid movie anyway. It's not even scary."

"Talk about not scary, Melody. *Hocus Pocus*? It has musical numbers. Are you twelve?"

I snorted.

"You'd think it would scare you more since you're the only virgin in the room, Gary. Don't light any candles tonight."

Mom whacked me again.

"I am *not* a virgin," he mumbled.

High five from Mel.

"One more for *Hocus Pocus*," Marco muttered without looking up from his sketchbook. I don't think he really cared what we watched, but antagonizing Gary, the antagonizer of all, never got old.

"All right, two for *Halloween*, four for *Hocus Pocus*, and one creeper for *Friday the 13th*."

Aunt Tess scrunched up her face and hissed.

"So, I guess Bette has it." He popped the DVD into the tray and squished himself into the recliner with Mom.

We were right in the middle of Bette Midler's rendition of "I Put a Spell on You" when the power cut out. We sat in the silence for a minute, looking at one another, the sounds of Halloween parties or possibly growing riots carrying from downtown across the river to our house.

I texted Sam.

Your lights just go out?

No answer.

Andrew and Bill went out front to look around.

"Looks like the blackout is all over," Bill said when they came back. "Pitch-black out there, streetlights and all."

With no further information to go on, the parents agreed that Tess and family would stay the night. As soon as it was decided Gary catapulted off the couch.

"You said we would be home by ten," he complained, "I've got a Halloween bash to hit up back in Coeur d'Alene. Brandon's dad has a *six-bedroom cabin* on the lake." He crossed his arms over his neon yellow "U Mad Bro?" T-shirt.

"I haven't been allowed out in literally weeks and Gary has a party to go to?" I glared at my mom.

"I actually have a social life, Cate," said Gary. "I have a girlfriend *and* a side chick. You don't even have a boyfriend."

"That is so not the point!" I shouted. I stomped out of the room, enraged and embarrassed.

They would probably think I was just being dramatic, which I was a little. But now was not the time to come out to my family. I didn't know if there would ever be a time, really. I was starting to suspect not, but I knew damn well that this wasn't it. I lurked in the doorway while Aunt Tess tried to reason with my jerk cousin. Hoping he would be stuck there too, not because I wanted him around—of course I didn't— but because if I couldn't go out, neither should he.

"Honey, people are really scared of this sickness. And with the blackout..." She put one fully inked arm around Bill's waist. "You never know, it could be back home too. We'll just stay here tonight. I'm sure the party was canceled anyway."

"God, Mom, don't you know anything?" He threw his hands in the air. "That's the *theme* of the party! And who needs lights when there's a bonfire? Do you have any idea how many slutty nurses you're keeping me from?"

"What? Your girlfriends busy?"

"Shut it, Melody." He put his phone to his ear. "*Great,*" he said, "Dylan's not picking up. There goes my backup ride." Under his breath, he added, "This wouldn't be an issue if you'd got me the truck I wanted."

"Too bad about that low-C average," Marco interjected quietly.

"Shut up!" Gary shouted.

Aunt Tess rolled her eyes and ran a hand through her short, orchid-purple hair. Gary was so unlike his parents. Both Tess and Bill were quiet vegetarians who always dressed for comfort and donated to every conservation charity known to man. Gary ate steak three times a week and wore bejeweled jeans that would be too tight even for Mel.

"If you're so desperate to go," Marco said, "you can always hoof it. You should probably leave right now, though."

"Who asked you, *freak*?" Gary sneered. He turned back to my aunt. "Mom, Mommy, come on, just gimme the keys. I'll be back before sunrise. I promise."

When it was clear that no amount of his begging would change their minds, I slunk back into the living room just as Gary flopped down on the couch. He proceeded to drain his phone's battery by shining the flashlight in our eyes until, to everyone's relief, he fell asleep.

Andrew pulled his phone out, suggesting we all do the same to try to figure out what was going on.

"Perfect," he said under his breath when the phone's screen lit up. "Battery's about dead."

Mom sighed as she picked up her phone off the coffee table. "You should have uploaded that battery thing Melody told you about."

"Downloaded, Mom," I corrected her.

"Well whatever." She waved a hand dismissively. "The point is that if you had, your battery would be full like mi—" She stopped and clicked her tongue. "Nothing."

I was never so grateful for a 52 percent charge in my life. I scrolled through my news feed once more, finding nothing new, and sent Sam another text: *Power out still, turning my phone off. Come over if you can. I'll wait up.*

After ten more minutes with no reply, I powered my phone off, trying hard not to let my anxiety run away with me. Sam was fine. Of course she was. Even still, my heartbeat gave a familiar thump. I slowed my breathing, inhaling for four seconds and exhaling for eight, quietly trying to ground myself. She was fine, I repeated in my head. She was fine.

Everyone else's phones died within an hour of the blackout, mostly due to their nonstop scrolling. They sat silent except for the occasional recitation of anything having to do with either the sickness or the blackout, motionless except for the constant flicking of thumbs, their faces illuminated by the glow of tiny screens.

But not Marco. He took one of the candles we'd bought only days before, sat at the dining room table, and flipped almost maniacally through a little brown notepad from his backpack, turning the same several pages back and forth, back and forth.

"You're not going to check your phone?" I murmured as I scooted out the chair across from him to plant myself on. "Don't you have any friends you're worried about?"

Marco didn't lift his gaze from the notebook. He just kept flipping the same pages back and forth. "Don't have one," he said. *Flip, flip.* He stopped for a second and added, "A phone, not a friend. I have a couple of those." He resumed his three-page blitz.

"You don't have a *phone*?" I asked as though it was the craziest thing I'd heard all day. Talk about a lack of perspective.

Marco smirked, a little condescendingly, and marked a place with his thumb. Then he looked up at me with only his eyes. "I don't have one because I don't want one. They breed dependence. They're the most widely accepted drug of the twenty-first century. And they're useless now, aren't they?"

"Useless *for* now, you mean," I guessed.

He just smirked again in reply. How aggravating.

It was going to be cramped with all four of them staying with us; I'd have to move into Mel's room to make space for my aunt's family to sleep in mine. While I unloaded some of my stuff into her room, Mel and I expressed our mutual dread at the thought of sharing our one bathroom between eight people, especially when Gary called up the stairs that he would need an hour in the morning to "do the *do*."

"I'll tell him where he can stick his *do*," I mumbled as I spread out some blankets on Mel's floor.

"Relax, Cate," Andrew said, sticking his head into the room. "It's just for now."

Isn't it strange how you can sit and watch something unfold on the news, a bombing or a standoff or something, and you know it's real, but you're somehow removed from it? I think that's how it was for us. Probably for a lot of people. Everyone knew something was changing; for days before the lights went out, we'd watched entire cities consumed by chaos on TV. But from the comfort of our home, surrounded by food and family, things didn't seem so bad. We continued to munch Halloween candy and told some spooky stories by candlelight. We effectively stuck our fingers in our ears, pretending nothing had changed. Trying to pretend.

Two hours after the power went out, our incredibly old neighbor, Mrs. Minkin, came knocking at the back door. It wasn't uncommon for her to come over through the back; Andrew had even installed a gate in the fence between our properties. She'd been coming around for years to babysit my sister and me, and even after we were old enough not to need a sitter, she would come over at random times to borrow this or that or to have a cup of this bitter dandelion tea that Mom kept around just for her.

She was wearing a thin pink old-lady nightdress and no sweater. Her arm was badly injured and bleeding profusely. My sister put her pre-degree nursing skills to work while Mrs. Minkin told us what happened.

"I was going to bed," she said in her thick Russian accent, "when a trick-or-treater came to my door. I thought he was a straggler, maybe. He did not knock. But I happened to see him in my front window. He was a young boy, teenager. He wore a penguin costume… When I opened the door, he came after me! I hit him wit' my cane and run out the back door. But before I am outside, he bit me." She held out her forearm, now bandaged. "So odd… He never spoke."

She'd shut him inside her house. She had no idea why he hadn't just opened the door and run after her, and we were too busy with her to think much of it. We told her to stay with us that night, bringing the total number of occupants to nine. Mel shoved a grumbling Gary off the couch, and we made Mrs. Minkin a bed there. She was feverish and complaining of stomach pain by the time everyone went to bed, but Mel assured us she didn't need help. It was most likely the stress, she said, that was making her sick. I said good night and told Mel to wake me if she needed me.

Marco caught me on my way up the stairs. He had the little brown leather-bound notebook he'd been reading earlier.

"She was bit," he said.

"Yeah," I whispered back. "People are going nuts."

"People aren't the problem," he said, glancing back at Mrs. Minkin. Then he moved in so close I could feel his breath on my face. It smelled like cigarettes and spearmint. He looked me dead in the eye and asked me, "You know what's happening, don't you?"

The way he asked sounded like I ought to know, but I didn't. I had no idea what he was talking about. "No," I whispered. "What—"

Marco suddenly backed away from me, his expression going from expectant to guarded and even a little hostile. I turned around to see Gary sauntering toward us. He yanked on Marco's long black hair and put an arm around his shoulders.

"What're you doing now, creep?" Gary goaded before turning his attention to me. "Don't encourage him, cousin. He's, you know—" He raised his eyebrows and mouthed *crazy* not-so-subtly.

Marco kept his eyes on me, his mouth set in a flat line.

"Something big is going down. You know I'm right." He hefted Gary's arm off himself, pulled his mane into a ponytail, and went outside.

Gary watched him go with a look like he smelled something awful and then turned back to me, a derisive grin plastered across his face. "*Something big is going down,*" he mocked in what I assumed was supposed to be Marco's voice. "Foster kids, am I right? I dunno why my parents insist on taking in these degenerates." He rolled his eyes and stomped upstairs to my room.

I shuffled up after a minute to crash on Mel's bed, but not before checking my phone once more. No reply. I lay there, staring at the ceiling for a while, Marco's words playing over and over again like a chant in my head until I eventually fell into a fitful half sleep.

You know I'm right.
You know I'm right.
You know I'm right.

Three: It's probably zombies.

In my dream, I was wading in a river. I could feel the current pulling gently at my legs as I made my way across. Sam held my hand, smiled her dazzling sparkly smile, and we went deeper. Our knees went under—she smiled. Our hips—the smile grew. But when the water reached our shoulders, she screamed. I tried to backtrack, to pull Sam back with me, but the current intensified and her hand slipped out of mine. Before I could even call her name, she was lost under the white rapids and I was alone.

Mel woke me up at half-past midnight.

"Cate."

"Mmnh."

"Cate. It's Mrs. Minkin. Come on."

Mrs. Minkin was lying on the couch, groaning. Her wound was infected. The veins around it had gone black, the blackness spreading all the way up her arm under the sleeve of her powder-pink nightie. Her fever had continued to rise all night; it had been 107 last time Mel checked.

"The news mentioned something about the black wounds, didn't it?" I asked.

"So?"

"So do you think this is, you know...*the* illness?"

"I've never seen an infection like this," Mel whispered, dabbing Mrs. Minkin's forehead with a damp towel. "None of my classes have even touched on it. But it doesn't matter. If her fever doesn't go down pronto, it could damage her brain."

Mrs. Minkin muttered to her dead husband between these horrible wet hacking coughs that hadn't been there before. She went between speaking English and Russian until she wasn't speaking any language anymore, just murmuring softly and scrunching her face in pain. All the while, the blackness was spreading.

She died just after one in the morning. I dialed 911.

"All dispatchers are busy," said a computer-generated recording. "Please stay on the line."

I tried twice more, just in case, with the same results. But we couldn't just leave her on the couch, so we woke our parents. After some head scratching, Andrew woke Uncle Bill, and they carried Mrs. Minkin's body out to the backyard.

"If there's no one coming," Andrew said as they set her in the far corner, "this is the most sanitary option."

We covered her with an old red-and-white checkered tablecloth from the tool shed. After Mom said a few kind words about Mrs. Minkin, everyone but Mel and me went inside, agreeing to figure out what to do in the morning.

"Remember when she got that cat?" Mel whispered. "The hairless one?"

I shuddered. "No?" I did not recall ever seeing one of those things in person, though they'd always given me the heebie-jeebies.

"I guess you wouldn't remember. You were maybe three or four. She got this hairless cat and named it Dave. Anyway, Mom brought us over the day after Mrs. Minkin got Dave. You took one look at that cat and wailed like your head was on fire. That was when Mrs. Minkin started coming to our place to babysit."

I smirked. "Well, now my fear of hairless cats makes sense." My face fell. "She was a good lady."

Mel sniffled and hugged me close. "Let's go to bed, Cate. It'll be better tomorrow." Mel stopped halfway across the yard. "Doesn't look like anyone is in there."

"He's in there." Marco's voice from the back porch startled us. "And you can't leave her like that." The glowing red ember of his cigarette moved up and down as he took a drag.

"We know that, Marco," Mel snapped. She didn't much care for Marco. She said he was too quiet not to be up to something. Called him sinister on more than one occasion. "We tried the police three times. The line's busy. We'll try again in the morning."

He jumped off the porch and walked into the moonlight. "She'll be up before morning."

"What's that supposed to mean?" Mel yelled. "Mrs. Minkin is dead! I checked her pulse myself, twice!"

"I know," he said. "You know I'm right, don't you?"

He was looking at me now.

"Right about what?" Mel demanded.

I suddenly became very interested in my own shoes.

"Look," Mel sighed, "I'm exhausted, and our neighbor's dead body is under that tablecloth. I don't have time for—" She was interrupted by a soft gurgling sound.

It was coming from under the tablecloth.

Then the tablecloth moved.

"Mrs. Minkin!" Mel cried, running to her. She threw the tablecloth aside and knelt down beside our neighbor. "I'm so sorry, I thought you were... Well, it doesn't matter. Mrs. Minkin?" She stopped. Checked Mrs. Minkin's pulse. Dropped her hand. "Cate, come here."

Marco took my hand. "Don't."

I pulled my arm away and crept toward them. Mrs. Minkin's eyes were closed, and her breathing, raspy and watery, almost didn't sound like breathing. Go figure.

"There's no pulse," Mel whispered to me. Then more loudly, "Mrs. Minkin? Mrs. Minkin, can you hear me?"

Mrs. Minkin's eyes fluttered open. The whites were bloodshot, and the once-brown irises were milky white; pupils too. She moved her head from side to side, opening and closing her mouth just like the man in the viral video.

"Water," Mel said, "she needs water."

We both ran back toward the house.

Mrs. Minkin sat up.

"Try not to move, Mrs. Minkin," Mel said.

"We'll be right back with some water," I reassured her.

"She doesn't need water," Marco growled. "You really don't get it?"

Mrs. Minkin stood up slowly, awkwardly, like a newborn calf.

"Mrs. Minkin?" Mel called.

She stumbled across the yard with her arms outstretched, a feral growl tearing out of her throat. She slashed at Mel's face with her obscenely long fingernails. She continued to struggle; they both went down. Mrs. Minkin was gnashing her teeth at Mel, who was crying out in confusion and panic.

"Cate, do something!" she yelled. "Mrs. Minkin, what are you doing? We're trying to help you!"

"Move!" Marco called from behind us. He shoved me aside and kicked Mrs. Minkin hard in the ribs, eliciting a loud *crack* and knocking her off Mel.

Mel scrambled to her feet. "Are you out of your mind?! She's eighty-four years old!"

Marco ran into our tool shed and came out a second later with a screwdriver.

"What are you doing? Cate, what is he doing?"

But Marco didn't even look back at us. Mrs. Minkin was standing again, seemingly unfazed by a kick that had to have broken some ribs.

Marco staggered his footing, assuming a loose fighting stance just as she charged him. She swiped at his face; he dodged. She tried again; he jumped back. She kept coming for him, swiping and lunging. He side-kicked her square in the chest, and all she did was get back up.

"Do you understand yet?" he growled. He ducked under Mrs. Minkin's arm, took her by the hair, and buried the screwdriver handle-deep into her right eye. She fell to the ground in a heap. This time, she stayed down.

Mel was in some sort of shock, sputtering half words and pointing at Marco, Mrs. Minkin, and Marco again. Marco paid her no mind as he pulled the screwdriver out of Mrs. Minkin's head and wiped it off on the grass, unnervingly stoic until he suddenly doubled over and wretched onto the grass. But a second later he stood, wiped his mouth on his arm like nothing, and went into the shed again. He returned with another screwdriver and a hammer.

He handed Mel the hammer and me the screwdriver. "You'll need these." Then he grabbed his backpack off the porch and started toward Mrs. Minkin's house. He looked over his shoulder when he reached the gate.

"You coming?"

"Coming where?" Mel cried. "With *you*? Not a chance! You killed our neighbor!"

"That wasn't your neighbor anymore," he said. "Now come on. There's at least one more next door."

I hardly gave it a thought.

"Cate, where are you going?" Mel called after me.

I ignored her. Marco obviously knew something, though how he knew anything was still not clear.

Four: It's never that easy.

I'm standing in my backyard. It's night. Mrs. Minkin's light is on next door. Leaves crunch under my feet as I walk toward her house. I know what I'll find inside, know I shouldn't be going over there unarmed. I can see what's happening, but I can't control it. Mrs. Minkin appears in the window, only it isn't her. It's dead Mrs. Minkin, the pale, white-eyed zombie woman.

The light goes off. When it comes on again, she's gone. I tiptoe closer. Why don't I have a weapon?

The light goes off and on again. But there's no sign of Mrs. Minkin. Off, on, off, on, off, on. Suddenly, zombie Minkin is right in front of me. She takes a long, slow swipe at my arm. I can't dodge; I can hardly move at all. The air is viscous, the consistency of molasses. It travels down my throat, cutting off my vocal cords. The light continues to flicker. Off, on, off, on, off, on...

I don't open my eyes right away after the dream ends. Through my closed lids, it looks like the flickering light has followed me from my nightmare into the real world. At first, I assume it's just the foliage moving overhead, letting sunlight through every so often. But when I blink away the blur of sleep and see a bunch of seagulls circling like vultures, and one particularly brave bird picking at my arm where dream-

Minkin scratched me, I jump up and start waving my knife like a madman.

"Get the hell out of here!" I shout, probably a little too loudly, considering our rather exposed state, but sometimes, I can't help myself. "Go on, go! God!"

The birds scatter instantly, squawking their displeasure.

Mel wakes up, yawning, just in time to see me waving my arms at thin air.

"Cate?" she croaks, slipping her glasses on.

I plop down on the ground and rub the raw spot on my arm. "Seagulls."

We watch them watching us.

"What do you think made them like this?" Mel asks as we pack up our meager belongings.

"Hell if I know."

"I mean they've always been scavengers, right? They'll eat anything."

"Right, but I don't think people were ever on that list."

"I read somewhere once that they could unhinge their jaws to choke down larger prey." She shrugs into her backpack. "I guess it's lucky they aren't bigger."

As we mount our bikes (that truck only lasted a day), I glance up at the several watermelon-sized predators still lurking around us. Were they always that menacing? Maybe I never noticed because they were still basically below me on the food chain.

I shudder.

"They're plenty big."

"Maybe they turned man-eater to survive. Do you think? It seems like only some of them do it, though."

"It's a theory. I just wish we only had one man-eating subspecies to worry about. Hey, wait a sec." I look around, dismount my bike, reach into my backpack, and pull out two toothbrushes that have both seen better days and a very-nearly-empty toothpaste tube. I grin and make my eyebrows do a little dance. "We've got time today."

"Oh, sweet!" Mel launches off her bike and snatches her brush out of my hand.

We have to cut open the end of the toothpaste tube in order to get any out.

"That's it for the toothpaste," Mel says as she hands it to me.

"We'll find more." We always find more. Either oral hygiene is not high on the priority list of most survivors, or there simply aren't that many living people around anymore.

We're both lifting our toothbrushes to our mouths when we hear the telltale cracking of a zombie stumbling over the forest floor toward us. Chaz growls, slinking behind my bike and me, and lets out a little "boof."

"What a chicken," I chuckle, handing Mel my toothbrush and taking out my knife.

"Shut up. He's plenty brave." She puts on her baby voice and scratches his ears while I take care of the zombie, which was so old when it died that it had no teeth left. "You just pick your battles, don't you, baby?" She coos. Then she stands up. "Are you done with that thing yet?"

I flip a chunk of zombie gunk off my knife and onto her shirt.

"*Caaaate!*" she whines, brushing it off frantically. In retaliation, she throws my toothbrush, overhand, more at me than to me. I fumble, catching it barely a foot from the ground.

"Overhand?" I narrow my eyes. "Wow."

"Serves you right. Zombie brains on my only—literally my *only* shirt?"

We brush slowly, savoring the minty goodness. It's weird the way things change when your life is all about surviving. It used to take me half an hour just to roll out of bed. Now I'm lucky if I have five whole minutes to get up, pack up, and brush my teeth or wash my face. Never both. But on the rare morning when we wake up and *don't* find a hungry zombie headed our way, we get to partake in a fraction of the hygiene practices we used to take for granted. Otherwise, we usually forget to do it at all. Priorities shift, I guess.

"Well, goodbye, old friend," says Mel, dropping her toothbrush back into the bag. "I miss brushing my teeth twice a day."

"Same," I answer. "I'll take him first."

Mel hitches the dog's trailer up to my bike.

"You know what else I miss?" says Mel as we turn out onto the highway.

"Deodorant?"

"I miss my bed," she continues as if she didn't hear me. "Also my fuzzy pajamas... What is that?" She squeezes her bike's brake. "Is that a backpack?"

"Looks like it."

"See anybody around?"

"Nope."

We pull up next to the fat blue backpack. I unzip it and begin to rifle through the contents. Nothing good, just a little water, a nude magazine, and a LOT of ammo for a shotgun, which we don't have.

Chaz growls behind me.

"Cate," Mel says.

"Mm?"

Behind me, there's the *click-click* of a shotgun being loaded.

"Hands up," a gravelly voice calls from across the road. "Nice an' slow."

Damn it.

We do as instructed, both turning around. A bearded older man, surprisingly muscular for his age, stands across the road holding a shotgun pointed directly at us.

"Kick over your weapons," he says, "then drop your bags and go. Do it or I'll fill you and your mutt with lead."

Mel drops her hammer. My axe is in my belt loop, but all I can do is stand there. I can't reach for it, can't think about anything but the gun pointed at us.

He's standing still, favoring one leg. There's a tear in his jeans that's soaked with blood.

"You're hurt, right?" Mel calls, holding her hands up. "I'm a nurse. I can help you."

"No shit," he says. "You wanna *help me*, do you?"

"Well, no, but I can. And I will. Just let us take enough food to live for a day. The rest is yours."

"You tryn'a pull a fast one on old Roy, ain'tcha?"

"We just want to go in peace," I reiterate. "Please, let her help you and we'll be on our way."

He lowers his gun an inch. I can see the wheels turning in his bald head.

"All right. Tell you what. I got a gun, and you ain't. So you're gonna fix me anyway, and I'm still gonna take your shit."

"Let us take our weapons," I plead. "We can't survive without those. If you take our weapons and our food, you may as well kill us yourself!"

Roy snorts and spits on the street.

"I just might once you fix me up. Now you—" He points the gun at Mel. "—get your skinny ass over here. And best not talk back if you want a shot at livin' through today."

Something moves in the trees behind him.

"Hurry up now, no bullshit, or I'll shoot the dog first. Can't believe I found me a medic! Of all the dumb luck." He starts to laugh as Mel crosses the street.

His laughter is abruptly cut off and replaced with a sick gargling sound as a zombie lunges out of the trees and clamps its jaws onto his throat. He tries to scream, but it comes out as garbled choking as his vocal cords and esophagus are torn out and swallowed. He clutches at what used to be his throat, his eyes bulging in terror. Blood soaks his dirty shirt, and soon he isn't making any sound at all. He falls to the ground twitching, and the zombie goes down with him, making quick and gruesome work of eating its kill.

Without a word, Mel and I put our weapons and backpacks back on and run for the bikes. Chaz hops into his trailer quietly, and we jam out of there. We ride a long time before either one of us speaks.

"Did you ever think—" Mel pants as we pedal. "—that a zombie would save us?"

Five: You don't have to be brave, just be quiet.

"You said earlier that I should know what's happening," I whispered as I caught up to Marco. No idea why I was whispering after all the commotion.

"You should," he replied, vaulting over the four-foot gate instead of just opening it. Show-off. "It's all over the place. It's in movies, on TV, and in books. It's basically pop culture now. Aren't you afraid your sister is going to go snitch to your dad?"

If he could do it, I sure as hell could. I took a little run at it, planted my hands, lifted off, and fell flat on my ass on the other side.

"He's not really my dad," I said, dusting myself off and half jogging to keep up with his freakishly long strides. "My dad left before I was born."

"So are you afraid Melody is going to snitch to *her* dad?"

"No," I whisper. "She's not like that. Sister code."

We stopped outside Mrs. Minkin's back door. Marco put a finger to his mouth and tried the handle. The door swung open without a sound. In fact, as we tiptoed inside I noticed the depth of the silence. Marco held the screwdriver in front of himself like a weapon, rounding the corner from the kitchen to the hallway.

"Marco, what are we doing here?" I asked.

"Shh!" He turned to me with a fierce glare that was so unlike his demeanor a second before that it jarred me. "Do you want to find it, or do you want it to find you?"

"Find what?" I asked, lower volume. "And what happened back there?" In fact, the more I questioned the situation, the more I wondered if I should really be alone in a house with Marco, who I hardly knew and who had broken into my neighbor's house like it was nothing. The same neighbor he had just killed.

There was a quiet gurgling sound in the living room. A boy about my age wearing a penguin costume came around the corner. He staggered like he was drunk, which in my mind explained the biting. The boy slashed the air with his penguin flippers and lunged at Marco. What happened next took no more than five seconds: Marco shoved the kid against the wall, pinning him with his forearm, and stabbed him through the eye. The boy slid down the wall and slumped over.

My jaw went slack, and I was once again acutely aware of being alone with a boy who, in addition to his other acts of mischief, had just killed two people.

Two that I knew of.

I backed away silently toward the door, which we had left ajar.

"Where are you going?" Marco asked.

I didn't speak. I just turned and ran for all I was worth. But Marco was much faster than me. He grabbed my arm to stop me and yanked me around to face him.

"Let go of me!" I shrieked.

"Cate, you gotta calm down," he said, holding me in place. His other hand still held the screwdriver and was that the *eye on it*?!

I used to entertain the idea, and I think most people do, that in a situation like this I might be the type to retain some of my cool. Maybe stare bravely in the face of danger and maybe, possibly, even have something witty or badass to say. It turned out I was not that type.

"Please don't hurt me!" I begged. My legs went limp with fear, and I very nearly peed myself. "Please!"

"Hurt you?" He let go of my arm. "Cate, why would I hurt you?"

"You just... Mrs. Minkin, and...and that boy..."

"You're not one of them," he said. "You're not a threat. Now come on, please. We need as many supplies as we can find, and you know this place better than I do. Look—" He put the screwdriver into his backpack and held up his empty hands. "—now you really have nothing to worry about."

But I couldn't make myself move. I was not a threat, but an eighty-five-year-old with a bum knee and a kid in a penguin costume were?

Marco didn't seem to notice my shock. Or if he did, he didn't care. "You knew this lady pretty well, right?" He walked into one of the bedrooms. "Does she have any weapons? Tools, maybe? Firearms are all right too, though not ideal." He looked at me expectantly.

"Yeah I know her," I said, "or I knew her. But I haven't been inside her house since I was a—oh no."

Marco turned around impatiently.

"What now?"

"Her cat."

"Cat's name Dave?"

"Yeah. How did you know?"

He dug through bedside table drawers and moved quickly to the closet.

"I heard you and your sister in the yard. There's also a big flat stone in the flowerbed by the fence with a cartoon cat and *R.I.P. Dave* painted on it. So I'm guessing Dave is dead."

I followed him from one bedroom to the next.

"All right, Sherlock... Well, now that I know you are capable of explaining things," I called as he brushed past me and walked down the hall, "mind explaining what you're doing, and why you killed my neighbor and that kid?"

Marco looked back over his shoulder like I was the world's biggest idiot. "You still don't get it."

He had that right.

He took the little brown notebook out of his jacket pocket. "Look, this isn't the first time this has happened. There's a reason there are stories about it. They dramatize everything for entertainment, but it's all rooted in fact. Think, Cate. Think about what you saw tonight." He flipped it open to the same page I'd seen earlier and handed it to me. On one page was a lot of scrawling handwriting in bullet points. On the other, a drawing of a face with pale, vacant eyes.

I stared at him, and then at the drawing, trying to remember every detail of the last few hours.

All at once, it clicked.

"You're talking about zombies?" I half expected to be wrong, for him to make fun of me for such a ridiculous guess.

"Bingo." He opened up the cupboards and pantry and stuffed everything edible into his black backpack. When it was full, he grabbed two reusable grocery bags that were hanging on the wall and handed them to me. "Here, hold these."

I scoffed and handed his creepy journal and the bags back to him. "Zombies, really? Marco, those are *fiction*." It was my turn to be condescending, and it felt better than it should have. "This is a sickness, a new super virus or something. And why are you stealing all her food?"

"Why? You think she'll need it?"

I pressed my lips together so hard they started to go numb. "Mrs. Minkin died of an infection from that arm wound. Actually, no, she didn't. She died when you put a screwdriver in her brain!"

He pocketed the journal and put the bag back into my hands. "Wrong. She did die from the wound, but it wasn't an infection. It was *the* infection." He took my hand and led me to Penguin Boy's body. "Do you see the blood around the mouth? And the eye?"

I looked despite my better judgment. My stomach lurched twice when my gaze skated over the eye hole. But there was blood around the boy's mouth. I looked up, trying to remain nonchalant.

"Yeah, she said he bit her."

"And that doesn't strike you as odd? A teenager biting a random old lady? This is a sickness—you're right—but it's not new. Last recorded case was in 2005. I don't know how it got reintroduced on such a large scale, but this thing is about as old as people are."

"But the news said the first infection was a kid in Little Rock."

Marco gave me another look. "Don't even get me started on the news. You can't believe half of what they say. Now come on, I'll explain while we raid."

I still had some misgivings about collecting Mrs. Minkin's property like we were grocery shopping, but Marco was right about one thing: she wouldn't be needing any of it anymore.

I grabbed some expensive cutlery, but Marco said it was a waste of time, explaining that the blades would dull extremely quickly and once that happened they'd be useless.

"The screwdriver is fine until you find something better," he said, gesturing to the flathead I still had tucked into my belt loop. "Speaking of weapons, can you think of anywhere she might have any? Your tool shed leaves a lot to be desired in the deadly weapons department."

"Well, pardon me for not preparing for the damn zombie apocalypse," I muttered, and then louder: "Her husband was in three wars, used to hunt too. Mel and I were never allowed in the basement, so that's probably a good start."

I was right. There was an entire wall of tools and weapons: three small one-hand axes, a samurai sword, an old cutlass, an older crossbow, three handguns, two rifles, and around ten knives of varying sizes. I walked straight to the cutlass and picked it up, swishing it around like a pirate.

"That's no good."

"Why not?" *Swish, swish.* "It looks like a pretty deadly weapon to me." I stabbed the air. "Yah!"

"Unless you have extensive sword training, it's as deadly to you as it is to them. It also requires tons of maintenance to keep it in working order. And it's too big to carry easily. Like I said, no good."

"Okay, fine," I said, putting the sword back. "What *are* we looking for?"

Marco pulled one of the axes off the wall. "These are dual-purpose—skull splitter on one side, skull crusher on the other. And they require almost zero maintenance. Exceptionally portable too. You could carry this in your belt loop." He put one in his belt, one in the bag, and handed the smallest one to me. The handle and head were all made from one piece of steel. It was surprisingly lightweight.

I pretended not to be impressed.

"Are you going to explain your zombie theory or not?" I asked a little petulantly.

"Of course," Marco replied without taking his attention off the wall of weapons. "Hand me that bag."

I gave him one of the reusable grocery bags, and he pulled every knife off the wall and dropped them all into the bag.

"I think that'll do it," he said, backing away from the wall.

"What, no crossbow?" I asked sarcastically.

He shook his head. "That's another one that requires a lot of training and maintenance. Plus, retrieving arrows isn't always possible. It's impractical at best and a deadly mistake at worst. It's made for hunting big dumb animals, or at least for people who know what they're doing."

"Okay, fine. Now explain. And you're going to have to do a hell of a lot better than 'zombies are real' to convince me."

We ascended to the main floor.

"First off, I don't care if you're convinced or not. But let's face it, you came with me for a reason, right?"

I didn't say anything.

"There have been over sixty documented cases from all over the world, dating back to 600 BC. And that's just the ones that were properly documented. Some of the more recent ones have been covered up, swept under the rug, chalked up to drugs or mental illness. Remember bath salts?"

"The drug that made people try to eat each other?" I asked.

He scoffed. "Exactly. Now why is that more probable than zombies?"

"I guess it's not. But *zombies*?"

"You're getting hung up on the wrong thing. The word *zombie* originated in Africa centuries ago. It's just a word. Let's go. I think we've picked this place clean."

"What should I get hung up on then?"

"You should get hung up on zombies themselves, not what you call them. Zombies, biters, corpses, living dead, undead. No matter what you call them, they'll rip the flesh off your bones while you die screaming."

Jesus.

"Say I believe you," I said, trying to sound like I didn't. "What about fictional representations? What's real, what's not?"

"Well, they are reanimated corpses, and they are soulless, if you believe in souls. I myself do. They've been known to attack close family members, even children, with no recollection of life. No mercy."

"And destroying the brain is the only way to kill them?"

"Only way. The rest of the body is dead. They only walk because the virus attacks the brain, which controls the body. But the nerves are dead so they can't feel anything, which means any other wound is useless."

I couldn't believe the conviction with which Marco was talking about zombies, like a textbook, as though we were talking about gravity or the tides. But it sounded somewhat credible at least.

Another question occurred to me, and I wondered why I hadn't asked it first. "And how—"

"Cate!"

Andrew stood on our back porch, looking furious. "Come inside."

He wasn't alone. Mom, Aunt Tess, and Uncle Bill were all standing on the porch too. Mel and Gary were inside, peering out the kitchen window. So much for sister code.

"We need to talk," I called as we approached.

"Damn right we do," he said. "Melody told us what happened." He glared at Marco. "Step away from my daughter."

I took Marco's arm. "No," I whispered. "If this is all true, we have to make them understand."

Marco shook his arm free and stepped back from me. "They won't understand until they're ready."

It took several hours of convincing, showing them the bloody-mouthed Penguin Boy and Mrs. Minkin, how his eye was the same as hers, and after we pulled aside his costume, we found that their wounds were the same. Gary took issue with the whole thing, pointing to Marco's comic book collection as the reason for this wild idea.

"So what's your theory?" I asked, to which he had no answer.

Andrew and Bill buried the body that had once been Mrs. Minkin in the farthest corner of her backyard. We were going to burn her—it—but decided the fire would draw unwanted attention from the rioters, who were still going strong across the river, or possibly any more zombies (Mom still insisted on calling them "sick people") that might be lurking nearby.

Mom and Tess wanted to leave right away. By first light, Andrew had us packing the car and taking turns with one last quick shower. We would take ten minutes each, just long enough that everyone got hot water from what was left in the tank. If I would have known how long it would be before we saw another shower, I would have appreciated mine a lot more.

It felt like I had been showering for a minute and a half when Mel tapped on the door. I stepped out of the warm spray and felt an immediate chill. When I heard shouting downstairs, I threw a towel around myself. Or three quarters of the way around myself. It was one of those not-quite-hand-towel, not-quite-bath-towel towels, one that would probably wrap around Mel twice but barely went around me once. I tugged it down and up, trying to make it cover as much as possible as I inched out of the bathroom, clinging to it and my old clothes because, classic me, I'd left my clean clothes in Mel's room.

Mel was waiting outside the door, looking exhausted in her fuzzy pink bathrobe. "'Bout time," she mumbled. She looked me up and down. "My God, you're pale," she said. "Ever heard of sunlight?"

I rolled my eyes and tried to think of a witty comeback to do with her tanning-bed habit but came up with zilch. Instead, I tilted my head toward the noise. "What's going on down there?"

"Who knows," Mel yawned. "I've been in my room waiting for the shower." She shuffled past me into the bathroom.

I crept to the top of the stairs.

My uncle was standing with his back to me. He shifted his weight, and I could see Marco staring him down.

Marco put his hands out, palms up.

"You have to trust me, Bill! Leaving is the worst thing we can do! We need to fortify and stay put."

Uncle Bill sighed and leaned his elbows heavily on the kitchen counter. "I do trust you, Marco. I do. But you have to explain to me why the farm won't be safer. Explain why we shouldn't pack up and go to Connell tonight."

"It might be safer there," Marco conceded. "But everyone and their mom is leaving town right now. Every highway out of here will be packed. And when we do go, we shouldn't drive anyway."

Everyone noticed me at once.

"Catherine, what are you doing? Put some clothes on!" shouted my mom.

"We need bikes," Marco continued as I tiptoed into Mel's room. "They're more sustainable."

When I came out, Aunt Tess was hugging Marco tightly.

"That's so mature, Marco," she was saying, "but it's *our* job to protect *you*."

No one argued anymore about staying put. Marco was right; neighbors had been packing up and leaving since the minute the lights went out.

So we stayed. We sorted supplies, each took a weapon, and fortified the house. We didn't see another zombie until the next afternoon. Andrew, Marco, and Bill were in the living room covering all of the windows with furniture and sheets. Mom stood behind them clicking her tongue.

"We're going to put everything back when this is all over, aren't we?"

Andrew took a break and wrapped his arms around her. "As soon as we can," he said, kissing the top of her head.

Just then two costumed zombies stumbled into the yard, a sexy nun and a Viking. These were the first zombies we'd seen in daylight. I recognized both of them from various neighborhood events. They still looked like people but with pale skin and those horrible white eyes. Both of them had some sort of festering wound and blood around their mouths. They saw us eventually, of course, and began banging on the glass.

"Okay, who's coming out with me?" Marco called on his way to the front door. "They'll break that window any second. Bill?"

Bill followed Marco out.

Marco split the Viking's head, plastic helmet and all. The nun rounded on Bill, hobbling on one stiletto heel and one very broken ankle. He shoved it back.

"Just aim for the head," Marco reminded him.

Bill raised his hammer and brought it down on the thing's habited head once, twice, and the third time finally did it.

That day Marco taught Mel and me to use our weapons effectively, one of Mr. Minkin's little axes for me and a very small sledge-type hammer for Mel. We practiced aiming our blows by drawing targets on logs from the gigantic pile of firewood in Mrs. Minkin's backyard.

We all took turns cooking and cleaning, except Gary who was just as lazy as he was obnoxious, and at night, we entertained each other by candlelight. First Andrew and Uncle Bill traded off stories from their youth. Andrew told his spider-in-the-socks story that made Mel and me shiver even after hearing it a thousand times. Uncle Bill's tale of how he got his pilot's license was a little *too* unbelievable, especially with Aunt Tess shaking her head behind him. Uncle Bill also had a real talent, we found out, for mash-up impressions. One night, he sang "Billie Jean" as Elvis, doing Elvis hip-thrusting and Mom and Aunt Tess doing a really bad moonwalk behind him. We laughed until our faces hurt; I even powered my phone on to snap a picture. When no text from Sam popped up, I sent one more, hoping I wasn't coming across clingy but wishing even more that she would just reply.

Please come over, I typed. *Bring your mom. Dunno what you know, sickness is not a sickness. It's way worse. You're safer with us than alone. I love you.*

I erased the last part—we hadn't even said it in person yet—sent the message, and powered my phone off again, hoping there was still cell service and that the message went through. Hoping Sam was safe, wherever she was, wondering why I hadn't heard anything from her since the blackout, and fearing the worst had already happened.

Six: Safety in numbers.

It seems warm for September. Hot, even. The sun is beating down on us, making me sweat through my several layers.

"Hold up, Mel." I brake, peel my jacket and my long-sleeved shirt off, and stuff them into my backpack. I take a good, long drink from my water bottle, which—*ugh*—tastes like it needs a bit of a scrub-out.

"You should at least leave something on," says Mel. "Some kind of protection."

"Why? You know I don't need to."

Mel gives me the look to end all looks, but then her eyes focus elsewhere. "Do you hear that?"

She does this every few miles. At this rate, we'll be in San Francisco by next year. I humor her, though, because you never know. But it's quiet.

"Sounds like a whole lot of nothing."

"Swore I heard someone screaming." She shrugs. "Guess not. Anyway...what about Willem Dafoe?"

"He's alive for sure; probably in command of a gang. Bruce Willis, Lucy Liu, Samuel L. We'll run into them in California I bet. What about Bieber?"

She makes a *psh* noise. "He died day one. What about that director you and Dad loved, Quentin something?"

"He's probably behind this whole thing."

This is one of our favorite pastimes. The mundanity of road life—riding for hours on end with nobody but each other and the dog for company—can be maddening. So about a week ago, we started this game where we name celebrities and decide if they made it or not, and if we decide they didn't, we imagine how they died.

"Okay, Brad Pitt."

"So dead."

"What! C'mon, Cate, he's been in, like, a hundred action movies."

"Yeah. Movies. He doesn't even do his own stunts. Bet you anything he died the first week."

"Do you think he sacrificed himself to save Angie and the kids?" Mel asks.

I chuckle. "They probably sacrificed him."

Mel laughs, followed by an epic snort, which gets me laughing so hard that we have to pull our bikes over. We have so few occasions to laugh that it easily turns manic.

But the soft squish-slurping sound of a zombie eating its kill effectively silences us. The victim is a woman with black hair and pale skin, made paler by death. Judging by the intact state of most of her body and the redness of her insides, she died recently.

"Must be what you heard," I breathe.

The zombie doing the eating has been undead for a while. Its one-sleeved, slate-gray suit hangs loose on its frame; its visible skin is black and gray and oozing except for the flesh on its sleeveless arm, which has been torn clean off. It continues to pull and chew on the woman's remaining intestines, unfazed by our presence. It's a common sight, zombies chowing down on fresh victims, which doesn't make it any less sickening.

About ten yards away from the woman, we see another similar scene, only this time it's a child zombie eating a man. Both the zombie and the man seem especially fresh. She's wearing flowered leggings and a jewel-pink cardigan. Jesus, she can't be older than ten. We ride on.

"I'm guessing the kid got bit and Daddy couldn't put her down," says Mel when we're clear of them.

"Idiots," I mumble, trying to keep myself from dry-heaving. There's something you can never prepare for, getting slowly ripped apart and eaten by your ten-year-old daughter.

"Could you do it?" I ask after a few minutes.

"Do what?"

"Put down a kid. Your kid."

"I wouldn't bring a kid into this world, first off," says Mel. Her eyes glaze over for a second as she considers. "But, probably not. I mean, you put so much effort into cooking them up and keeping them alive, and then what? One little scratch and you have to shoot your baby in the head? No, I don't think I could."

I shake my head to clear the bloody images swimming around inside it.

"Me neither."

We're way off the marked route. We're still in Oregon, or so the signs say. Long story short, Mel twisted her ankle in Florence, and we had to find a ride or stop for at least a week. We found a van, but the 101—aka the Pacific Coast Highway or PCH, the road we were supposed to stay on—was blocked in Reedsport. Since Mel couldn't bike, we took the only route accessible by car, assuming we would be able to get back to the PCH fairly soon.

We were wrong. Several weeks and many close calls later, here we are, biking through a lot of very small highway towns, scrounging for extra supplies. I take the opportunity to read the map and look for a way back to the coast.

"That turnoff in Grants Pass was our last chance to get back to the 101 before we hit California. If we backtrack, we can probably make it to the coast by sundown tomorrow."

Mel glances at the map for a second, and then me.

"Have you ever wondered if we're doing the right thing, sticking to the map? What if we're all that's left? What if we get all the way to San Francisco, miraculously find a boat, make it to Alcatraz, and none of our people are there?"

I fold the map. It collapses obediently back into itself along the worn, creased edges, and I stuff it into my back pocket. "It's all we have."

This isn't the first time we've had this conversation. We have it every time I pull out the map, which is every few days. I don't mention that every time she asks me that question, my brain kicks into high-anxiety mode, playing out all of the horrible deaths that could have already befallen our family, or what's left of it.

"That looks like a vet up ahead." I point. "Should we check it out?"

"I guess."

We stash our bikes around the back of the vet clinic and wake Chaz to tell him to stay put. He plants his butt on the ground. We know he will only come find us if someone—or something—approaches. He may be useless in a fight, but his cowardice has come in handy as an early warning.

The doors, made of glass, are locked. Mel walks back toward the road and returns with a fist-sized rock.

Crash!

We both swivel our heads around, but we're still alone.

She unlocks the door and props it open with a chair from the waiting room. The inside is relatively intact: photos of animals adorn the walls; the shelves behind the reception desk are stocked with high-end pet food and treats. We put several cans of dog food and a bag of biscuits into our packs, and when it seems like we've found everything that might be useful, we move toward the back.

It looks completely untouched back here. Everything is clean and in its place; a thin layer of dust has settled on all the surfaces. I open the first cupboard I see. Towels and linens.

Mel checks the drawers and tosses various medical instruments into the bag.

I meander over to the second cupboard. It's stocked with medicine bottles.

"Anything I should look for?" I ask Mel.

"Anything ending in *cillin*," she replies, and then she opens a drawer and says, "Ooh, bandages."

There are four bottles labeled AMOXICILLIN, 10MG. I sweep them off the shelf into the bag. Right next to where the pills were, there's a stash of scalpels. I touch one, pick it up. I haven't self-harmed since summer, but the urge to take one still tugs at me.

Just as I'm about to put it in my pack, a sharp *clang!* erupts from one of the exam rooms, breaking the trance. I put the scalpel back on the shelf as a lab-coat-clad zombie ambles out of the room toward Mel, whose arms are now full of dog accessories both necessary and frivolous. She yelps and jumps back, dropping all of it and hopping over a counter to barely evade the zombie's grasp. She draws her knife.

"Hey!" I practically shout. I drop my bag and rush the thing, putting a clean hole in its eye as it turns to look at me. It falls to the ground in a bony heap.

Mel holds her hand out for a high five. "Nice."

I smile despite the gravity of the whole thing and smack her hand. Then I bend down to pick up my bag and the pill bottles that spilled out.

"Check this out," Mel says. I turn to see her holding up a bright blue harness in one hand and a brand-new teddy bear in the other. She's got a big goofy grin on her face.

"I don't know if the bear's necessary," I say.

"Of course it is." She brushes past me toward the front. "It weighs like nothing, and Chaz needs a new thing. He doesn't understand that the world ended. Now let's check the reception desk and get gone."

I quickly rifle through the drawers. Pens, scotch tape, a mini stapler, a photo of a little girl proudly holding a snake. Nothing useful. I dig around in the back of the drawer, bringing the contents to the front. More pens, some loose staples, and *oh*!

Jackpot!

"Mel." I get her attention as she moves the chair that kept the door open. I hold up the two white-chocolate-macadamia-nut-flavored protein bars and make my own silly grin. "Our favorite flavor."

Mel pumps her fists in the air like duel pistons and catches the bar I toss her way. She unwraps a corner and takes a deep whiff. "Mmmmm."

We've both devoured their soft, crunchy, barely stale sweetness before we're even outside. That was a nice surprise; we haven't eaten since...yesterday? Two days ago?

Before we round the first corner outside, Chaz comes bounding up from behind the building. We drop our bags and ready ourselves for a fight. I grip my axe handle and Mel her hammer. We listen for sounds of approaching footsteps, the telltale moan, maybe the sound of a car engine. But there's nothing.

"Chaz, what is it?" I ask, stroking his head. He's obviously in distress. He paws at the ground and whines.

Suddenly, we hear it. It must have been too quiet before, only loud enough for Chaz to catch: two human voices. It's the first time we've encountered another person in a while. Normally when we can, we hide from people. Better safe than sorry. But when they come into view, we realize they're too close to hide from. It's a man and an old woman. His white T-shirt and her white hair contrast sharply with their dark-brown skin. He's running with long strides and a sure gait; she's having trouble keeping up. They're running from six zombies, four of them new. Brand-new.

The man picks up the woman and slings her around his back in one smooth, practiced motion. She wraps her arms around his neck like a koala. Mel and I hold position with our weapons in hand as they approach.

"Run!"

Mel looks at me with a raised eyebrow. I shrug. Run? From six zombies?

"Run!" he calls again. They're only about fifty paces from us now.

In a moment of horror we understand: there are at least twenty more zombies coming over the hill.

He stops in front of us and sets the old lady down. They look clean. His face and head are recently shaved, and the only dirt on her mint-green sweat suit is at the hems of her pants.

"Hurry," Mel tells them. "Get inside. We got this."

Do we, though?

The zombies are closing in, not half a block from us now. My heart is doing flips in my chest. Mel and I have handled near this many on our own, but never all at once. It will not be easy, but there are simply not enough of them to make us leave our supplies behind. Plus, the bikes are parked exactly where they're passing, and Chaz is in no shape to run for more than several yards at a time. It always comes down to this—fight or flee.

"Get inside, Nana," the man instructs the old lady. She pulls him down to kiss his smooth brown cheek and hurries inside.

He removes two large Bowie knives from some very professional-looking sheaths on his thighs. First, he holds them both with blades pointed the same direction, and then he tosses one in the air and catches it the opposite way. So he has a background with some sort of combat.

Good to know.

"Chaz, go on," I say. Chaz pushes his nose into my hand and follows the old lady into the clinic.

The first few are nearly in striking distance.

"How many can you take?" I ask him, planting my axe in a rotten head.

"As many as you need me to," he says, kicking one hard in the chest and slicing another's spinal cord.

Perfect answer.

"What's your name?" Mel asks, pushing her glasses up with her index finger.

"Calvin Waters," he says. Stab. "Cal."

He flashes two rows of perfect teeth at her, and she turns beet red.

"I'm Melody," she replies with a coquettish grin as I stab a freshie in the temple. If this were a cartoon, I suspect her eyes would have been replaced with little beating hearts. Is she serious?

I clear my throat and pointedly axe the last nearby zombie.

"All right," I say. "Nice to meet you, Calvin." Chop. "I'm Cate."

The rest of the horde arrives. Mel, finally back from la-la land, smashes the skull of a rotten one just before Calvin kills two freshies at once. Most of them are new, in fact. They look and smell like they couldn't have died more than a day ago. I split one skull, and then by complete accident, I crush the skull of the old rotten zombie behind me with the back of my axe while pulling it out of the first zombie's face. Mel stabs one in the eye socket and takes her hammer to another. Calvin is ripping through three times as many as we are. He is impressive with those blades. In a matter of minutes, a whole mess of zombies lay at our feet.

We all clean and sheath our weapons.

"You're amazing with those knives," says Mel.

"Dude," I whisper, jabbing her with my elbow, "ease up."

Mel grits her teeth. "Overkill?"

"Just a bit."

"But I mean, look at him, Cate!" she gushes. "He's gorgeous!"

Calvin marches toward the door, probably only pretending not to hear us. "You can come out now, Nana," he calls.

The old woman emerges with Chaz in tow. When she stops, he sits by her feet and wiggles his tail. She strokes his ears.

"I think I've made a new friend, Calvin," she says with a distinctly Southern accent. She looks at Mel and me. "You have a very sweet boy."

"Thank you." Mel beams. "I'm Melody. This is my sister, Cate."

The old lady nods in greeting. "It's nice to meet you, ladies. I'm Calvin's grandmother, Maebelle. Call me Mae."

Just then a zombie with a hammer-shaped dent in its face sits up and bites down hard on Calvin's right leg three times. Calvin stabs it in the back of the head and stands up. "Have you got any water?" he asks.

Mel's face drains of its rosy hue. "I'm so sorry," she says, handing him her water bottle. "I thought I'd killed it."

"It's not a problem," Calvin replies. He drinks casually, though it's probably the last drink he'll ever take. He offers the bottle to his grandmother, who takes a delicate sip and hands it back to Mel. Mel takes it wordlessly, still staring at the spot where he was just bit. The fabric of his pants is torn in two spots.

Why is there no blood?

"Weren't you bit?" I ask, though I saw it happen.

He studies our faces with a raised eyebrow. Keeping eye contact (with Mel), he drops to one knee and rolls up his pants to reveal a prosthetic leg that appears to be implanted straight into his knee.

"Titanium alloy," he says, knocking on the metal. "I'm good."

That is some impressive luck.

"Nothing's biting through that," I say.

"Nope."

Mel scoots herself just a little bit in front of me.

"So where are you two headed?" she asks.

Calvin shrugs. "We were headed toward Medford. When our community in Ashland was overrun a few days ago, we decided to try our luck elsewhere. Thought Medford might have a better chance of safety, being a bigger city."

"Medford is gone," I say. "Is it just the two of you?"

"There were seventeen of us when we started," says Calvin. His eyes shift for a second to the bodies strewn about the parking lot.

"Were these your people?" Mel asks.

Mae fondles the delicate gold cross hanging around her neck, meeting no one's gaze. Chaz plops down right next to her and sits so close he's leaning on her. She pats his head appreciatively.

"It happened last night," Calvin answers. "Someone must have left the door open at the house we were holed up in. They came in while we slept. It was a bloodbath. I got Nana out in time, but no one else had a chance. By the time we were running, our people were already starting to follow."

"I'm so sorry," I say.

"And you're all that's left?" Mel asks.

"As of this morning. You got people?" For some reason, I'm certain he's asking specifically if Mel has a person.

She tosses her ponytail over her shoulder. "Nope, just us."

"We're headed south," I say.

"You could join us," Mel pipes up. "There is safety in numbers."

"You seem like sweet girls," says Mae. She leans in toward Calvin and whispers, "I like this dog." She has been petting Chaz nonstop since they met.

Chaz yawns and stands up as if he knows we're about to get moving. But instead of going right to his trailer, he turns and watches the four of us, Mae in particular.

"Why not," says Calvin. "You two seem pretty capable."

Mel just about eye-flutters herself to death over the pseudo-compliment.

"Right..." I squint in offense to "pretty capable," at the same time feeling a blooming hope at the prospect of a team. "Mae, can you ride a bike?"

Mae's expression is both amused and insulted.

"Of course I can," she says, crossing her arms. "Can't you?"

I stifle a giggle.

"All right then. Let's find you two bikes."

Seven: B&E – Your starvation solution.

We ran through our food in a week. We hadn't exactly been rationing, each eating two full meals a day (and Gary not-so-sneakily sneaking snacks in between). We congregated in front of the pantry and stared at the barren shelves. My stomach growled in protest.

"We need to find food," Marco said quietly.

"No shit," Gary sneered.

"What I meant was, we should search the neighborhood."

"We could split into pairs to cover more ground," Mom suggested.

Andrew took her hand.

"Marion, you can't be serious. We're going to break into our neighbors' houses and what, steal their food?"

"Not just their food," Tess interjected.

"Not helping, Tess."

"It's not like they'll need it," I said.

"Guys, I know it seems shady," said Marco, "but it's also our best option."

Gary snorted.

"You would jump right to stealing, you criminal."

"*Enough*, Gary." Bill placed a fatherly hand on Marco's shoulder. "Your head's in the right place, Marco. I know you're only looking out for us. But you're talking about breaking several laws."

Was he kidding?

I spoke up. "Uncle Bill, there is no more law. At least not for now. Has anyone heard any sirens? Seen anyone official since Halloween?"

"This really seems like our best bet," sighed Aunt Tess. "And if by some miracle we find someone, we'll bring them back here with us."

"And if someone's not themselves anymore?" Andrew asked. His nose turned red. It quickly spread to his cheeks. "Do we kill more of our neighbors? Bury them next to Mrs. Minkin? This is absurd."

"It's better than burying our heads in the sand, Dad!" Mel snapped, throwing her arms in the air. I had expected her to side with Andrew.

Bill and Andrew exchanged a long, uneasy glance.

"Fine," Andrew finally said. "We'll split into pairs." He glanced at my mom, who was visibly pleased to see her idea put into action. "And each pair will check one house at a time. If anyone has any trouble, yell."

"Everyone keep doors open so you can hear and be heard," Uncle Bill added, making eye contact with each of us. "Got it?"

Everyone agreed.

"We'll meet back here in fifteen minutes," Marco suggested, checking his watch.

Andrew and Uncle Bill checked theirs and nodded.

"And if anyone sees any birthday candles," Mom chimed in, casting a glance in my direction, "grab them."

"It's the seventh, isn't it?" Mel asked no one in particular. Then, "Happy birthday, Cate!" she gushed, "Wow, seventeen! Next you'll be graduating!"

Awkward glances all around.

"Or, you know...whatever."

"Happy birthday, honey," Aunt Tess said.

"You're growin' up too fast, kiddo," Uncle Bill added. "Knock it off."

"Happy birthday, Cate," said Marco.

"Dad," Mel cut in before I could thank anyone, "didn't you and Mom have that *special gift* for Cate?"

"Oh!" Mom exclaimed. "Wait here!" And she dashed upstairs and returned a second later holding a tiny box wrapped in purple paper. She handed it to me and stood next to Andrew.

"Happy birthday, honey," said Andrew.

"We found this in a thrift shop when we went to LA in March," Mom said. Then she hastily added, "The engraving was Andrew's idea."

She was always trying to give him extra dad-points for my benefit, as if she needed to. They had been married since I was little, and sometimes, I felt like he understood me better than my mom.

I tore the paper from the box and pulled the lid off. My breath caught when I saw what was inside: a skinny platinum wristwatch. Inside the face, I could see delicate gears, but they were still. There was a little window with the date, already set correctly to the seventh of November. Engraved on two of the links near the face were the words "Love Always, M&A."

"Mom, Andrew," I whispered, "thank you."

Andrew took it out of the box and gave it a little shake.

"It's kinetic," he explained, "powered by motion. It'll start working as soon as you put it on, and it won't stop until you take it off. Waterproof too," he added with a wink. He slipped the watch over my wrist and clasped it. Of course, it fit perfectly.

Before we went out, we each grabbed a large receptacle and went over priority items (food, water, weapons, medical stuff), as well as things that might seem useful but were ultimately unnecessary. Marco took point on the discussion because, let's face it, he knew his stuff. He ended by reminding us that for the most part, we didn't know what we were doing (which offended Gary more than it should have, especially considering that he'd spent exactly ten minutes practicing with us) and that our best shot at safety was to evade, not to fight.

"Fight only if you have to," he said, handing each of us one of Mr. Minkin's hunting knives, "and if you do, aim for the head. Eyes, temples, nape. Get in, get out."

We paired up: Mel and Gary, Mom and Andrew, Aunt Tess and Uncle Bill, and Marco and me. He and I had already raided Mrs. Minkin's house, so we took the house to the other side, the Coopers' place.

"Car's gone," Marco pointed out. "Windows are dark too. They probably left."

"I would've hated to have to kill them," I said. "They were nice people."

"Like you could."

"Shut up."

It turned out Marco and I made a decent raiding team. In five minutes flat, we were wheeling our loot back home on the seats of the two bikes we'd found. As we parked the bikes next to our own, I could see Gary through the picture window of his and Mel's assigned house. He was sweeping the entire contents of the mantel—three framed pictures and two silver candlesticks—onto the tile floor. I could hear the clatter from where I stood. Mel came running in from another room, arms full of food, saying something I couldn't make out.

Gary kicked a porcelain swan off of the coffee table.

"Gary!" she yelled.

He picked up a lamp and threw it through the huge front window. Both shattered into a thousand pieces. Mel continued to shout at him while he casually destroyed everything in sight.

"What are you *doing*, Gary?"

He eyed her as he knocked over a bowling trophy. *Thud.*

"We have to get supplies!" she yelled, stuffing food into a Batman backpack.

He slid two picture frames off a side table, one by one, keeping eye contact with Mel as he did. *Smash. Smash.* It reminded me of those videos people post online, or used to, of petulant cats sweeping things onto the floor.

"Gary! Gary, this is serious!" Mel was yelling.

"What the hell is he doing?" Marco growled. "He's going to attract every goddamned zombie around."

And sure enough, as if on cue, zombies started to emerge from everywhere all at once. Three came from inside one house while two more came from the neighboring house's backyard. Four from the next house, more than twenty from the big house at the end of the street. Two from another house, one from another. Most of them were still in Halloween costumes. There were kids too, some as young as five or six. Witches, little princesses and superheroes, clowns and vampires of all ages, and, ironically, a few zombies. They came all at once, too many to count, all gurgling and moaning, all decaying.

All dead.

All hungry.

I looked at Marco, ridiculously stoic Marco, and for once, he was every bit as scared as I was.

"Go!"

We slung the bags over our shoulders and hopped on the bikes we'd found. Marco sped toward the house Aunt Tess and Uncle Bill were in. I rode to my parents, who were in the house closest to the approaching horde.

We barely got out in time to run. Mom had found two bikes, the last two we would need, so Bill and Andrew rode home with Mom and Tess on the handlebars.

Marco was the last to arrive.

"You!" he shouted. He vaulted off his bike and charged Gary. They hit the ground, and Marco landed one solid blow to Gary's right cheek before Uncle Bill yanked him off.

"Whatever this is, it is not the time!"

"We have to go," Andrew yelled. "Grab what you can and meet back here in sixty seconds! Go!

Everyone else ran inside, but I was frozen in place. My heart raced; my vision went black and sparkly at the edges. I couldn't catch my breath.

"Cate?" Mel called from the doorway. "Cate, we have to go. Come on!"

But I couldn't make my feet move. I could hear my pulse, feel it in my throat and in my head. Pounding. My breathing quickened and became frantic, desperate. It felt like someone was sitting on my chest.

Mel was next to me in a split second, rubbing my back in little circles like she'd done since I was small. "It's okay, Cate," she said in a low, soothing voice. "We have a little time. Just breathe—in four, out eight. Here, drink this." She handed me a bottle of water.

I concentrated on counting and breathing. In four, out eight.

My hands shook so badly Mel had to unscrew the top. I sipped a little water. A little more. *They're coming! You're going to get everyone killed!*

In four, out eight.

I felt myself coming back. Throat opened up, heart rate slowed. Another sip, another breath. I sighed and blinked away the tears that had pooled up in my eyes.

"You all right?" Mel asked, her eyebrows knitted in concern.

I nodded. "I'm sorry."

"Let's go."

The others were outside again. We jumped on our bikes. The zombies were already crossing into our yard. We rode away, carrying all we could. Hoping it was enough. No one heard the little *plink* sound of my mom's bike chain snapping a few feet from home. I don't know why she didn't yell for us. We stopped at the end of the block and found her standing a hundred feet behind us with this helpless expression on her face.

"Mom, run!" I screamed.

She dropped the useless bike and stepped over it. But before she could start running, they were on her. A clown sank its teeth into her shoulder. She shrieked. Within seconds, there were four more, biting and chewing and ripping her apart.

Andrew yelled her name, over and over, while our undead neighbors consumed her. Then he turned to me.

"I love you, Cate," he said, kissing me on the forehead. He kissed Mel and held us both close. "I love you, Melody. Take care of each other. I'm going to get her."

He rode straight for them, pedaling so fast that his baseball cap flew off his head and landed in front of Mel.

"No!" Mel and I both screamed. He knew what they were. He knew what they'd do, what they'd done. He just kept riding, straight into the writhing wall of bodies. I covered my eyes just as he was tackled off his bike. Mel didn't; her screams almost drowned out his.

I dropped my bike and fell to my knees. If I'd been able to keep it together until we got away, if I hadn't wasted precious seconds having yet another panic attack, my mom would have had those extra few seconds to run after her chain broke and my parents would both still be alive. I put my head in my hands and sobbed. This had to be a nightmare or some sick Halloween prank. It could not be real.

"We have to go," Marco said not even a second after the screaming stopped.

I looked up to tell him that he was a heartless bastard, but suddenly, I was yanked to my feet and swept into a bear hug.

"I'm sorry, kiddo, but we gotta go," Bill murmured, squeezing tight and steering me to face my bike.

Shaking, I picked up my bike. Then I looked at Mel. Her face was drawn, cold with grief. I nodded at her, and she nodded back. She bent down to pick up her dad's hat—his favorite hat—and put it on her own head, looping her ponytail through the back while silent tears fell down her face.

The six of us rode south.

No one felt safe camping along the highway. We didn't want to take a chance in one of the few towns in between, either, so we rode through the night, stopping for several minutes every couple of hours to give our legs a rest. Probably none of us could have slept anyway.

Uncle Bill had had the foresight to bring a roll of duct tape, so before the sun went down, we fixed the four flashlights we had onto my bike, Marco's bike, Mel's, and Gary's. Marco was right as well. There were three separate traffic backups on the way down. Some cars were empty, but many were occupied by the dead and the undead. We rode through as silently and quickly as possible, which was made easier by our makeshift headlights.

We hardly spoke, except to communicate when someone needed to stop. I didn't say a word the whole way. My brain was too occupied with regret and pain and anger to form any actual words. Why did I have to have an attack right then? Why did the bike chain have to break? Why did Andrew have to make that suicidal decision, abandoning us, *orphaning* us? *But he wouldn't have had to make that decision*, my anxiety-brain whispered, *if you could have held yourself together. It's your fault and everyone here knows it.*

Mel stayed silent too, but every once in a while, I would catch her looking at me while we rode. Did she blame me too?

I tried to convince myself that Connell might have been spared. A farming community with a population in the upper five thousands, I mean, talk about peaceful living. Maybe the virus just never made it there.

I realized how irrational that notion had been as soon as we rode into town. The streets were deserted. The shops were closed. There wasn't one living person in sight. We passed a doctor's office and saw the doctor, a nurse, and several patients inside—all dead. Undead. They were trying to get out, banging on the glass door, attracting the attention of two other zombies that were wandering the sidewalk.

"Jesus," Tess said as we rode by, "how could it have gotten this bad in a *week*?"

Aunt Lucy's farmhouse was on the far southern side of Connell. Memories of my summers with Lucy—helping milk the cows, warm summer air, trips to the farmers market—all wove sweetly into the fabric of my childhood. Despite crippling exhaustion and the elephantine weight on my chest, I knew seeing the old place would somehow mend some of the broken pieces inside me.

But the house we found was not the same house at which were made the memories I so desperately clung to now. The cows were gone; dogs too. The big picture window in the living room was shattered from the outside. And the front door was wide open, swinging on its hinges.

Marco offered to go inside with Uncle Bill while the rest of us waited outside.

"Just in case we...find something you wouldn't want to see," he explained.

No one said a word while we waited. With my mental barriers broken down by exhaustion, images of death swam around in my head unabated. Blood, gnawing, biting, tearing. Screams, more screams. Theirs, Mel's, mine. They filled my head. Had I told my mom I loved her recently? Or what a beautiful, inspiring person she was? Had I told Andrew how much he meant to me; that I could never imagine a life in which he wasn't my stepdad? I squeezed my eyes shut and tried to picture anything but their horrifying end.

"Found three dead inside," called Uncle Bill as he and Marco came out. "No Frank, no Lucy."

"I saw this on the fridge," Marco said, putting something into my hand. "I thought you'd probably want it."

I looked at what he'd handed me. It was a photo-booth strip from the last time we'd visited Connell, over summer break. My mom, Tess, and Lucy had all squeezed into the booth together. The first picture had been a dud, with most of the frame being taken up by Tess's hand as she tried to steady herself. The second was of the three of them laughing as Tess finally decided to perch on my mom's lap. The cackling that had erupted out of that booth when the second picture snapped had made Mel and me blush. We always made fun of the childlike joviality that would take over every time the three sisters were together. The third and fourth pictures were variations of the same pose, the three of them having finally found a comfortable position, all smiling into the camera. The only difference was the bunny-ears Mom gave Tess in the last shot, and the devious grin on her face because of it.

My eyes welled up as I folded the strip in half and slipped it into my back pocket. "Thank you, Marco."

"No car keys in the dish," Bill said. "My guess is they got out."

"But where?" asked Marco.

"Probably the church," said Mel. "I mean, they practically live there already."

"Which church?" Marco asked. "We passed at least ten on our way here."

I had forgotten he'd never been here; the last time we all visited had been a specifically girls-only trip for Tess's birthday. The men, including Lucy's husband, Frank, had gone on a fishing trip for the weekend, taking Marco—but not Gary, who hated the outdoors—with them.

"It's east," I told him, pointing, "like a mile from here."

"They're probably all dead by now," Gary said.

Suddenly, Mel shoved him hard in the chest. He barely budged.

"Shut your mouth, Gary!" she yelled.

"Shut your own, Melody!" he shouted back. "That shrill crowing will wake up every dead farmer in the neighborhood!"

She glared at him. I wouldn't have been surprised if she'd hauled off and hit him. I wanted to. But she just quietly seethed for a minute. With a steely voice she said, "You would know about waking up the neighborhood, wouldn't you, Gary?"

So she didn't blame me. At least, not fully.

"What do you mean, Melody?" Aunt Tess asked quietly, blinking her sparkly blue eyes like she didn't know what a monster she'd raised.

"It was *his* banging around and breaking that window that brought on the zombies in Spokane!" She rounded on Gary again. "If you didn't have to be such a delinquent, we'd still be home, and Marion and my dad..." Huge, choking sobs shook her whole body. I took her hand and stroked the back of it with my thumb. She squeezed in reply.

Tess hugged Mel, but her eyes were on Gary.

"You broke a window?" she asked over Mel's shoulder.

"Was that why you hit him?" Bill asked Marco.

Marco hesitated. He looked at Mel, Gary, and me, and nodded.

Bill looked at Gary, saying nothing.

"You're gonna believe the *reject* over your own *son*?" Gary put a hand to his chest, like he was shocked—shocked!—that we would think to place one iota of blame on him.

"It doesn't matter now." I forced icy calmness into my voice. I looked Gary right in the eyes for the first time since my parents were killed. The bruise from where Marco hit him was an angry reddish-purple. I held his gaze, letting all of my pain and rage spill into my stare. He wasn't to blame for all of it, of course, but he sure as hell had a role in their deaths. I spoke my next words slowly, deliberately. "My parents are dead no matter who killed them."

"But Lucy and Frank might still be alive," Tess said, holding Mel at arm's distance. "And no matter what, you've got us."

Sympathetic nod from Uncle Bill.

Mel wiped the tears from her cheeks with her sleeve and nodded.

It took a minute and a half to get to the church. There were signs on the main road that directed us to what looked like a giant shipping container. It was made of steel or whatever, with very few high-up windows and only two doors, one in front and one in back. That shot a bolt of hope through me. Maybe we'd all be okay now.

Lucy and Frank were there along with about fifty others, parishioners and their families. They seemed to have a pretty organized security system. Connell was a prison town; most civilians had guns. Everybody had brought as much food as they could, so there was no shortage of that either. The pastor, a tall, broad man by the name of John, welcomed us into the church with a tired smile.

We told Lucy and Frank about Mom and Andrew, leaving out the details. It had been real before—how could it not be?—but as we sat on the tan berber carpet with what was left of our shattered family, we finally got to mourn. All of us, together. After what felt like hours, the sleep deprivation finally took over and I curled up on one of the benches, which had all been pushed against the wall to make room for everyone to sleep, and I sobbed until my throat was raw, until my abdominal muscles and my face hurt and my eyes were nearly swollen shut. Someone—maybe Pastor John— put a rough woven blanket over me at some point. I cried quietly, not wanting to disturb anyone, and because by that time my voice had been reduced to a raspy whisper. I passed out like that, curled into myself, sometime during the afternoon.

I didn't know how I came to be on the floor, tucked into one of the sleeping bags we'd brought, but I awoke in the pitch-dark church to whispers coming from the far corner of the main room.

"If we stay, we'll be dead inside a week," someone whispered.

There was some inaudible mumbling.

The same voice whispered: "There's barely enough—" More mumbling. "—minimal security at best."

Marco?

"It's made of metal," someone protested. A woman. "High windows, plenty of guns..." Then she said something I didn't catch.

"Guns make a lot of noise. All it takes is for one zombie to come wandering around, and boom. Someone shoots it and attracts every other one for miles."

I propped myself up on one elbow. It was Marco. He was huddled into a tight circle with Mel, Bill, Tess, and Gary. Between the five of them was one long-stick candle, burned down almost to a nub. Wax pooled on the sheet of newspaper they'd placed under it.

How long had they been sitting there?

"We can train them," Mel protested. "Like you trained Cate and me. It is an option, is it not?"

It sounded like they were discussing, or rather arguing, the possibility of leaving. *Already*? I scrunched up my face like a little kid pre-tantrum. My emotions, wrecked by exhaustion, had turned against me. We'd just gotten there! How could we leave? A fat tear rolled down my cheek.

"I trained you for a week," Marco said, shaking his head. "That's nothing. And these people have probably been in here since just after it started. I doubt more than a few of them even know they need a head shot to take one down for good. Besides, there are places out there that not one single zombie can get us. And not just for us; we can bring everyone who wants to come. We can all be safe."

I was starting to see a pattern in Marco's plans, or suggestions of plans: they were rational, if a little idealistic. I climbed out of my toasty cocoon and crept over to the little group. They didn't notice me at first. Marco was still making his case.

"I'm telling you, it can work. We can pull this off. If we cooperate, we can make new lives for ourselves."

"And where would we go?" I asked, startling Mel so much that she nearly kicked the candle over.

"It's a nice idea, honey," Tess said in her very best mom-voice, "but where would we be free of...of these..."

"Zombies," Bill finished for her. "May as well call it like it is, sweetheart."

"Well, anyway, where could we possibly go?"

By the way he was watching all of us, the wheels in his head clearly not spinning, I suspected that Marco might already have a place in mind. I narrowed my eyes at him.

"You've already got an idea."

"I do."

"Well?" Mel whispered.

He took a deep breath.

"Alcatraz Island."

Eight: Stay together.

"I think they're gone," whispers Mel. She pokes her head around the corner of the RV we're hiding behind, but immediately yanks it back and flattens herself against the side, eyes wide. "Nope."

"How many more?" Calvin asks.

But I don't listen for the answer. I let my mind wander back to before for a minute. I would be going back to school this week probably. When is Labor Day again? School always starts right after Labor Day. I haven't seen my friends in almost a year. I wonder if anyone else made it. I wonder if Sam is somewhere out there, hiding from a herd of zombies with her mom just as we are now.

Suddenly, Mel is poking me hard in the arm.

"Cate." Poke, poke. "Cate. Coast is clear. Let's go."

"Sorry," I mumble, flipping up the kickstand on my bike.

"Cal, would you mind taking the dog?" Mel asks, already moving to hitch up the trailer to Calvin's bike.

We only left Phoenix two days ago. It took a while to find two working bikes. But we've made up for it. Sort of. We found a working rig that fit all of us and the gear this morning. We drove back through Medford on side streets, with no map to rely on, winding our way through countless loose throngs of the undead and back to the highway. Mel's uncanny navigational savvy surprised and impressed Calvin, much to Mel's satisfaction.

Now we're somewhere just west of Grants Pass on the Redwood Highway, which happens to be the only road that will lead us back to the coast. The cars are so tightly packed in that we can't even ride our bikes on the road. We've been walking along the side of the highway for a little over an hour now. It's not wholly unpleasant; the heat wave has finally subsided, and the familiar chill of September is setting in. But redwood roots are huge, girthy things that roll unexpectedly out of the knee-high underbrush, so it's slow going.

As we walk along the highway, we talk about Alcatraz (which Mel spilled the beans about on the first day), life before, favorites, anything to keep ourselves occupied. I mostly listen, occasionally spacing out and tuning back in to utter a quick "uh-huh" if prompted.

"One thing I didn't know I would miss—" Mae sighs. "—is the taste of a good strong cup of coffee."

"Oh, *God*, yes!" Mel agrees.

"That's my favorite car," Calvin says, pointing to a vibrant green Mustang.

"Really?" says Mel, squinching up her nose.

"Why? What's yours?"

She tosses her ponytail over her shoulder.

"Audi R8."

"You're joking."

"Better than a Ford!"

"The maintenance alone..."

Through the window of the Mustang, I can see a suit-and-tie-clad body that may have once been a zombie, but it's hard to tell now. After baking in the sun for however long, the body is almost completely decomposed. I can't even imagine what the inside of Calvin's favorite car smells like. I feel like I can smell it from here.

Mel and Calvin also find, over a very long six or so minutes, that they have the same favorite food—steak, rare, with green beans and potatoes. They go on a bit about missing real food. My stomach makes all sorts of embarrassing noises that I'm glad no one else can hear. Mae changes the subject, thankfully, saying she has over fifty bowling trophies back home, the first one from 1967.

"Where is back home?" I ask Mae.

"I'm from Georgia originally, moved to Mississippi when Calvin's grandfather got his first teaching job. My Charlie was the best teacher in the world. He died four years ago, cancer. I was a mess. That's when my Calvin came back home. Charlie and I raised this boy from birth. He went straight to college when he graduated high school. He traveled all over, can't tell you exactly where he went. But when I needed him, he came right back home. We'd still be there now if it wasn't for his cousin Tara's wedding."

"How long was he gone?" Mel asks.

"Well, let's see now. If he left for college when he was sixteen…"

"You graduated at sixteen?" I ask.

"I was gone seven years," says Calvin. "And yes."

Mel swoons so hard she almost trips over an exposed tree root.

"He got a full scholarship. Proudest day of my life."

"Athletic scholarship?" Mel asks.

Calvin looks sideways at her, cringing a little bit. She doesn't notice. "Academic," he says after an awkward beat.

"Arts or science?" I ask.

"Science. Computers, mostly."

"But he still won't tell me everything he did while he was away," says Mae.

Chaz trots next to me, elated to be able to walk for an extended length, off leash, for the first time in days. Occasionally he drops his ball and nudges it toward me with his nose, my cue to pick it up and toss it back to him.

"So what did you do before the end?" Calvin asks Mel.

"I was a nurse," she says. "Well, almost. I wasn't sure I'd made the right choice when I started the hands-on stuff—it can be a thankless job—but I suppose now I'm grateful. Now being trained in any kind of medicine is helpful. More helpful than my other career choice would have been."

"What was that?" Calvin asks.

Dry chuckle from Mel. "Advertising."

"What about you, Calvin? What did you do?" I chime in. That's something I've been wondering about since we met them. A guy who fights like that, graduated at sixteen, and traveled the world must have a pretty interesting story.

"I traveled."

"But what did you *do*," I pry, "you know, for work?"

"I'm afraid I'm not at liberty to say."

Mae glances at Calvin.

"Can you even be not at liberty to do anything anymore?" I ask.

Calvin shrugs.

I'll revisit the time-abroad topic later on. After all, if we have a lot of anything, it's time. Constant, unrelenting, life-sucking time. Long stretches of silence come and go; sometimes, I forget how long it's been since anyone spoke, or what it was even about. I look ahead. The packed-in cars go on and on and on as far as I can see. Some still have undead passengers inside. There are several with actual, never-turned dead inside too, people who couldn't bear to face what was outside their vehicles and chose the final escape.

I had a therapist once who told me that suicide is a permanent solution to a temporary problem. She said it all the time, in fact. I remember thinking that depression felt anything but temporary. I don't know why I think of her now, passing by an SUV with the back windows splattered so thick with blood and gray matter that it's impossible to see inside until I pass the front. Had the person who'd once owned that car thought of their problem as temporary? Scores of the living dead right outside their car with no one to help, nowhere to run? How can you see the other side of that situation? When you're in that moment, submerged in the thick ooze of doubt and paralyzing fear, how do you remove yourself enough to think clearly? That feels like a very on-the-nose metaphor for depression: no help, no escape. Feeling hopeless and sick with your own self-doubt.

I wonder if my therapist is still alive.

Mel stops. Everyone else stops, except Chaz, who continues to wander up toward the front and plops down by Mel and Calvin.

"*What?*" I mouth when she turns back to Mae and me.

Mel points to our right, away from the highway.

"What's up?" Calvin says.

"I think Melody heard something," Mae whispers.

There's a distinct rustling in the trees not far away.

Calvin holds up a finger in signal for us all to wait, and then he kick-stands his bike and marches toward the source of the rustling.

Mel and Mae obediently stand still as he disappears through the trees. Not me. No one protects me better than I protect myself. I lean my bike on a tree and swiftly tiptoe after him, congratulating myself on my stealth. He hasn't even noticed me, and I'm only two yards behind him.

"Cate," Calvin suddenly whispers without turning around. "Go back."

I narrow my eyes.

"I don't know who you're used to ordering around," I hiss, "but it's not me."

He's just about to argue when a newish zombie finds its way through the trees and ambles toward us. There are wicked slashes across its face, and its flesh has been gnawed away from the knee down. Calvin draws a knife and drives the blade into its eye, treating it more as an annoyance than a threat, and then he turns back to me.

"Listen, Cate. I—"

He's interrupted by another zombie, and another. Soon we've got five on our hands.

"Damn it all," he says. "Hold that thought."

We handle them quickly enough; I can't help but get a little competitive. I kill one with the blade of my axe and another with the butt while Calvin takes on two at once with a sweet double temple-stab maneuver with both of his thigh-knives. When four are down, we both race for the fifth. Calvin raises both Bowie knives, probably to stab the temples again, which seems to be a preferred move of his, but just before blades meet flesh, I swoop in behind the thing and split its skull with my axe. It falls straight down like a marionette that's just had its strings cut, leaving Calvin looking at me with a raised eyebrow, neither impressed nor concerned, even though I could have taken some of his fingers off.

"You're pretty confident with that thing, huh?" he says as he sheaths his knives. "Who taught you to swing an axe like that?" The way he says "confident" smacks of condescension.

I shoot him a grin that's half adrenaline, half defiance.

"I'm not at liberty to say."

He cracks a smile.

"You're all right, kid," he says.

"Who are you calling kid? What are you, twenty-one?"

"Twenty-four."

"*Oooooh.* Well I'm seventeen, so. Yeah. I'm no kid."

His grin widens.

"Sure you're not... Well, you've got some fight in you, and you know what you're doing with that axe. To a degree. But you're no warrior."

I squint my eyes at him and square my posture.

"I'm no *warrior*?" I repeat. "What does that even mean?"

"It means you think you're all that, some defender-slash-tactical whiz. But you stomp like a bear when you walk, you take criticism like a toddler, and your fighting form is messy and inefficient as hell. I think you've had a little weapons training, probably recently. I figure that's mostly what's kept you and your sister alive."

I cross my arms and stay silent, grinding my jaw.

"I also know you love your sister more than the world. I know you feel the need to protect her even though she's older. Because she's not like you. She's tough, but it's a different kind of tough. She probably had to adapt to survive. That's one kind of person—the kind who had to change when the world went down." He gestures to the zombies at our feet. "But if I'm right about you, you're the other kind—the kind who hardly had to change. In fact, you probably became more yourself when it ended. I think the fighting instinct comes naturally to you. Which is also why you're such a combative pain in the ass."

I don't know what to say. His insights are unnervingly accurate. I try for a neutral-but-skeptical expression. Never let 'em see you sweat.

He walks right up to me and puts a hand on my shoulder. "If you'll let me, I can help you."

"Help me how?" I ask suspiciously, ducking out from under his hand.

"All I'm saying is, we're a team now. It's okay to act like—"

Chaz barks behind us. Mel and Mae come through the trees with Chaz. "We have to move," Mel whispers so quietly I almost can't hear her. "Get your bikes. Hurry. Chaz barked at a squirrel, and now there are like a hundred zombies coming. They came out of nowhere."

Calvin curses and earns a slap on the head from Mae.

"Okay," I whisper, "we'll be right back. Don't move. Last thing we need is to get separated."

We return less than a minute later to find Mae standing in the forest where we left her.

"Where's Mel?" I ask.

Mae looks over her left shoulder, deeper into the forest.

"Chaz ran off before we got the leash on him. Must have heard something. Melody ran after him, that way."

My gaze darts around. I wait for Mel to burst out of the trees, laughing. *Joke's on me!* But nothing happens. My heart thunders in my ears and stomach. Anything could have happened to her! A list of scenarios runs through my head, none of them good. All of them bloody.

Calvin pulls out a knife. "Cate, let's move out. Nana, you have to come with us. Corpses are too close for you to stay here. Leave Melody's bike for now. Hopefully, we can circle back."

As quietly and quickly as we can, we head deeper into the woods.

"Mel!" I whisper as loudly as I dare.

No answer.

Calvin bends down and touches a bent bit of foliage at knee-level that I would never have noticed. After no more than a second, he's up and we're moving again.

"What was that?" I ask.

"That meant someone or something has been by here," he says.

We call for Mel and Chaz, but they're either not in hearing range or Mel is not able to call back. Either way, it's going to be dark soon. A few yards later, we find a footprint that apparently looks fresh and about Mel's size, pointed a little left of where we're currently headed. We change course accordingly. Calvin also finds a set of dog paw prints that I never would have noticed, and more bent foliage a little farther up make it clear that we're on the right track.

Calvin stops at the next human track and fingers the loose dirt around the boot print.

"What?" I ask.

"She was running."

I crouch beside him and run my own finger along the loose dirt.

"Something's not right," says Calvin. He stands and looks around, hands on his hips. "Shouldn't be so much exposed dirt around the boot print. The ground should be covered in undergrowth..." His face goes blank. "Oh no."

"What is it, Calvin?" asks Mae.

"The dirt here is exposed because it's a well-worn trail. Nothing has a chance to grow."

"What does that mean?"

"First time I saw a trail like this was a few years back," Calvin says as we pick up our pace, "but it's not necessarily the same thing." He slows, but doesn't stop, to examine another bent branch. "We were trekking the Amazon rainforest and my, ah, colleague and I ran across a similar trail." More boot prints. "See how these are deeper, Cate?

Messier?" He barely stops long enough for me to look. "Come on, we gotta move." He speeds up so that Mae and I are stumbling down the path—which has suddenly gone from level ground to a steep downward incline—struggling to keep hold of our bikes, trying to keep up with him. We're about to ditch our bikes when the ground levels out and the trees abruptly give way to a small clearing.

"Melody!" Calvin calls, making no effort to whisper.

The zombies are so close I can hear the din of their collective moans. What the hell is he thinking?

"Calvin!" I whisper.

"The corpses are the least of our worries," he says. "Trust me."

"What's worse than a hundred zombies heading directly this way and you ringing the dinner bell?"

"That's what I'm saying. This trail, it's—"

He's interrupted by a thundering bark that can only be Chaz. We run toward the source, somewhere across the clearing, Mae trailing a little way behind. We stop short at the edge of a huge ravine. Mel is on her hands and knees at the bottom, hair full of leaves and sticks, patting around for her glasses and hat. Chaz is leashed, barking viciously at something we can't see in the trees beyond. The trees part with loud cracks and we see it—a huge black bear about a hundred feet from Mel. The thing is a monster.

"Bear trail," he finishes. "This is a bear trail."

The bear just stands there at first, sniffing the air. Then it starts slowly lumbering toward Mel and the dog. Mel is sitting now, and she's just noticed the bear. She screams and scrambles backward.

Ninety feet.

Calvin sighs and utters an expletive.

Eighty feet.

"Mel!" I call. "We're coming!"

Seventy-five. It's not running, but it is interested.

Calvin's right about one thing: a bear is a much more immediate threat than a bunch of zombies. Zombies we can outrun. But a bear? I try to remember what you're supposed to do in this situation: did I hear somewhere that bears have bad eyes so you're supposed to be still? No. I'm pretty sure that's Tyrannosaurus Rex. Do you make yourself physically larger to intimidate them? Or is it that you get into the fetal position?

"Stay here," Calvin says, picking up his bike and Nana's bike, one in each hand. "Do *not* come down unless those things get too close." With that, he barrels down the steep embankment without a second's hesitation.

"What's he fixin' to do?" Mae asks me, looping her arm through mine for support.

I shake my head. I wish I knew.

Fifty feet.

Mel, who even without her glasses can see the bear headed her way, is frozen with fear. The bear has its eyes on her. Calvin jumps in front of Mel, hoists her up, and tucks her behind himself. Chaz is still barking madly, straining against his leash. The bear is about thirty feet from them and closing fast. Calvin lifts both bikes, upside-down, one seat in each hand, straight over his head. The bear rears up on its hind legs and then paws the ground in challenge, curling its lips to reveal finger-length fangs, growling ferociously. Calvin stands his ground, replying with his own throat-shredding battle cry. The bear charges, running straight for them. I hear Mel scream. Mae hides her face in my sleeve. Calvin roars again and shakes the bikes over his head. At the last second, not ten feet from them, the bear stops in its tracks. After half a second, it huffs in their general direction and turns its back on them and ambles off into the trees.

"Holy shit," I whisper.

Mae whacks me on the arm but lifts her head.

"What happened?" she asks.

"He did it."

I can hear my pulse pounding in my ears as Calvin sets the bikes down, turning his attention to Mel. He picks up her glasses, wipes them on his shirt, and hands them to her. She takes them gingerly, puts them on, and then flings her arms around his neck with a choked little cry. After she pries herself off, they climb back up the ravine and rejoin us with a few quick hugs. Mel is a little scratched and bruised, and there is a new hole in her pants, but she escaped basically unscathed, considering.

The zombies from the highway are close enough to see us, but not quite close enough to catch us. We get away in plenty of time, and even manage to find our way back to Mel's bike with the trailer still attached and only a few straggler zombies nearby, the rest of the horde having wandered by long ago. We head back into the trees, vowing not to split up again for any reason until we're out of the woods.

Nine: If you're still alive, stay that way.

"Alcatraz?" Aunt Tess repeated. "As in, *Escape From*?"

"Think about it," Marco whispered. "It's an island, so extremely finite zombie supply. It's a prison; what better security is there? There's a medic station, probably well stocked because the island's been a national landmark for years. There's even a library."

"He has no idea what he's talking about," Gary accused. "Foster kids don't take trips to San Francisco."

"Really?" I shot back. "How would you know that? And name one flaw with this plan."

"We can't just run to an island and start over. This is not the movies. And just because freak boy made a few right guesses doesn't mean he knows jack shit else. All we can hope for is survival. This place is as good as anywhere else."

"You're more than welcome to stay behind, Gary," I muttered.

Uncle Bill shot me a look.

"We stay together no matter what we decide. I think Gary is right to some degree. This building is secure, and I'm sure if we explain what's really going on out there, people will listen. There's something to be said for safety in num—"

"*Plus,*" Gary interrupted, "what's the point of going to Alcatraz if we lose half our people on the way down?"

No one had an answer for that. After going in circles a few more times, we decided to table the discussion and revisit in the morning when we were all better rested.

I suppose most of them got the rest they needed, despite the ongoing competition for loudest snore. For me, the sounds were far away. I was on my old street, watching as my mom's bike chain broke. Watching us fail to notice until it was too late; watching Andrew riding away. The costume-clad zombies closing in, the subsequent screams—hers and then his—the sights and sounds of my parents being ripped apart.

Mom... Andrew... My heart sank like a stone in the water with each new memory, over and over. Deeper and deeper into cold darkness. I closed my aching eyes and pushed my thumbs into the sockets. How could they just be *gone*? If I refused to accept its realness, would it cease to be? Would I open my eyes and see my mother's face?

No.

Suddenly, the snores were deafening. I sat up and reached for my axe. I had to get out of there. Keeping silent except for the cracking of my knees, I stepped over several strangers and made my way outside.

The air outside was fresh and chilly. Really chilly. Frost was beginning to form on the grass. It crunched softly under my feet. The repetitive sound was almost therapeutic as I slipped my axe handle through one of the belt loops in my jeans, turning right and beginning a slow lap around the building. I thought of the day I'd gotten these jeans, a back-to-school shopping spree the previous month. My mom had already bought me coffee, lunch, new school supplies, and a few outfits. But I'd begged her for these pants, despite her assertions that they were way too expensive (which they were), ultimately resorting to a petulant pout-fest until she eventually gave in for fear of further embarrassment.

What a brat I'd been. Selfish and immature.

I looked down at my watch, not noticing the time. The little parts moved around each other, and I imagined my parents picking it out. I wished I could thank them one more time for the watch, and the flowers Andrew would send to me at school on my birthday. For Mom taking care of me when I was sick, or baking four-dozen cupcakes the night before a bake sale because I'd been too self-absorbed to mention that I needed them beforehand, for every silly little thing they'd ever done for me, just one more time. My whole chest felt empty when I imagined her smile. *Mommy.* The black hole was growing, sucking in all traces of warmth and light.

The screaming started again. Their wordless cries of fear and pain. It overtook the sounds of my feet crunching the frosty grass and grew even louder, enveloping my senses. I took a few more slow steps but couldn't catch my breath. I stooped, hands on my knees, gasping.

In four, out eight. Tears blurred my vision. I let them spill, concentrating on my breath. Watching each little cloud form and dissipate.

In four, out eight. How was I supposed to do this on my own? Why didn't I do something to stop them from dying, especially when I had basically caused it? I dug my fingernails into my arm, dragging them across the flesh over and over.

The screaming in my head took on a new quality. Something about it was suddenly very real, very guttural. I turned to see a zombie wandering around the corner toward me. Its overalls were baggy on its bony, shirtless body. I put a hand on my axe, fully prepared to take it out of my belt loop, but something stopped me. What exactly was the point? So what if the zombie bit me, turned me, ate me like the others had eaten my parents? So *what*? I searched my psyche for an urge to fight, a will to live, and found nothing. Nothing to hold on to.

It would probably hurt, I figured, but only for a minute. But there would be no more of this scraping by, no more watching my family get ripped away from me. No more pain. In a sort of half trance, I held out a hand the way you'd offer it for a dog to sniff. Limp, but available. It reached for me.

I closed my eyes.

Crack!

I opened my eyes. Marco yanked his weapon out of the fallen zombie's skull and wiped it on the frosty grass, never taking his eyes off me. His brows crinkled as he retrieved a bent cigarette from his pocket, lit it, and took a long drag.

"What the hell was that?" he asked point-blank.

My whole face burned red. Shit. I didn't know whether to feel embarrassed that he'd seen that or unnerved that he'd followed me out there in the first place or angry that he'd stopped whatever would have happened from happening.

"Were you following me?" I asked.

He snorted. "No." Short drag. "Too noisy to sleep in there." Exhale. "Plus that giant crucifix on the wall freaks me out. The fake blood just seems unnecessary. Now you gonna tell me what I just came up on or what?"

"That's a disgusting habit," I said, deflecting again. "And for someone so hell-bent on surviving, you should probably know those things kill you."

He seemed to get the hint that I didn't want to talk about it.

"Preachy, preachy," he said as he dropped the spent cigarette and snuffed it with the toe of his boot. "I'm well aware of the effects, thank you." He shuffled his feet and looked at the ground. "Anyway, I've been trying to quit."

"Should be easier now that there's a finite supply..." Ahem. "Sorry. I didn't mean to be rude before."

"No big," he said with a shrug. "This is my last pack. After this one, I'm not going to look anymore."

"Probably wouldn't find any anyway."

"Oh I'd find 'em. I can find anything. But I have a feeling that sometime in the very near future I'll need to run more than twenty feet without getting winded." He huffed a laugh at his own self-deprecating joke.

"Is that why you don't take your boots off?" I asked. "You left them on at my house on Halloween too; that's when I first noticed. But then you didn't take them off here either, not even after lights out." I also thought I'd seen him crawl into his sleeping bag with them on, but didn't want to admit I'd sort of watched him in the dark, because how creepy does that sound? Was this entire question kind of creepy?

He looked at me sideways. "I always have an exit strategy. If I don't feel completely secure, shoes stay on. Easier for a quick getaway." As he spoke, he let his hair loose. It hung down his back in thick black waves.

I wasn't sure what to say about the shoes. After what had happened, I had to agree with the mentality, but thinking about it in broader perspective, it was sort of sad.

"So you really think Alcatraz might work?" I asked after a minute of dead silence.

"I don't know," he admitted, running a hand through his hair and yanking at a tangle he found. "It has to be better than this. These people, they don't know us. We're not their people. They would feed us all to the zombies if it meant saving their own skin. But I'd probably do the same to them."

"That's not funny," I chided.

"No, it isn't. But it's true."

"You'd let someone else die if it meant you would live?"

"Only some someones."

I was only surprised for a second. Mom had said that Aunt Tess once told her that he'd been to juvenile detention three times before he was sixteen.

"How can we trust you then?" I asked. "If you're so willing to give up another person's life to save your own, how do we know you won't do that to us one day?"

"Don't," he said sharply. "Don't say that."

My face must have reflected my feelings, a mix of jarring confusion and surprise to see any authentic emotions coming from Marco. When he spoke again, his composure— which I was starting to suspect might be somewhat artificial—was back, his voice much softer. But his eyes still burned.

"Your family, you, you're good people. Your aunt and uncle treat me like their own. Like actual real family. That in itself is enough to make me care for you all. And you..." He cleared his throat. "Bouncing around like I do, I don't have a lot of friends. But I consider you a real friend."

I could see him blushing even in the darkness.

"Wow, Marco" was all I managed to say. Wow, did that sound rude or what?

"Shush. What about you?"

"Me?"

"I mean, how do you feel about Alcatraz? It sounded like you were open to it earlier."

I took a few breaths before I answered, still processing his uncharacteristic display.

"See, I wish we could stay here. Even with that horrible bloody crucifix. We've lost enough, and leaving means that some of us will definitely die. But I have this feeling that if we stay much longer we'll lose a lot more than a few people."

"Exactly," Marco murmured, "and I don't think this family can take that."

"Well then, I guess we need to convince a church full of people that Alcatraz is our best shot for a new life."

I swore I saw a smile through his curtain of hair.

We continued to walk a while, talking about what we might say to convince people that his plan—our plan—was the best plan.

A biting autumn wind picked up, and I started to shiver.

"You want to go back inside?" Marco asked.

When I thought of the lonely darkness that waited inside, my parents' faces swam to the surface again.

"No. I need to stay out here a little while longer. Don't know when we'll have another chance for a peaceful walk."

"Then take this." He stopped and removed his leather jacket, then the green canvas jacket he wore underneath, and held it out to me. Normally, I would have refused on principle. But I really was freezing. So I slipped my arms into the sleeves. The inside was still warm. It smelled like cigarettes and spearmint chewing gum, like him. It wasn't a bad smell.

"You should probably just keep that."

"What about you?" I asked. "You just have the one now."

"It's no big deal. Really. This one is plenty."

I nodded and thanked him again. We walked on in silence for a long while.

"And, Cate?"

"What?"

"You don't have to talk about...whatever that was before. But if you ever feel like that again, come find me. Because I get it. I know how that feels. That sick emptiness, like you're breaking away from yourself and you'll never be whole again. And you probably won't be, not totally. But your family needs you. You matter." He took my hand. "Okay?"

I blinked. Heat smoldered under my cheeks. I never knew what to do when people were so direct. In fact, it usually made me pretty uneasy. But what he said, that I mattered, that he understood, felt good to hear.

"Okay," I said.

Ten: They all die the same.

Mel and Calvin seem to be sort of an item. Their flirting was barely tolerable before he saved her from that bear; now it's teetering on the edge of ridiculous. They bantered and teased nonstop through Redwood, Wonder, Selma, and into Kerby. Somewhere between Wonder and Selma, I told them to get a room—jokingly—and that night, they zipped their sleeping bags together "for warmth."

For the last week or so, Mae has ridden in the trailer with Chaz. Since he's skinny and she's tiny, and since they are now each other's favorite, they were both favorable to the idea of riding together. We ditched her bike once it was clear that this would be a permanent arrangement, but not before I put the comfy seat on my bike and Mel took the basket.

"Let's stop and hydrate," Calvin calls as he pulls back from the front. "Cate, will you take the trailer again?"

"No problem," I lie. In truth, my legs are still burning from my last turn several hours ago. You wouldn't think it would be all that difficult, towing one skinny dog and one little old lady, but it is. It's kicking my ass.

We pull into the parking lot of a general supply store and hitch the trailer up to my bike.

"May as well re-up on supplies while we're here," Calvin says. "Mel, Nana, stay here with the dog. Cate, with me."

We park our bikes under a white awning, out of the late-autumn drizzle, and creep inside. As the door closes, Calvin leans over and rubs his thigh gingerly.

"Bad today?" I ask. This is the fourth or fifth time I've seen him doing that.

"Rain makes it ache," Calvin mutters. When he straightens up and walks farther in, I can see a little limp.

The place looks deserted at first, but we know better than to assume anything. Calvin claps his hands and whistles loudly. Two seconds later, several zombies are coming out from all around us. A quick headcount reveals five. No problem.

"I've got the two in the back," I tell Calvin as I speed-walk toward the back of the store.

I hear Calvin dispatch two zombies in quick succession behind me, but it sounds like the third is proving a little more difficult. He'll be fine, though, and I've got two of my own to handle. I take down one with little issue. The last one is farther back, almost all the way in the back of the Costco-sized store. I finish it just as I hear Calvin finish with his, but as he's about to open the door to let the others in, I hear something that makes me hiss and put a hand up.

I shake my head *no*, and point toward the back corner of the store. The telltale shuffling sounds out again. I turn back to Calvin, raise my axe as if to say "I've got it," and tiptoe softly back toward the sound. The store is pretty dark, but not too dark to see. I close in on the source of the sound and find one more zombie, a child that was no older than four or five when he died, at the very end of an aisle. The thing is facing the corner; I assume I can easily sneak up and put it down. Which is lucky, because I'm not sure I can put my axe in a kid's face, no matter how gruesome and lifeless. But when my shoe squeaks loudly on the floor, the boy zombie turns its head around to face me. Its chubby cherub face is covered in blood. And judging by the amount of blood down the front of its coveralls, I wouldn't be surprised if it had made at least a few of the other five zombies in here. It's definitely not newly dead; its flesh is putrid, and its light-brown hair is matted and plastered to the side of its face with, you guessed it, more blood. It continues to turn around, its posture sort of slouched as they tend to be, its dead eyes focused on nothing in particular. But as soon as I take another step closer, the little zombie does something totally unexpected and frankly terrifying. It straightens its posture and looks right at me. Full eye contact.

I quickly chalk this off to the zombie's instinct directing its focus on me rather than thinking it's actually *looking* at me. But then it charges me, this tiny used-to-be-human in an all-out sprint coming right at me down the long aisle. It's about as fast as a normal kid, however, so I still manage to grab it around the middle, restraining its arms as you would with an actual child who was throwing an epic tantrum. Its tiny hands claw at my jacket and jeans, penetrating neither. I slide my knife into the base of its skull, a choked, horrified cry escaping my throat as I drop to the floor still holding the little body. Even after I stand and step away from it, I'm shaking.

The raindrops pound insistently on the store's metal roof in the silence that follows. My hands fumble with my knife as I put it away. I've seen my share of child zombies. Hell, a couple of them took part in destroying my parents. But this was my first actual, up-close encounter, and I have several nagging questions swirling around in my guilt-stricken mind.

Did the zombie really run? And was I hallucinating, or did it *look at me*? Do all child zombies have different abilities or whatever you'd call that? I try to remember if I've ever seen a child zombie running or making eye contact.

"What the hell was that?"

I turn around, still thoroughly spooked. Calvin is behind me, standing at the end of the aisle with the same facial expression I probably have, one of fear and bewilderment.

"Did you see it too?" I ask.

"You mean did I see it run?" Calvin asks. "Yeah, I saw that. And did it, did it look at you before?" Even as the words are coming out of his mouth, he sounds unsure of what he's saying.

I shake my head and cast an involuntary glance at the little zombie, a fresh pang of guilt stabbing me in the gut. "I don't know," I whisper. Its eyes are still open, and when I look more closely, my heartbeat quickens again. "Hey," I call, gesturing for Calvin to come over. He does, and I point to the zombie's eyes.

"I thought the eyes were always white," Calvin says, backing away a little.

"They are," I answer. "At least as far as I've seen."

"But his eyes are blue, like a person."

"Do you think it's some sort of abnormal zombie? Like a mutation in the virus or something? Some sort of evolutionary thing?"

Calvin shakes his head and crosses his arms over his chest. "I don't know." He sighs.

We decide not to tell Mel or Mae, both of us agreeing that since we aren't 100 percent sure about what we saw (though I think we both are), it would only cause them undue worry. We drag the bodies into a pile in the back office before letting the others in.

"It's about time," Mel says a little irritably. "It's raining cats and dogs out there, you know."

While Mae plays fetch with the dog and I cruise the aisles looking for clean, dry clothes, Calvin leads Mel to a shelf of twine. He picks up a ball of the thickest stuff.

"What's the twine for?" Mel asks.

"Defense," Calvin says as he stuffs two balls into his pack. "I'll show you later."

"It's sweet, isn't it," Mae murmurs to me. "Even in this mess of a world, those two managed to find each other."

"Yeah," I agree somewhat absently while I change into a new pair of socks and discard mine gratefully. After two months, they're more grime and hole than sock.

We pack up to leave the store an hour later with new clothes, several extra pairs of socks, two balls of twine, a bunch of protein bars, though not the good kind, and eight cans of dog food. The dog will probably be disappointed since he's had nothing but fresh fish and squirrel for weeks now.

"Too bad we couldn't sleep in here," Mel mutters.

"No way," I say. "The front is practically made of windows."

"Tell me why outside is better than a wall of windows?"

"Okay, fine," I say. "But what about the smell?"

"It's not that bad," Mae says.

"We can air it out," Calvin adds. He tosses his pack on the ground. "Cate, help me get the bikes in and then we'll prop the door open with a shopping cart."

Once we have everything set up, Calvin slips outside with a ball of twine. I follow him out. He crouches next to a neighboring door and ties some twine to the handle. "What are you doing?" I ask.

Calvin answers with a bit of twine between his teeth. "Making a perimeter." He ties it in a knot, runs a length of it to a nearby street sign, ties it off, and sets the ball down.

He grins when I pick up the twine ball.

"Will you show me?" I ask.

"Thought you'd never ask. See, look at how I tie this." He points to the knot he just tied. He unties it and reties it slowly. "Loop under, then pull. This is a useful knot. Easy to tie, easy to untie." He pulls the end of the string, and the whole knot falls apart. Then he hands it to me. "Try."

Loop under, pull.

"And you pull this one to undo it?" I ask, holding the length of string hanging from the knot.

"Correct. It's the perfect knot for quick setup and quick tear down. This perimeter won't keep the nasties out forever, but it will give us time to defend ourselves or escape, depending on what the situation calls for."

I tie and untie the knot a few more times.

"Are you two going to play with string all night," Mae teases from inside, "or will you come inside and have some of this delectable meal I've prepared?" She holds up an open can.

The four of us split two unheated cans of peas and talk until cold air has filled the store. When we're finished, Mel takes the shopping cart out of the doorway, and everyone retires to their respective beds: Mel and Calvin to their shared bed, Mae and Chaz to the trailer. I stay up, tying and retying the knot I just learned in a short piece of twine.

"Aren't you going to sleep?" Mel whispers.

"Soon."

After a long stretch of quiet, Mae lifts her head. "What time is it, Cate?"

"Nine thirty-five."

"You know, this is the exact time Calvin was born. Seven pounds, three ounces. The littlest baby you've ever seen." After stealing a quick glance at Calvin, she settles back into the trailer with Chaz, stroking his ears with her tiny hand.

When my fingers are too cold and stiff to work, I climb into my sleeping bag. Even with my shoes and jacket on, I shiver.

"It's odd, isn't it," Mae says after another minute, "that I can remember things like that off the top of my head, but I can't remember when my mother died."

An image of my mother flashes in my mind, her body being ripped apart by a horde of hungry dead. I wish I could forget that. I turn away and squeeze my eyes shut, trying to replace the image with one of happiness. I force myself to picture something innocuous from my past. Friends. School. Homecoming. Sam. I went to every dance from sophomore year on with Sam. We would get ready at each other's houses, donning sparkly dresses and high-top tennis shoes, and then we'd rent a limo with our collective allowance money.

The pleasant image stays with me for but a minute, until I realize that she is almost certainly dead. Probably every friend I ever had is dead. Not all of them are really dead, though. Some had to have come back. Some of them are likely chewing on live flesh as we speak, or aimlessly wandering an alley somewhere. And even if they're not dead, I'll never see any of them again.

I concentrate on my breathing—in four, out eight—trying to bring myself back to now.

"What's your sister's story?" Calvin asks Mel. "Sometimes it seems like she expects it all to go wrong."

"We've been through a lot this year," Mel whispers back. "Cate had some problems before, and after our parents, then the church... She was never a giddy kid. But now, I don't know if she'll ever be totally okay." She takes a breath, and I hear their bedding shift. She's probably listening to see if I'm asleep. I make my breathing steady and even. She continues. "She sort of had someone."

My heart skips a beat. Does she know about Sam? Has she known all along?

"Our aunt's foster son, Marco," she continues. "They got really close before we were separated."

"They were together?" Calvin asks.

"No, not like that," whispers Mel, "but they...understood each other somehow. On a level I don't even think I understand her, Marco did."

I tune them out after that. I haven't heard his name in almost a year. I wonder all the time if he's still alive, where he is. But hearing someone else say it out loud makes my insides ache for my lost friend, for all of my friends, and for Samantha, which makes them ache even more in guilt. Do I have the right to grieve anyone else when my parents are dead?

I bring my watch up to my face just before I fall asleep. The moonlight is just enough to read the face.

Today is Halloween.

Eleven: Killing zombies is tough. Practice.

We stayed in the church for another day, and another. We were safe, sort of. Marco and I made a ritual of our nighttime walks, agreeing that it was the only way one could sleep in the "bear den," a term Marco had used to describe the symphony of snores that played out every night. We would only walk a few laps around the church at first, but our radius grew each night until we were walking a mile or more. We'd usually stay out until we either got tired enough to sleep or encountered enough zombies that it was no longer worth the trouble. In those cases, we would run farther away from the church, just far enough to lure them away and lose them, and then we'd circle back and go to bed.

Our third night at the church, we ran into four zombies only a few blocks into our walk. We could have run. I wanted to, but Marco insisted that this was nothing compared to what we might face on the road to San Francisco. He'd added in his annoying way of always being right that every dead zombie was another zombie we didn't have to worry about later. When the first one got close enough for me to take a swing, I chickened out and shoved it backward just as

Marco killed another. My zombie came back, of course, and reached for me. It got hold of my jacket—Marco's jacket— and I froze as it pulled me closer to its jaws.

Suddenly, an axe clove the zombie's skull in two.

"You take the next one," Marco huffed as he put his foot on the zombie's head and yanked his axe out.

It came at me faster than I expected, but I swung my axe hard and managed to hit its neck. The only purpose that served was to make the zombie look even more terrifying, with its head hanging halfway to one side, nearly headless. It kept coming too, completely undeterred, chewing and clawing at the air. I swung again, this time burying my axe in the side of its face just below the eye. It crumpled to the ground.

It took me a good thirty seconds and a ridiculous amount of effort to remove the axe. By the time my weapon was free, the last zombie was practically in my face. Marco brought his axe up.

"I want this one," I said, a little out of breath.

I decided to try out the butt of my axe, which Marco had mentioned as an effective weapon. I swung hard, the connecting hit making a sick crunching sound and sending the zombie to the ground. But it was sitting up again in an instant. Panicked, I glanced at Marco, who just jutted his chin out at the zombie as if to say "Go on, finish it." I swung again, hitting the thing's cheek and then the top of its head with the blunt part of my axe. It fell again, and again, it tried to get up.

Are you kidding me?

I swung two, three, four more times, each hit connecting with some part of the zombie's head until it was nearly crushed into oblivion. When it finally went down for good, I dropped my axe with a loud *clang* and stood there panting for a second, hands on my knees, thoroughly embarrassed at how much that had apparently taken out of me. But I felt little shivers of adrenaline and triumph as well: my first official zombie kill!

Well, kills.

Marco congratulated me on my progress with the axe, to which I replied, still huffing loudly, that it was *not at all* like the chopped-wood target practice. He smirked and offered me a drag of his very last cigarette, which he'd been saving all day for our late-night walk. Something about the way my heart was pounding made me feel invincible and dangerous. I accepted the offer, taking a slow draw with my eyes half-closed like they do in old movies, wondering if I was doing it right and how cool I looked. As soon as the smoke entered my lungs, I coughed and wheezed and choked and coughed some more, pathetically trying to catch my breath. I could feel my poor incinerated lungs burning like tissue paper. My eyes watered. I was going to vomit. Any second. But nope, just more coughing. When I finally got a handle on myself, wiping the tears off my face with my sleeve, my head pounded.

"Is that how you always feel when you smoke?" I asked. "Like imminent death? What the hell's the point?"

In lieu of an answer, Marco threw his head back and laughed so hard I could have counted all his teeth if I'd wanted to. It was odd to see him so unbridled. It only lasted a few seconds before he was stoic Marco again.

"You've never smoked?" he asked, wiping laughter-tears away from his eyes as we turned back toward the church.

"Have so!" I said, reminding myself of a whiny kid.

Marco watched me patiently.

Here comes dweeb-status. I'd only had one other experience with smoking, and that was also not a cool moment. I soldiered on anyway, my words tripping over each other as they tumbled out of my mouth.

"Last year. My best friend Charlotte found pot in her parents' room when they went away for the weekend. But neither of us really knew what to do. So we had to google it." When I peeked sideways at him, he was looking at me like I was a stick insect in an exhibit. I continued, crossing my arms self-consciously. "The joints kept falling apart, so we did that thing with the soda can."

"And?"

"And, nothing. Neither of us felt much of anything except hungry and a little tired. We laughed a lot. Then we ordered like six large pizzas and went to sleep. We probably didn't do it right."

Marco snorted. "No, that sounds about right."

"So what about you?" I asked, desperate to redirect the conversation.

"What about me?"

I jabbed him with my elbow. "Y'know, drugs. Alcohol."

He shrugged. "Just the usual, I guess. I'll try anything once, but I never liked the feeling of not being in control. Drugs make you hazy. Liquor too. I wanna know that when the feces hits the fan, I can handle myself."

There was that mentality again. The same reason he kept his shoes on, or at least in the same vein.

"You just expect stuff to go wrong, don't you?"

"Well." He shrugged again, gesturing around us.

I got the hang (more or less) of putting down zombies throughout the next several days. Marco and I began to spend a lot of our nighttime walks seeking out corpses to drop. That sounds dangerous and ill-advised, but don't judge. Living in such a cramped space, day in and day out, with so many people—none of whom had access to more than a washcloth bath every few days, and most of whom somehow felt entitled to a position of leadership—let's just say it got tense *often*. Tense and rank. We didn't always actively seek out zombies, but there were many nights when both of us needed to recalibrate, and there is no better way to blow off steam than culling the zombie population.

Also, is it still called a population if they're dead?

"You're quiet," Marco said as we wandered. "Out with it."

"I'm fine."

He made a face. "Quit it."

I wrapped my arms around myself. Closed my eyes. "I really miss my girlfriend. We were supposed to go to Homecoming this weekend."

"Girlfriend?"

"Yeah. Samantha. Sam." I pulled my phone out of my pocket—I had been carrying it out of habit, but just then it seemed ridiculous—and switched it on. "This is her," I said, opening a picture of Sam and me from September. It was the last picture I had taken of her. We'd spent the night at her place, dying her hair, and in the morning we'd gone dress shopping for Homecoming. Under the crappy dressing-room lights, with her tongue sticking out and her hair a mess, she was so fucking beautiful. It made the center of my chest hurt.

"She was pretty," Marco said. His use of past tense made my stomach drop.

"I feel selfish missing her, though, especially after my mom..."

Marco watched me. I could hardly believe I was telling him about Sam, but it felt kind of validating to finally tell *someone*.

"My family doesn't know about her. Actually I'm lying. They know she's into girls. But they don't know about me or us. Andrew found out by accident. He was fine, but I couldn't figure out how to tell anyone else."

"What do you mean?"

"I mean, it would be so easy for my mom not to accept it. That's what I thought. I never trusted that she might just support me. Sam wanted me to. She didn't pressure me or anything, but I could tell. And now I'll never get the chance."

"Well," Marco said after a second, "you can still tell your sister."

"Not likely."

"Why not?"

"I'm not sure how she'd take it, okay," I said, wishing he'd change the subject already, trying to think of any other subject to steer toward.

"Who cares how she takes it? It's who you are. Do it for Samantha."

Suddenly, I couldn't think of a thing to say. So I pointed at the gas station ahead and asked, "Have we checked that one out yet?"

Marco eyed me, chewing his cheek. Looked ahead. "I don't think so. We haven't been out this far yet."

Inside, it was deserted. Marco hopped behind the counter and ducked down to suss it out, looking for any weaponry or ammunition first, as always. He stood up a second later with a pack of cigarettes.

I scowled reproachfully.

"I thought that one the other night was your last."

"It was." He sighed and set the pack down like he was Frodo putting down the One Ring. I repressed the urge to make fun of him. "Bummer, though. Would have been legal to buy my own in a couple weeks."

"You're turning eighteen?"

"Yup," he said, stretching his back and vaulting back to my side of the counter. "Would have been legal to buy cigarettes, but also probably homeless. So."

"Homeless? Tess and Bill wouldn't let that happen."

"Right," he said, "you're probably right. But these families never last long. Even the nice ones get sick of you. I've been with—" He counted silently to himself. "—eight foster families in six years. Nine including this one."

"And when you're not in a home, where are you?"

"Group home. It's not so bad. Most of the kids were around my age. Little ones get adopted like that." He snapped his fingers.

"Why didn't you?"

"Me? I wasn't even in the system until I was twelve. When you're that old, they're lucky if they can find a foster home for you. No one wants an ugly twelve-year-old with behavioral issues when they can adopt a toddler and mold it into the perfect kid. I'm damaged goods, babe." He smiled, but there was something profoundly lonely about it.

"You lived with your mom until you were twelve? What happened?"

"Y'know, life. Mom got busted for cooking meth after she lost her job. One night, a fire broke out in the kitchen. Methsplosion. Next day, a lady in a gray suit came to the door with two cops. Cops took my mom, lady took me. I spent the night in her shitty office pretending to sleep so I wouldn't have to talk to anybody. Day two, group home. Couple months later, my first foster home. That one only lasted a month. They said I was too angry." He let out a short, bitter laugh. "Like a twelve-year-old is supposed to be fine with suddenly having no mom. I mean, she was obviously not winning any awards. But still." He sighed, sending a wispy cloud into the air. We both watched it disappear.

"Jesus, Marco. I'm so sorry." The words felt hollow and meaningless.

"It's all right." He shook his head. "Really. I've been lucky. Only been beat up twice. Some kids die in their foster homes. And I've met some cool people. My favorite foster mom was my last one. Cindy. I was with her for two years. She even kind of looked like me." Marco seemed lighter somehow as he described his life with Cindy. "She was an honest-to-God scatterbrain, always losing stuff, and rarely was our dinner not takeout. She was a chain-smoker too, probably the reason I picked it up to begin with.

"She was a news reporter for one of those off channels. She would excuse me from school when her assignments took her out of town. We went to Canada, Seattle, once all the way to New York. She'd work for a couple of hours a day, but the rest of the time, we had to ourselves. My favorite trip was to San Francisco. We watched *Escape from Alcatraz* the night before we left, and as soon as it ended, she handed me two plane tickets and asked if I wanted to see Alcatraz for real. She always did stuff like that. She had a flare for the dramatic."

We took stock of our loot—three energy drinks, all the same terrible flavor, one airplane bottle of vodka, which we agreed probably had some medical use, half a roll of duct tape, six partially used pencils—three of which Marco pocketed for himself—a box of ten heavy trash bags (excellent rain ponchos), and five maps of the West Coast. We stuffed it all into his backpack and headed outside.

"She put me in martial arts right after I moved in with her too. I came home with a shiner. She iced it and enrolled me that night. When I got my orange belt, she hit the ceiling. That's not even halfway to black. You should have seen her when I got my black belt."

"You're a *black belt*?" I asked.

"Yeah. I earned it a few weeks before...before I left Cindy's house."

"What happened?" I asked, half expecting him to tell me to mind my own damn business, which I probably deserved.

But he didn't say that. It would have tainted our unspoken pact of absolute honesty, a pact that had been in place since the night he effectively saved me from myself. Instead, he took several deep breaths, and when he spoke again, his voice had lost every ounce of its buoyancy. He spoke in short, clipped sentences.

"She died. Last September. You must have heard about it."

I was surprised to realize that he was right. I had heard about it. Cindy Sanders, the murdered journalist. Her picture was all over the papers and local news for months and months, with headlines like, "Journalist Killed in Home, No Suspect Named," "No Leads for S.P.D. in Sanders Slaying," and then, months later, "Murder Suspect Identified by Sole Eyewitness." After the arrest was made, it all went surprisingly hush-hush. There was talk of the direct involvement of a minor being the reason.

Marco pulled a magazine out of his backpack. It was a Spokane local magazine, unfussy in its design, the pages matte instead of glossy. On the cover was written the last headline I remembered seeing about Cindy Sanders, a memorial piece published after the trial had wrapped up and most of the city had long since moved on: "Cindy Sanders, Signing Off: A Daring Life in Pictures." He flipped open the magazine to the center.

Spread across the entire two pages were pictures of Cindy doing all sorts of things—reporting a story on a sailboat, life jacket and all, and one of her sitting in a tree, one dancing at what appeared to be an outdoor wedding. There were a few pictures with Marco in them as well. In most of them, he was just a sullen-looking kid sitting in the background, but in the bottom-right corner was a quarter-page picture of Cindy and Marco, strapped into a parasailing chute, both grinning right into the camera. Their pale legs dangled down, her toes barely brushing the water, his feet fully submerged. Both of them had their hair down, billowing and intermingling freely around them, and in the windy moment the picture was taken, you couldn't tell whose hair was whose.

"I took that one," Marco said, pointing to the photo in the center, the focal point of the piece. It was a snapshot of Cindy reporting the news, microphone in hand. The shot was candid, with Cindy on the left and the cameraman and his camera on the right. "That was in New York. Right before she met Brandon."

The way he said "Brandon" triggered my few scant memories of the stories about her trial. Brandon "Ace" Buckner was the guy who'd killed her.

"Were you there when it happened?" I felt immediately guilty. "You don't have to talk about it," I hastily added.

"It's okay," he said. "My shrink told me it's healthy to talk about it. I was the only other person there that night. She'd gone out with him. I was in bed before they came back. I woke up to shouting, and there was this repeating sound. It was like... I don't know. You read comics?"

"Once or twice."

"Okay, so you know in a comic book, when someone's getting hit and they use words like *crack*? It was like that. *Crack, crack*, over and over. When I got downstairs, I saw Brandon standing over Cindy. She was on the floor covered in blood. When he saw me, he bolted. She was choking, couldn't talk when I got to her. Her face was..." He took a deep, ragged breath and pulled a half cigarette out of his pocket with a shaking hand.

I opened my mouth to ask where he got that, and hadn't he quit, but thought better of it.

He continued talking while he lit it. "She died before the paramedics got there. But when CPS came for me, I told them I could identify him. They took ages to find him. The prosecutor said my testimony would put him away for life. Apparently, it wasn't the first time he'd done something like that, just the first time there had been a witness. I spent a couple of months back at the group home, and then your aunt and uncle took me in. They're good people. They put me in counseling. Not my first shrink, but I like this one okay." He took a long drag off his cigarette and exhaled, adding, "He lets me smoke in the office. Or, let me."

When he stopped talking, his eyes were focused on something far away. No wonder he didn't trust anybody. No wonder he always expected the worst.

When he finished his cigarette, he dropped the butt on the street and snuffed it with his foot. "That was the last one, I swear."

"I'm glad you ended up with us," I blurted without thinking.

He looked sideways at me but didn't say anything. God, was I insensitive.

"I'm not glad that you had to get through so much pain to be here," I backpedaled, "but if anything at all had been different, you could be anywhere else by now."

"I don't think so," he answered quietly. "I think I would have ended up here regardless. Do you believe in that stuff? Destiny or whatever?"

"I don't know, sometimes."

"I do. I know it's cheesy, but it helps to have something to look forward to, especially when shit gets real."

"It sure is real now," I muttered, "and about ankle-deep most days."

"Gross." He chuckled.

A soft dragging noise made us both turn. A few yards away hobbled a quiet zombie that was missing a foot. When it got closer, I noticed that its throat had been ripped out, which explained the lack of the moaning zombie lament. The thing was so slow that stabbing it in the eye with my knife was probably more automatic than necessary.

We walked a little way farther, back toward the church, until we came upon an old black truck a few blocks from the building. We'd used this truck as a stopping point many times already. As I hopped in, Marco pulled out two of the maps and handed one to me.

"Scoot," he said as he slid next to me, chucking his backpack to one side.

I scooted.

"I think we should take the coast," Marco said, clicking on a flashlight. "Highway 101."

I glanced at the coastal route Marco suggested. "It's a lot longer than the route that goes through Nevada."

"The route that goes through Nevada will have extremely limited fishing at best, and you're basically riding through the desert most of the way. The 101 provides better tree coverage, which is good for both sun and rain, more access to fresh water, more vegetation, and more cities to collect supplies."

"Okay, so we take the coast. When do we take this plan to everyone, and what do we need to gather before we go? I feel like if we get what we can and come to them with a rock-solid plan, it may go over more smoothly."

"Maybe, but a lot of what we need we'll have a better chance of finding on the road. Fishing pole or poles, tackle, enough knives or melee weapons to arm each person who isn't already armed—"

"Melee weapons? What is this, a first-person shooter?"

"Shush. That's what they're called. Oh, and food. We need a *lot* of food. We'll need to consume twice as many calories as we do now once we're riding all day every day."

I slipped a hand in his jacket pocket, which made him jump a little.

"Pencil," I said sheepishly, and started writing the list on the blank blue of the Pacific Ocean. *Fishing poles + tackle, knives/melee, FOOD...* My stomach growled as I wrote it, circled it, and underlined it. "What else?"

Marco ran his fingers through his hair and tied it back into a ponytail. Suddenly, I had the strangest urge to run *my* fingers through his hair, but the feeling disappeared as soon as it formed.

"Medical stuff. Tents, or at the very least, sleeping bags..." I wrote as he spoke. *Med supplies, tents/sleep bags.*

"When do we talk to everyone?" I asked.

"Tomorrow?" Marco said. "No reason to put it off."

A zombie not too far away caught our attention. Marco clicked off the light, and we slid down into the truck bed and lay on our bellies to wait for it to pass. Hardly worth the trouble of getting up just to kill one zombie. Especially since it was heading away from the church. We fell asleep waiting for the zombie to move on.

I woke up first. I sat as slowly as I could, trying not to disturb Marco, whose arm had found its way under my head sometime in the night. The sun was barely peeking over the trees, but the light was diffused by the dense fog that surrounded the truck. The air was still and quiet except for the sounds of a few birds singing.

"Morning." Marco's voice startled me. It was heavy with sleep. He sat up and stretched his arms over his head with a loud yawn.

A familiar gurgling groan responded from somewhere out in the fog. I grabbed the backpack and hopped out of the truck. Marco was right behind me.

"Today's the day," he said as we jogged back to the church. "You ready to pitch Alcatraz again?"

"I'm ready to get out of here." I yawned, and then winced. "God, I would kill for a travel tube of toothpaste. Tastes like something died in my mouth."

"Well, that I can help you with," Marco said. He gave a big all-teeth-on-deck grin and held up a finger comically, like a performer about to do a big reveal. He reached into his coat pocket and pulled out his empty hand. Then he waved the other hand over it and produced a pack of spearmint gum from thin air. He removed two sticks and offered one to me in a flourishing bow. "Milady."

I snatched it and popped it into my mouth. The minty explosion almost burned my taste buds as it washed down my throat, the closest thing I'd had to proper toothpaste in two days. "Mmmm." I sighed. "Thank you." I blew a little bubble and burst it with my teeth.

Pop!

A moan drifted out of the fog in reply. I figured it was probably the same zombie, much closer this time.

"We'd better get a move on. That sounded close."

Marco shook his head and took out his knife. Seconds later, the zombie came lunging out of the mist. It gargled and slashed with its putrid fingernails, nearly cutting Marco's face. He ducked and came back up swinging. First, a punch connected with the zombie's face, whipping its head halfway around. Before it had a chance to straighten itself out, Marco slid his knife into its temple.

Squish.

"Now we can go," Marco said, wiping and sheathing his knife. "You know, I think if everything goes smoothly, we could be out of here by tomorrow morning."

"Let's hope," I agreed, and we jogged back toward the church.

Twelve: Take necessary precautions.

"One...two...three...four!" Calvin's voice reverberates off the sides of every house around us.

I move through the formation to his count.

"One!"

I duck. This move is to evade zombie claws, which are generally the first attack.

"Two!"

I roll to the side—further evasion. Calvin says direction doesn't matter, but I always end up rolling left.

"Three!"

I spring into a loose crouch, drawing my knife as I come up. This one took a few tries to master. Calvin made me use a stick before using a real knife, which at first offended me greatly ("What am I, six?"). But after I stabbed myself in the leg with the stick a few times, I was grudgingly thankful for the training wheels.

"Four!"

I swing my leg to take the imaginary assailant out at the knees. Calvin insists I use my right and left legs alternately so as to attain equal skill with both.

"One!"

This form was easy to memorize, albeit not so easy to complete smoothly. I swear Calvin made it up on the spot when I asked him to show me how to fight like him. But even still, this is an almost foolproof routine for maximum zombie kills and minimal injury.

Suddenly, Calvin holds up a fist, signaling for me to stop.

"Got one on your nine," he says.

He doesn't make a move or even touch his knives.

My hand is barely around my axe before a skinny grandma zombie grabs at my arm. It misses, its fingers hooking into the hair tie at the end of my braid and snapping it. Damn it, that was my last one! I stumble-jump backward as it closes in, nearly falling on my ass.

"Cate!" Calvin booms. "One!"

Right! Duck. Okay. Duck, roll, crouch, swing. The zombie is on the ground in seconds. It begins to sit up, snarling, reaching for me, and is met with an axe to the forehead. I yank the axe back (with one hand!) and wipe the blade of my axe on her—its—blue-and-green dress. My mom had that same dress. She wore it on her last birthday, unintentionally matching the cake we'd bought for her. My gut twists and my eyes prickle.

In four, out eight.

It takes me a second to stand back up.

"One!" Calvin shouts as soon as I'm standing.

"Hang on a minute," I call to him, holding up a hand. I tug Marco's jacket off and lay it gently over the banister of a nearby porch. "Hot," I lie. He doesn't need to know about the dress or my reaction to it. I whip around as fast as I can into a loose crouch and tuck my wayward hair behind my ear. "Okay. Ready."

Calvin eyes me with disapproval and a hint of *are you kidding me?*

"This is not about your comfort, kid… One. Two. Three. Four! You think those undead assholes will stop trying to kill you because you're a little warm? Use your fucking head!"

"Calvin. Language!"

"Sorry, Nana. Cate, remember this—survival is priority. One. Two. Three. Four! Next comes sustenance, shelter, loved ones, and about a hundred other things before comfort. Next time you stop for anything less than a zombie invasion, it'll be knots all night. Got me? One. Two. Three. Four!"

I hate knots. The tedium makes my brain numb.

He takes a knee.

"Foul!" I cry, springing back to my feet. "You just got on me about comfort two seconds ago and you're kneeling?"

"Tell you what," Calvin says without moving, "when a shark removes your leg from your body, you rest all you want. Now, lose the entitlement or you get knots until your fingers bleed."

"Seriously? A shark?"

"One. Two. Three. Four!"

Duck, roll, eye roll, crouch—almost eat it—swing.

I know he wouldn't make me do them until my fingers literally bleed; that only happened the one time, and really it was the nasty hangnail that did it. But he'd absolutely have me tying and untying rope, twine, and my least favorite, fishing line, for hours.

We crossed the California border a week after my birthday. I didn't even realize it had passed until I looked at my watch on November 13. I was glad it had slipped by unnoticed. The only memory that day lends itself to now is one I'm trying to stuff deep down into my unconscious, one that keeps clawing its way desperately back to the forefront of both my waking thoughts and my dreams. It doesn't need any help being remembered.

To hell with that day.

We're in a little beach town called Trinidad now. It was a slight detour, but we were low on supplies. We found this little old restaurant on the ocean with a café inside. Much to Mel's dismay, every last coffee bean had already been pilfered. I guess caffeine is a valuable commodity in an apocalypse. Or would it be *the* apocalypse?

After we (Mel and Mae) decided to spend a second night in Trinidad, I started to feel a familiar restless twitch. Calvin must have noticed, because he insisted we put the time to good use. I have to say, passing the time with a little training has been a lot better for my mental health than glancing at my watch every fourteen seconds for the next however long. Speaking of.

"One. Two. Three. Four!"

Duck. Roll. Crouch—I try to sneak a glance at my watch, resulting in a sloppy swing.

"One, two, three, four!" His count quickens when he notices my attention straying.

I match pace.

Mae watches from nearby as usual. She tosses the ball to Chaz and clasps her hands together. "My stars, Cate, if I hadn't been here these past weeks watching you, I'd swear you've been at it for years!"

I grin through my roll.

"One, two, three, four!" Calvin says with a little edge in his voice.

I execute near perfection.

He's very serious when we're training, doesn't approve of distraction, but he'd never argue with his nana.

"One, two, three, four! Get lower, Cate. If you're not flying under the radar, you're liable to get eaten."

Lower duck, roll, crouch, swing.

I know he's right. Most of a zombie's attacks are straight-on, which means the lower I get, the less likely I am to get hurt.

"One two three four! Get lower, Cate. Fly under the radar."

Low-low-duck, roll, crouch, swing. My legs burn.

"Lower! One two three four! Onetwothreefour!"

On the last four-count, I lose my balance and tumble.

"Cal," I call when I regain a vertical posture, "nobody can go that fast. And how low am I supposed to get? My ass was nearly touching dirt!"

"Language!"

"Gimme a break, Mel!" I pick the sticks and leaves out of my tangled mane.

"You'll get a break when you show me some gumption, kid," he shoots back, zipping up his jacket.

I huff, embarrassingly loud, trying to catch my breath. We've been at it for weeks. We started small with things like different ways to establish a perimeter and which everyday objects could be used as weapons in a pinch (rocks, sticks, even the metal buckle on my belt if correctly wielded). Then we got tactical—how to evade a predator if I suddenly find myself without access to a weapon. How to remain unseen if there are unfamiliar people in the vicinity. How to signal from a distance with smoke or mirrors, even a well-shined coin.

He still won't tell us where he got his training, and Mae, always with a mysterious wisp of a smile, swears she has no idea. It almost doesn't matter, though. Who we were before everything ended, what we did, none of it matters except the skills that might be useful now. Mel's medical training and Calvin's survivalist training are at the top of that very short list. I often wonder what I bring to the table other than my mediocre fighting skills.

"All right, soldiers," says Mel, "it's time we head out."

"You got it, baby," says Calvin. He hefts the largest of the three packs over his shoulders and helps Mae into the trailer. Chaz crawls into the space next to her and curls up with his head in her lap.

As I walk by the trailer, Mae grabs my hand.

"You just ignore that old stick in the mud," she stage-whispers. "By the time we get to Alcatraz, I expect to see you whoop his behind."

Calvin takes the lead, hitching the trailer to his bike first. We're through Trinidad and back on the highway in seconds. Outside the protection of the houses, the biting winter wind howls in my ears and whips my hair around my face. I keep my gaze down directly in front of me. I almost don't see Calvin pull off to the side.

"Hey!" he calls over the roar. He says something else, but his words are snapped away.

Mel shakes her head, looks at me, shrugs, and veers off toward him.

I growl under my breath. This had better be worth it.

It is so worth it. Parked off to the side of the road, nearly concealed by fallen branches and debris, is a small RV.

Though I can't hear her, I clearly see Mel's mouth say "Oh my God" just before she heaves off her bike and gives Calvin a neck-wringing hug.

I practically cry with relief; I can't think of a more welcome sight. While Mel gives the engine a cursory once-over, Calvin and I take care of the three zombies inside. As we're dragging out the last one, the wind dies down. With my eyes suddenly free of hair, I notice a band of black elastic around its wrist. I slide the hair tie off the dead wrist and tie my own rat's nest into a ponytail. *Finally.* The way it's been living in my eyes and mouth for the last several miles, my hair was in very real danger of being shaved off tonight.

When I look up, Calvin is eyeing me with what looks like a squeamish face. "Are you, uh...taking that?" he asks, wrinkling his eyebrows.

I shrug. "My last one broke. And it's not like she's gonna need it."

"You guys ready?" says Mel as she slams the hood closed. "I did what I could, but this heap is seconds from breaking down permanently, so we'd better get going."

We all pile in, tying our bikes to the top, which Calvin makes me do with a semiserious "No pressure, but it's on you if we lose the bikes."

Despite the frigid cold, we keep the windows open.

The road south is relatively deserted. There are more zombies than there were in the forest, some just aimlessly wandering the way zombies do (more slowly now that it's cold), some chowing down on a recent kill. We raid a few convenience stores along the highway, mainly looking for food, which is getting scarce. There are more shops in Eureka than on the highway, only some of them useful. We hit up a grocery store that's mostly picked over but still has a few boxes of macaroni (and only a couple of zombies). There are lots of places we don't even bother to stop at—a huge apartment complex, a sandwich shop with about ten zombies inside, a Chinese restaurant with no windows that we decide isn't worth the risk, and a novelty gift shop with a display of red flannel blankets and Thanksgiving decorations in the window.

Just outside Eureka, we hit another roadblock. There's a collective groan as we unload our aching, frozen bodies from the slightly warmer interior of the van and take down the bikes. Chaz whines before climbing rigidly into his trailer and curling up into a shivering ball. Mae hugs him tight, but she's freezing too.

"Hang on a minute," I say, and I ride back to the last little shop we passed by, the novelty gift store. I pull one of the red flannel blankets from the display and then one more for good measure.

"Thank you, Cate," Mae murmurs as she takes one and tucks the thick flannel around herself.

Chaz licks my face as I lean over him to wrap the other around his body. When they're both tucked in, they're nothing but a couple of heads sticking out of a bright-red blob.

"Well, that's adorable," says Mel.

"It is, isn't it?" I say. I dig my phone out of my pack and turn it on. Forty-seven percent. "Smile," I say as I snap a picture.

Snow falls delicately as we ride through the roadblock. In front of me, Mae's little hand sticks out the side of the trailer. I smile as I realize that she's trying to catch a snowflake. I get Mel's attention and point.

"I didn't think it snowed this far south," says Mel as we carefully pedal through the thickening slush. "Weird that it's happening now."

"End of the world." I shrug. "All the emissions and stuff suddenly stopping had to have some impact."

"Whatever it is, it's sure pretty."

"We need to get inside," Calvin calls back to us. "Snow's not stopping anytime soon."

We duck into the next building we pass, a little mom-and-pop place just off the highway. Its windows are plastered with flyers for various services and lessons, the better for concealment from anyone—dead or alive—that might wander by. But in truth, we see far fewer living people than one would expect. We come upon the occasional former campsite, a pile of ashes that was recently a fire, or maybe a sleeping bag or two left behind in a hasty escape. But as far as actual, living people, we've only seen a handful of them, and we never make our presence known.

Inside, the little shop is bare of anything really useful. We don't bother to take our shoes off; we'll be gone as soon as the weather permits. I raid a few shelves, finding nothing but some stale candy, which of course I help myself to. Then I see a familiar object, just one, green and rectangular with the words "spearmint * sugar-free" written on the front in cursive white lettering.

I trace one edge with my finger and pick it up gingerly, imagining that maybe Marco came through this way, and that at some point recently he was holed up in this same little shop. I immediately dismiss the notion. If he came through here, there would be no gum left. I pocket the pack, wondering if he even made it this far.

Behind me, the bathroom door slams shut.

"Mel?" says Calvin. He looks at me and we both shrug.

"I'm sure she's fine," I offer. Even so, the hairs on the back of my neck stand up. This is the second time this week Mel has been sick.

Three long minutes later, she comes out, searches the aisles, and darts back into the bathroom and slams the door.

Mae sits behind the cash register on a stool, reading a year-old Sunday paper. Chaz, relishing his time out of the trailer, alternates between sitting outside the locked bathroom door and rolling his ball back and forth up the aisles. Neither of them seem worried.

"I miss reading the funnies," says Mae when I sit on the counter next to her and Chaz. "They were my favorite part of the Sunday paper. Calvin used to sit on my lap, and we'd read them together over oatmeal and chocolate milk. That's how I taught him to read." She smiles over the paper at

Calvin, who is still standing vigil outside the bathroom door. He smiles back distractedly. "His favorite was that little boy with the tiger." She watches Calvin for a long minute. "Melody will be fine. All this stress isn't good for a person, that's all. But she'll be just fine in no time. Just get her some water and a sports drink if you can find one. She needs electrolytes. Yellow, not the sugary kinds."

"Thanks, Mae," I say as I spring up, grateful for something to do with myself.

Calvin knocks softly on the bathroom door.

"Mel," he calls, "how are you feeling?"

"I'm okay, I'm...I'm—" Her words are cut short by gagging and vomiting sounds.

Liar.

"Mel, can I come in?" I ask. "Do you need anything?"

"No!" she shouts. "No, stay there. I'm coming out."

When one of us was sick before, Mom would send us to bed with chicken soup and make us take handfuls of vitamins and drink gallons of tea. I begin to scan the aisles for boxes of tea with no real idea of what kind to give to a sick person or if this is even a sickness that tea would help. I say a silent prayer to my mom or whomever is listening.

I can't do this alone. I don't know what to do. Let her be okay.

The bathroom door opens, and Mel comes out. She doesn't look that sick anymore, which is a relief. But her face is...if I didn't know better I'd say panic-stricken. Like she just walked into a bathroom full of zombies with no weapon. I look down and notice she's holding a thin white something in her hand. She sees me looking and holds it up for me to see.

It has two little windows, one with one blue line and one with two.

No way.

"Oh!" Mae hops off her stool and shuffles over to Mel. "Melody, come here and let me hug you!"

Calvin looks from Mel to me, visibly flustered. "What's going on?"

"It's a pregnancy test," Mel whispers over Mae's shoulder. "I'm pregnant."

Thirteen: It's never just a scratch.

"I still think it's a bullshit plan," Gary snorted.

"If it's a prison we need," said Uncle Frank, "Coyote Ridge is right up the road. What makes Alcatraz any better?"

"Coyote Ridge isn't quite the same, Frank," Tess gently explained.

"Oh yeah? How?"

"For one, it's highly unlikely any inmates were released in the chaos of the initial outbreak," said Marco, "so best-case scenario, we have a prison full of zombies to deal with. Worst-case, there are survivors. Dangerous survivors. Alcatraz is well stocked, probably free of people, and it's surrounded by water."

No one could deny that the benefits outweighed, but the main drawback—getting there safely—seemed impossible to reconcile. Most of them regarded the new outside world with trepidation, and who could blame them? The majority of them had been holed up there since the beginning, making them uniquely sheltered from zombie contact.

The topic of zombies as a matter of fact had been another hard pill to swallow, even after we told everyone who would listen about our experience before Connell: Mrs. Minkin on Halloween; my birthday. My lungs refused to inflate when Bill recounted what had happened to my parents. And even after they heard every grim detail, some of Rob's people remained unconvinced.

"Idiots," Mel whispered as the arguing continued. "They're like sheep, all terrified and huddled in the back of their pen." She shook her head in disgust. "They're all going to die."

Hearing Mel—sweet, sunny Mel—talk that way gave me shivers unimaginable.

"But we're safe here," one of the sheep said from the back of the church. "We have food and water...guns too. Why would we leave?"

Gary picked that moment to speak up, the asshole.

"Exactly! I've seen what's out there, you guys." He addressed the church as a whole, stepping toward the center of the group and raising his hand dramatically to his chest. "And let me tell you something. It's ugly, really ugly. In here, we are *safe*. Why would we risk that for a *pipe dream* like Alcatraz?"

Before I knew what I was doing, I was across the room with my hand clamped around Gary's upper arm. I yanked it roughly, making him face me, digging my fingers in and secretly hoping that it hurt.

"Because soon enough it'll all run out," I seethed. "What then?"

Gary's face went red. He yanked his arm away from me and stalked outside. We both knew what he was doing, rallying people to his cause with fearmongering. *I see you, Gary.*

I turned to everyone.

"The food will run out first, maybe the water. Either way, once you start going out to get more supplies, your ammo will go, a *lot* more quickly than you think it will. And guns are useless, by the way, *useless* unless you get a clean head shot. And even if you do by some miracle manage to kill one zombie with *every single shot* you take, every shot fired will draw more and more." I could tell I was starting to get through to them, but I wasn't done. The metallic, acrid tastes of pain and rage mingled on my dry tongue, and I could feel my heart pounding in my chest and my ears and my head. "Hell, one shot or loud voice or slammed door or light shining or anything that attracts their attention could bring on a full-blown rampage! Don't you people *get it yet*? Even with all of the food and water and guns in the *world*, they are relentless. They don't sleep; they can't be hurt or deterred. Once they get a mind to claw their way in here, for any reason, they won't stop until they're eating someone or dead. I watched zombies kill my parents. They didn't stand a chance. And do you know what attracted all of those zombies? A goddamned window broke."

My voice cracked hard on the word "window." Hot tears spilled down my cheeks. Mel's arm was suddenly around me. I let her lead me toward the rest of our family.

People mumbled under their breath, shifting and looking sideways at one another. They were clearly afraid. Good.

But by noon, most of them had decided to stay. The people who had elected to go gathered at the front of the church to make a departure plan for the next day.

"First, we need able fighters," said Marco. "Ideally, half the group at least."

I raised my hand, as did Mel, Gary (ha!), Bill, Tess, Frank, and one woman and three men from the church whose names I hadn't caught.

"Okay, great. The rest of you will be in charge of carrying the bulk of the load. We'll all carry, but this will keep the fighters unencumbered. Bill, Tess, can you get what you can from Pastor John and divvy it up? Great, thanks. We'll also need to find, ah—" He counted silently. "—eight more bikes. If we all look, we'll find them in no time. We should make time to practice hand-to-hand. Cate, Mel, would you assist?"

Mel and I nodded.

"Then it's set. Here—" He reached into his backpack, pulled out the maps, and passed them out. "I've drawn out a route in case anyone should get separated from the group. We'll establish a basic buddy system, with the exception being Bruce's family."

The guy with a wife and two kids—the only kids coming with us—nodded as he took a map.

I sneaked a glance at Mel, who had a ghost of a smile on her hollow face for the first time since home. There was hope.

"Guys?" I said, scrambling to find my phone in my pile of stuff. "Can I take a picture of everyone please?"

Everyone shuffled into a few neat rows as I propped my phone up on the podium and set the timer. "Thirty seconds!" I called. I jogged to the place Mel had saved for me, trying hard to bury the bitter resentment that my parents were not there.

"Are you scared, Ryan?" Bruce's little girl asked her older brother.

"No. Fear is the path to the dark side."

"Well, I'm afraid," she muttered.

"I find your lack of faith disturbing."

"You're such a dweeb."

"One thing's for sure," Uncle Bill chimed in. "We're all going to be a lot thinner."

Amid groans and giggles, the shutter clicked.

By midafternoon the next day, we had divided stuff, packed, even trained a little, and found six bikes in the surrounding neighborhood; we were just waiting on Frank and Bill, who would hopefully return with the last two.

They came back around an hour after the rest of us. They'd found the bikes.

"It got a little hairy out there," Bill said. "Frank had a run-in with one of them. He's okay."

Frank stumbled in, fanning himself with his cowboy hat. A bead of sweat rolled down his bald head. Lucy sat next to him.

"Just kept comin' at me," he huffed. "Relentless, that's the truth. Bill saved my ass. Almost managed the whole thing without a scratch."

My stomach dropped.

Almost?

I felt the tension crackle to life, electric and buzzing, like the air before a lightning storm. Everyone was suddenly very restless, except Frank and Lucy.

"What does he mean, *almost*?" Tess hissed at Bill.

Bill's eyes widened.

"I didn't know," he said, panic in his voice. "It looked like a close call, but I thought he managed to get away in time."

"What's the problem?" Lucy pulled up Frank's sleeve and turned his arm over. "You mean this little thing?"

Frank let out a loud gunshot of a laugh. "Ha!" He slapped his knee. "I've injured myself worse trippin' on a shoelace."

No one said anything at first. Then Gary stepped forward and drew a gun, which until now none of us had known he had. Wonder who he filched that from.

"Sorry, Uncle Frank," he said, and pointed the gun at Frank's head.

"Gary!" Lucy cried out. "What do you think you're doing?"

"He's infected, Aunt Lucy," Gary answered without moving except for his shaking hand. He cocked the hammer. "There's no cure. This is the only way."

Tess placed a hand on Gary's arm.

"Gary, lower it. You're scaring people."

"This is the only way," Gary repeated. "You know that's true!"

"*Put the gun down*!" Bill roared, getting the attention of most of the parishioners. He looked around, mortified, and grabbed the gun out of Gary's hand. "We will *talk* about this outside. Like normal people."

The six of us filed outside, leaving Lucy and Frank inside.

"You know I'm right, Dad," Gary said as soon as we were outside. His tone was plaintive, a kid who knows he's in trouble. "He's as good as dead already."

"Stop it, Gary!" Tess yelled.

"There's no cure, Mom!" Gary yelled back. "You're living in a dream world!"

We argued for about half an hour, mostly Gary and Bill taking turns shouting. Tess cried, went on about the possibility of a cure that we just didn't know about yet. After all, she'd said, we were in the country. There was bound to be someone somewhere in a bigger city who could help us.

"There probably isn't a cure," Marco said quietly. "I'm sorry. Frank isn't going to be around much longer, and when he goes, we'll have to...take care of it. Before he comes back."

He looked at me. "You should go inside and spend whatever time you have left with him. Prepare your aunt if you can. When the time comes—"

He was interrupted by a shout from inside.

Lucy.

"Tess!" she shouted. "Tess!"

Inside, Frank was lying on the floor with his head in Lucy's lap. He was as pale as a sheet, his skin slicked with sweat.

"He has a fever," she whimpered. "He's burning up."

"Get him some water, Cate," Mel instructed.

I did. He drank a little, thanked me, and laid his head back down.

"What's wrong with him?" Lucy asked all of us.

I gave Gary a look that said *shut up*, and I explained it as delicately as I could—necrotic wounds (pointing out his now blackening wound and surrounding veins), fever, death. Reanimation. But how delicately can you explain that to a sixty-five-year-old woman? She didn't want to hear it. Just shook her head and stroked his face. We left them alone, all in silent agreement to keep a close eye.

Marco waited at the far side of the church with the other parishioners, who were now openly watching the scene unfold. I think he probably felt out of place with us. But I knew without asking that when the time came, he'd be there.

The fever took Frank in minutes.

"Gotta get up, Luce," said Tess gently, offered her sister a hand, and led her away. Then she murmured to Bill, "Do we bury him or—?"

"You still have to, you know," muttered Marco apologetically. I hadn't even seen him come over.

"I'll do it," Gary offered.

"Okay, psycho," Mel whispered loudly to me.

"All right," said Bill, "over here with this." He herded the family toward the back door.

"*Because*," Gary continued, "none of you girls should have to do it, and I hardly knew him."

"You came here every summer!"

"Okay, *Melody*, I'm trying to do a service here."

"Whoever does it, it needs to be now," Marco said, stepping between Mel and Gary. "Let's take Frank outside and decide—Tess!"

A sudden hot spray erupted over my face.

Blood?

Then Mel screamed.

Fourteen: Plans change. Roll with it.

Spring has sprung in northern California. The corpses have thawed; the world smells like flowers and rot. And there's something in my eye. It feels like a grain of sand the size of Wisconsin is lodged between my upper eyelid and cornea and is slowly, steadily working its way through. I blink furiously, which only exacerbates it.

"Mel," I call, stopping the convoy of bikes. "Something in my eye."

She rides back to me. "Seriously?"

"Just look, will you?" I pull my eyelid away from my eyeball.

She looks for a millisecond and shrugs. "Nope, don't see anything."

"Well, it's in there and it's killing me. Gimme some water to rinse it out."

"No way, Cate! This is all we have until we find more." She takes a swig and puts the bottle back into her bottle holder without offering me any. "Just blink a lot. And keep your dirty fingers out of it! Your body will produce the tears necessary to reject the foreign object."

She tosses her ponytail over her shoulder, turns around, and rides back to the front of the convoy.

I mimic her haughty tone under my breath. "Blink a lot, bleh, foreign object, ooh." Ever since she got pregnant, she has been extra rude. "How long until the baby's here?" I ask pointedly, hoping she'll get the hint.

"About twenty to twenty-two weeks."

Swing and a miss.

That's another obnoxious habit she's picked up. She measures time in weeks instead of months now. No explanation, no reason, just suddenly the second she knew she was pregnant, it started happening. Mae (who insists that Mel and I call her "Nana" now that we're going to be a family) does it too, though it's admittedly a thousand percent less annoying coming from her.

"What's the date, Cate?" Mae calls back to me from the trailer.

I pedal up so I can see her. She's adorable in a sweet-old-lady sort of way, all cozied up with Chaz in the little trailer, stroking his ears just the way he likes.

"April nineteenth."

She stretches her hands over her head.

"That was the longest winter of my life. There was this one winter in Mississippi. Charlie got frostbite. Don't ask where. But this year, there were a couple times there when I thought we might well and truly freeze to death."

Winter was harsh and cruel, almost as bad as last year even though we were considerably farther south. The zombies had all but frozen by January, but the real danger in the winter isn't zombies. It's exposure. We spent January and February in an abandoned barn by the Oregon border, just trying not to freeze to death.

"Ain't that the truth," Calvin mumbles. "That old barn saved our asses. Even with those ten—"

"Twelve," I correct him.

"Twelve zombies we had to put down, that barn was worth it. How long were we in there?"

"Eight and a half weeks," says Mel.

I have to actively stop myself from smacking her as I ride by.

"So in normal people time, about two months."

"Remember before the barn? How many days in a row did we eat crackers and questionable berries?" asks Mel.

"Too many," answers Calvin.

"I was this close to eating dog food," I say.

Calvin chuckles. "I think we were all pretty close to eating dog food at one point or another. It's not ideal, but it will probably get you through in a pinch."

"What about pee?" I ask. "Those survivalists on television are always drinking their own pee."

"As dehydration progresses, toxin-to-water ratio increases. So you're kind of slowly poisoning yourself if you do it more than once."

"So no?"

"Only in the most dire circumstances."

"Did your circumstances ever get that dire?"

Calvin side-eyes me as he rides past. "Once," he says, "in Madagascar."

"I am never kissing you again," says Mel.

We've moved at a decent pace since we left the barn. We're in some neighborhood of a town in northern California now, just passing through.

"Let's try these ones over here," says Calvin, pointing to a neat little cul-de-sac of nearly identical houses. "Remember—"

"Water is top priority," I finish his spiel for him, "food second, and meds if we see any."

"Right. Cate, you're with me. Nana, Melody, keep an eye out. Call us if you see something. Only fight if you can't run and—"

"Don't use the guns." Mae places a hand on his arm. "Calvin, we know. Let's go."

Mel nods and unconsciously rests a bony hand on her belly. With her other hand, she adjusts her glasses, wiggling them around and peering through them like an owl. It's times like this, when she's not measuring anything in weeks or acting like queen of everything, that I find her particularly endearing.

We move toward the first house as a silent unit. There are no immediately apparent noises or movements inside, so that's a good sign. The door is ajar, though. Calvin pushes it open slowly and creeps inside.

"Looks clear," he says after a second.

"Got six on our six," Mel whispers.

Calvin and I both utter a quiet expletive as we turn. Sure enough, six zombies in varying stages of decay are coming around the corner.

"Far enough to run from?" I ask Calvin.

"Nowhere to run," he mumbles. "Damn cul-de-sacs. Get inside," he calls to Mae and Mel as the zombies close in.

We hop off the porch and fight them off one by one—crushing, stabbing, shoving, decapitating, splitting skulls. I lodge my axe into the crown of one of the last ones—a freshie that was recently a paunchy little old man—and try to yank it loose, finding that I can't.

"Cover me!" I yell.

He continues to deal with the remaining two, shouting at Mel to go back inside when she scrambles out of the house with her hammer drawn.

I finally dislodge my axe and stand, panting, just in time to see Calvin dispatching the final zombie with a quick blow to the base of the skull. It drops and he looks over at me, smirking a little.

"Good timing, kid."

I stick my tongue out as I wipe my axe on the bottom of my shoe and yank my pants up. "Check yourself," I shoot back. "By my count, that was three-three. Which means I managed as many as you even with my—"

A scream erupts from inside the house. We run full speed to the front door, throw it open, and find Mel on the ground, crying, barely keeping off a zombie that has her utterly pinned. Her hammer and tiny pocketknife are across the room, presumably knocked out of her hand when the zombie bowled her over. Mae is beating the thing over the head and back with what seems to be an iron candlestick, not deterring it at all. Chaz growls ferociously from the corner he's hiding in.

"Nana, move!" Cal bellows. He wraps one arm around the zombie's neck, yanks it off Mel with one quick, angry jerk, and smashes its head against the hardwood floor until it stops moving (that's another thing about zombies that you wouldn't know until you found out the hard way—their heads don't just squish like watermelons if you stomp on them or throw them on the ground; their skulls are just as thick as ours, so it takes a fair amount of effort—at least a few good whacks—to thoroughly crush a zombie head).

It all happens in a matter of a few seconds: the scream, the bust-in, the kill. Then we're all standing around the lifeless corpse, Mae and Mel wiping frightened tears away, Calvin practically breathing steam through his flared nostrils, and me with my mouth wide open.

"That zombie..." Mel stands, shaking. "Its eyes were *normal*. Brown, like mine. When it first came down the stairs, I swore it looked at me. I thought it was a person. It moved so...human. Didn't make that sound either. And I couldn't be sure, but when it saw me, I swear it *ran* at me. They don't run, though, do they?"

She looks around at each of us, waiting for an answer.

Calvin and I glance at each other, and I'm sure he's remembering the little-boy zombie we saw in Kerby, the one with blue eyes that definitely ran at me.

But instead of answering Mel's question, Calvin says something I never would have seen coming.

"We're not going to Alcatraz."

I'm stunned for a beat before I formulate my one-word reply. "What?"

"You heard me," says Calvin. "We're not going. Things like this are only going to keep happening the longer we're on the road."

I'm not sure if he meant things like the running zombie or zombies in general. But I'm not having it.

"What the hell do you mean, we aren't going?" I shout, throwing my hands in the air.

"Cate," Mel chides me.

I ignore her. "Alcatraz is our best chance of escaping things like this! It's our only shot at a real life!"

Calvin raises his voice too. "Cate, I said we aren't going. It isn't safe and you know it. Please, think about someone other than yourself for one damn minute! Think about Melody!"

"Were you thinking about my sister when you knocked her up in the middle of the fucking apocalypse?" I yell, and feel guilty immediately. That was a low blow.

"Stop!" Mel yells a bit more loudly than either Calvin or me. "Cal, honey. Alcatraz has always been our plan."

"Since before we met you."

"So—" Mel gives me a look. "—if you want to talk about changing the plan, that's fine. But you can't just change it."

"We can't talk about it either," I say, crossing my arms. "It's not up for negotiation."

Calvin squares off, something I know he only does when he's feeling pretty threatened.

"That's my woman and my baby. We're family now, and it's my job to keep you safe."

"Your job?" I practically shriek. "Please, keep your testosterone to yourself. We've had this plan since way before we met you. We've had close calls before. It's fine. We're fine. We have to keep going."

Calvin finally starts all-out yelling. "Fine? You're fine? Mel can't keep this up, Cate! She's weak! Five months ago, she'd have had that thing dead in two seconds! You know I'm right!"

Chaz barks and paces around the room. I lower my gaze and breathe as quietly as I can, counting. In four, out eight.

Calvin lowers his voice. "You can keep going, Cate, but you'll be alone."

Mel looks at both of us, her eyes pleading. "Cate? You're not going to go, are you?" Huge, fat pregnancy-tears start rolling down her cheeks.

I think for a second, weighing my options. Then I sigh. "No...no, Mel, of course not." I'd never leave her, not in a thousand years. Even if it means giving up on Alcatraz, the one thing that's been keeping me sane, at times keeping me alive, I can't leave Mel.

She smiles, a sad, apologetic smile, and rests one hand on my arm and one hand on her slightly swollen abdomen. "At least until the baby's born. Believe me, I won't be weak forever. As soon as I'm me again, we'll get back on the road. Okay?"

She looks up at Calvin, who gives a curt nod. When I don't say anything, she looks at me.

"Fine."

"Now that that's settled," Mae calls as she comes back into the living room. None of us noticed her leaving. She's wearing a *Kiss the Cook* apron that was made for a much larger person. It nearly touches the floor. "Let's eat a real supper. I found herbs and spices and enough food to feed us all like kings tonight!"

The next day, we ride south again. Not to Alcatraz, though. Not anymore. Now we search for a shelter that can house us all safely for now. We spend six days checking every abandoned structure we find for viability. We move very slowly in doing so, but I guess it doesn't matter now. None of the places we find suit our long-term needs until we find a cement building, some sort of small warehouse, on the southeastern outskirts of Santa Rosa on the seventh day. It has only one south-facing window and two doors. There's even a small creek that runs right along the north side of the building. I hate to admit it, but the place is perfect.

We kill and burn the three zombies that are inside, one of which has human eyes that look right at us, and spend our first night in the new fortress talking about what we know of the human-eyed zombies, which we have taken to calling Abnormals.

"So you guys saw one in Kerby?" Mel asks, sounding a little offended that we didn't share that information earlier.

"A little boy," I say between shoveling bites of canned corn into my face. "It had blue eyes. And it ran, just like the one in the house."

"So they have some higher level of motor function then," Mel muses. "Interesting. Maybe it's some mutation of the virus. You think?"

Calvin shrugs.

"Either way, I think it's safe to say we should keep an eye out for Abnormals. No matter why they are the way they are, it makes them a hell of a lot more dangerous."

The first morning, Calvin and I check the surrounding area for zombies and anything useful. The only thing we find is healthy soil. So while Calvin and Mel clean up the inside, Mae and I suss out the possibility of a garden. After all, if we're going to be stuck in the same place for a while, we may as well make it somewhat sustainable.

Mae crouches in the dirt and picks up a handful. "Soil's good," she mutters more to herself than to me. "Remember that feed store we saw on our way here? They probably have a seed selection. Doubt many people would've taken seeds." She looks up and smiles.

"We'll go on a run later today," I say absently. I'm only half paying attention. I'm also scanning the area around us. There was movement in some nearby bushes out of the corner of my eye a second ago, and I'm trying to find it.

Mae says something about planting season, but I can't make myself listen. Because right in front of me, in the bushes a hundred yards away, there's a person staring at Mae and me. At least I think he's a person. He could be another Abnormal. He's short and skinny, wearing a red shirt and black ball cap. He's not moving. He's just watching us. I turn to Mae to ask if she sees him too, but she's still chatting merrily away about squash or something. I turn back to the man, but he's not there anymore.

"Hold that thought, Nana," I say. Then I take off into the trees. But my search turns up nothing. There's no one out here. We're alone again.

Fifteen: When it hits the fan, stay calm.

Tess kept screaming, desperate and wordless and almost inhuman, a scream I've only ever heard from those being devoured by the dead.

"Tess!" Lucy fell to her knees, sobbing.

Bill shouted and lunged at his wife, trying to tear them apart, though he must have known it was too late. Tess's throat was a ruined red mess, and somehow her nose ring had been ripped out. The whole ten-second scene had a surreal quality: brighter colors but hazy lines. The blood on my skin burned like acid. I couldn't accept that it was happening again.

Bang!

Before anyone could stop him, Bill put down zombie-Frank with a single, well-aimed shot to the head. Brain matter splashed out the back of his skull.

Mel bent over and wretched.

It was instant pandemonium. People were running, screaming, trying to flee. Several more shots rang out for no reason from all around the room.

Bang! A window broke.

Bang! A chunk blew out of the giant crucifix.

Bang! A woman fell to the ground clutching her knee.

"Please stay calm!" Pastor John shouted over the din.

"Quiet," Mel said. "Everyone!"

"Shooting and screaming will only attract more," Marco pleaded.

Bang! Bang!

"No!"

Someone threw open the front door and half the parishioners spilled outside, straight into the approaching zombies. Some fought for life, taking a few down before they met their ultimate gruesome deaths, but most of them, unskilled and without useful weapons, were attacked and killed immediately. The half-human screams erupted from all over as people succumbed to zombies, life to death. And each death inevitably would add to the zombies' numbers.

My chest tightened; I couldn't make myself move or even breathe. How could this be happening again? *Was* there anything else, or would this be it? Was there a point? They were quickly multiplying and surrounding the building; pouring in through the door that had been left open. I stood there, defeated. Catatonic with fear.

"We have to go," Marco called over the din.

I heard him, saw him waving his arms. Didn't move.

"Cate!" Mel shook my shoulders. "Catherine! Where's Lucy? Come on. We don't have time for this now. You gotta move!"

I dropped to my knees.

"No," I whispered, so quietly I almost couldn't hear myself.

"No?" Mel's face was anger and confusion. But determination took over. She slapped me hard across the face, jerking me back to life. "Cate, we're getting out of here. You're all I have left. Get your ass up and *move!*"

The haze lifted. My will to live, or at least to live today, forced my feet under me. Mel let out a choked sob of relief, just one, as I stood up.

"Cate, Melody," Marco called. "Grab what you can and meet me out back. I'll clear a path. Go!"

Mel and I each took a pack and crammed in all the food, weapons, and medical supplies that we could find. When we got outside, Marco was nowhere to be seen. There was only one lone zombie on that side of the church. When it was within striking distance, Mel distracted it, and I struck the base of its skull. Adrenaline coursed through me, making me feel shaky, hypersensitive, and strong.

One more zombie ambled around the corner. I hardly had time to process what I was doing. In a split second, I was in front of the fallen corpse, yanking (or trying to yank) my axe out of its face.

At the exact moment I finally pulled the axe free, Gary, hero that he was, came up from wherever he'd run off to and yanked Mel's backpack out of her hand.

"It's all about surviving now," he said, and he took off down the street.

"Damn it! Gary, you asshole!" I yelled after him.

Mel didn't say anything.

Five more zombies wandered our way over the next few minutes, one by one except the time two came at once. By the time the fifth corpse fell, it was beginning to get dark. The temperature was dropping pretty rapidly. Now it really felt like November.

Mel buttoned her denim jacket over her hoodie.

"How long do we wait, before..."

Marco sprinted around the corner carrying a bulging backpack.

"Where's your uncle?" he asked.

Mel and I shrugged.

"Lucy?"

"We were hoping they were with you," I said.

"Gary?"

Mel scoffed.

"He stole Mel's pack and took off that way," I said bitterly. "Some crap about survival and then he was gone."

Marco just shook his head. "We have to go before—"

Somewhere nearby, Bill was yelling. Marco ran to the front of the church. We followed and found Bill surrounded by five zombies, swinging his hunting knife wildly. He stabbed one in the eye, then barely dodged the claws (because when you use them like that, there's no other name for them) of another. That one got it in the temple.

"Uncle Bill!" Mel shouted.

Marco looked back at us. "Cate, take Mel to the truck. Wait there. Get your bikes if you can. Run!"

I looked back at Bill, who was still managing but barely. And there were about ten more zombies headed that way.

"You need help!" I protested.

"Cate! I'll be fine. I'll get your uncle, and we'll meet you at the truck by the gas station. Please go. He needs me. *Go!*"

Mel and I ran a block before we stopped and turned around. Marco had run straight into the mob that surrounded my uncle. He took three down in as many seconds. But more were coming, so many more. He turned and looked at me. He opened his mouth; was he saying something? I couldn't hear anything over the growling moaning bedlam. I blinked, and he was gone, disappearing into a throng of the undead.

I turned around to face my sister.

"We have to go back," I said. "Mel, they need us!"

Mel grabbed me by the arms. "No. We are not fighters. We can handle a couple, but that's more than a dozen! Marco and Uncle Bill can handle themselves. They'll meet us at the truck just like he said. But we have to go." She pushed her glasses up the bridge of her nose. "Now, show me where the truck is."

I nodded and led her in the right direction.

"Does it run?" she asked when we found it.

"I dunno. We never tried."

"We'll wait for Marco and Uncle Bill. Then I'll hot-wire it."

"You know how to do that?" I asked, trying not to sound too shocked.

Mel let a teeny-tiny smile tug at one side of her mouth.

"Remember Gabriel?"

Of course, I did; I remembered all of them. Mel's bad taste in guys was legendary. I shrugged. "Yes?"

"I saw him do it once or twice. Okay, a lot. And if I can't, I bet Marco can."

"What does that mean?" I asked as I opened the tailgate and we both sat.

"It means, you know, foster kids...just a hunch."

"Jesus, Mel," I said. "Way to generalize."

She clicked her tongue. "Cate. Language."

"Shut up."

But neither Marco nor Bill made it to the truck. After a couple of hours, probably because she knew I'd never make the choice on my own, Mel made the call.

"We have a map of the route to Alcatraz, and so do they," she said gently, fitting two exposed wires together. "If they survived, they'll stick to that route. We'll find them, Cate. We will. But we have to keep ourselves safe. It's time to go."

So we drove west for a few hours until we found Highway 101, which was mercifully clear as far as we could tell, and then we drove south.

Sixteen: Helping people is inherently risky.

We're surrounded. Someone is yelling at me to run. But my backpack and limbs are too heavy and the air too thick. Suddenly, I'm standing across the road as the zombies close in around Marco and Bill. I can't make my feet move; they're sinking slowly into the road, which has begun to melt. I open my mouth to call to them, to tell them I'm coming, but the words are mercilessly shoved back into my throat by an unseen force. I can't move. I can't speak. I can only watch as the corpses stumble toward them, the only family Mel and I have left.

"Cate, come on!" Mel takes my hand. She's shouting in my ear, but the sound is muted, deadened. Like I'm hearing it from underwater.

Then everything slows down. My uncle brandishes his knife, desperately slashing whatever he can, making one lethal hit in ten. A zombie that can only be Samantha dashes toward Bill, Abnormal speed. Marco kills one, two, three, six zombies on his way through the horde, but not her. I have to help them, but I can't move! My backpack seems to double in weight, pressing me down into a crouch.

My feet keep sinking into the sidewalk. It swallows my shoes, my ankles, my legs to the knees. Marco turns his face back as Mel pulls on my arm feebly. He opens his mouth to speak, but the snarling gargle of the undead crescendos until it's all I can hear.

I open my eyes, still trying to run from the nightmare. I can't move my legs! My heart thunders in my chest, and my stomach tightens into a knot. I sit up in a panic, thrashing my limbs, trying to escape the liquid cement. But it isn't cement; it's my blanket twisted tightly around my legs. Even after I push it off, my breath comes in ragged, shallow draws. Tears waterfall down my cheeks as I struggle to regain control against the waves of terror crashing over me.

Sam, my Sam!

Where's Bill? Marco?

Where am I?

I calm my breathing and try to take in my surroundings: a dark room, a table and two chairs behind me.

In four, out eight.

My pulse is pounding in my ears. There's a rocking chair with two missing legs lying on its side in the far corner; a fruit crate that will soon serve as a bassinet. Through the only window I can see a hundred stars in the black sky outside.

In four, out eight.

I blink and let my eyes adjust. I'm in the warehouse. Of course I am.

And Sam could be anywhere. Anywhere but here.

And Bill and Marco are gone.

Mel, Calvin, and Mae sleep soundly around me in a chorus of snores and deep breathing. Mae sleeps curled around Chaz on a pile of old pillows. Calvin sleeps on his back with Mel's head resting on his shoulder. Her round belly is pressed against his side. He pets her long flaxen hair unconsciously. It looks silver in the dark. She entangles her fingers in his new beard.

He stopped shaving after Mel's close encounter with the Abnormal, the day we decided to postpone Alcatraz. When I asked him why a few days later (it took me that long to speak to him again), he said, "I've come to find shaving to be a waste of time." I think what he really meant was that anything not having to do with Mel and the baby was a waste of time. Even Mae tends to dote on Mel. I don't think Mel minds.

Part of me doesn't want to go back to sleep, but part of me wants to lie back down and never get up. I'm exhausted, but I'm also not. I'm afraid to fall asleep, but I'm also afraid to get up and keep living. Sometimes, I wonder if the circumstances are the reason for the way I feel, if everyone feels hopeless most of the time, or if it's just me. Does everyone think so often about just giving up?

Eventually, I stand up, put my jacket on, and slip my axe into the well-loosened belt loop on my right hip. My shoes don't come off most days. Just in case. We've been here around three months—I check my watch—three months and ten days and not one major attack, human or zombie, has occurred in that time. So I suppose Calvin was right about this being safer until Mel has the baby. But you really never know when it'll happen, when a horde will wander by, or a threatening human presence will make itself apparent, so the shoes stay on anyway. Just in case.

I walk outside, starting along a familiar path around the building, and I pretend for a second that Marco and Sam are waiting just around the next corner. I put the collar of the green jacket to my nose and inhale, imagining that the faintest scent of tobacco and spearmint might still cling to the fibers. When I round the corner and find no one, I sigh and jam my hand into my pocket, letting the daydream dissipate. They aren't here; who knows if either of them is alive? If I had the courage to be honest with myself, I'd guess that he died that day and she died even before that. I pull out the second-to-last piece of the gum I found months ago and pop it into my mouth. It's unnaturally chewy, as old gum is. It falls apart in my mouth, dissolving into nothing.

I think there's probably a metaphor in there somewhere.

What did Marco say? The question burrows into my brain, the answer tugging at the back of my unconscious. His lips moved; he was looking right at me. But no matter how many times I have that nightmare, I can't make out the words. So when I dream that scene or any other that causes me to wake in a choked, sweating panic—which is about three times a week—I walk to calm my nerves, just like before. Yet another reason to keep my shoes on.

I hear the faint sounds of a zombie somewhere north. It sounds like it's close to the perimeter that Calvin and I constructed around the warehouse. I could leave it, since it will probably never get through. But I find myself speed-walking toward the sound anyway, drawing my axe from my belt loop before I even realize I'm doing it. I arrive at the perimeter, a makeshift security fence made up of hundreds of stakes pointed outward with an intricate web of twine woven between them, and stop just in front of the zombie. It's not quite to the perimeter yet, so I decide to watch and see how well our defense holds up to a hungry zombie faced with a fresh meal. I back up a few paces and wait.

The zombie ambles a little faster once it sees me. In the rapidly brightening light, I can barely make it out. It's obviously naked, though, except for a pair of tube socks. I have to admit, that's a first. It gets closer to the spikes, and

I fully expect it to either impale itself and get stuck or to be stopped by the twine. But neither of those things happens. The corpse, which is putrid and quite old, gets to the perimeter and stops dead (pardon the pun). It stands there for a second, doing what I can only describe as *looking* at the fence. It turns its shoulders and steps between two spikes, stopping again at the twine.

"What the—?"

The zombie slowly lifts its tube-socked foot and *steps over the twine*. It sort of wheezes as it lifts the other foot and begins to step over.

My axe is in its face before it gets all the way over. It lets out one gross and prolonged gurgle, and when I yank my axe free, it face-plants, its left foot suspended in the air by the twine. I stumble backward, staring at the felled zombie, shaking from head to toe. What the hell did I just see? The whole scene races through my mind, making less sense than it did when it happened. But suddenly, it does make sense. I step closer to the naked zombie and crouch down in front of it. I lift the head by its shaggy gray hair and examine the face. The blow destroyed one of its eyes, but the other is still intact. It's not white, but green.

I drop the Abnormal's head and walk back to the warehouse, dragging my axe through the tall grass to clean it, and resume my laps. I continue to think about the zombie, its human eyes and obvious cognitive abilities. In the time since we completed the fence, seven days after we found the warehouse, we've had exactly zero zombie breaches. Sure, we've had to dispose of plenty that got caught up in the fence, especially when we cook fresh meat, but there hasn't been one zombie inside in three months and three days. Until now. I can't even believe I'm pondering normal versus abnormal zombies, but there you go.

Out of the corner of my eye, I see movement in the trees. Another Abnormal? In my periphery, an Abnormal is exactly what it looks like. I spin around, all adrenaline and paranoia, just in time to see an owl landing in a tree. I keep walking, expecting the other zombie to come out of nowhere any second. But it never does.

When the sun peeks over the eastern tree line, I decide this will be my last lap around. Everyone will be waking up soon anyway, and there's no better distraction from my own brain than daylight and people. But as I'm rounding the corner closest to the entrance, I hear something far in the distance.

A voice?

"*Help!*"

I run inside and wake Calvin, who gently lifts Mel off him and lays her down again, brushing the hair away from her face. The corners of her mouth lift. He sits up, ruffled and still a little sleepy, his dense, curly hair sort of smooshed on one side.

"What's up?" he asks.

"There's someone out there," I whisper.

Calvin nods and bends down to put on his shoes. Then he takes his knives out from under his pillow and slides them into his thigh holsters.

The man is still shouting when we get outside. He's not far into the forest by the sound of it. We find him quickly and hide behind a huge tree to assess before we go any closer. He's middle-aged, alone, dodging four zombies around a little clearing and waving a pathetic three-inch pocketknife around uselessly.

"Does he realize he's attracting every zombie for miles?" Calvin whispers.

Between shouting, the guy says three names over and over, like a chant: "Martha, Rose, Donna… Girls. Please." He resumes yelling and swinging his knife at nothing. *Swish-swish-swish.*

"He has no idea what he's doing. Wonder how he made it this far."

"Three of those zombies are brand-new. And four sleeping bags? They must have been his people."

"Martha…Rose…Donna." *Swish-swish-swish.*

"Christ, Cal. Two of them are little girls."

"Man, that's rough. Doesn't look like we have any Abnormals, though."

"That's something, I guess."

He hums in reply. "So are we going in?"

I sigh. Four zombies, that's nothing. We could do it with our eyes closed. But the implication of us helping this guy is that we're also willing to take him in. And are we? I have to think about it despite the man's obvious plight. Eventually, I grimace and nod. He's alive, so of course we have to help him. We run out from behind the tree, and I take the first zombie's head almost clean off. The guy has to have seen us, but he's still screaming for help, please, help, over and over, swinging that rinky-dink knife of his for all he's worth.

"Calm down, would you?" Calvin whispers harshly as we get closer. "We're here to—oomph!" Calvin grunts as the man's pocketknife slashes his abdomen. He stumbles backward. A crimson stain blooms rapidly over his white T-shirt.

The guy stops, stunned for a second at what he's done. That's when the zombie that probably used to be his wife lunges, taking one of his cheeks into its jaws and ripping flesh from bone like a cheetah on the Discovery Channel. His scream changes then, a wordless cry, like an animal. The kid zombies close in. They chomp and chew indiscriminately until one of them finally rips out his throat, and he's silent.

The man's body is still twitching by the time I've put all four zombies down and get around to him.

Calvin grunts behind me. The blood is still pouring out of his side, and he's halfheartedly trying to staunch the flow with his palm. He tries to stand, but he falters and falls back down.

"Come on, Calvin," I say, sliding his knives back into their sheaths and forcing my shoulder under his unoccupied arm. I cannot push us both up. "Come on!" I yell through gritted teeth. "We have to go. I need you to get vertical! I can't get you back by myself." I try for an encouraging smile. "Hey, let's get you back to Mel, okay? She can patch you up no problem."

When I say her name, Calvin forces himself up.

"That's right—come on, Cal!"

The dead man's scream rings in my ears as I haul Calvin back to the warehouse. The sound someone makes when they're being torn apart by zombies is singularly unique. It isn't only the sound of excruciating pain—and believe me, it hurts like nothing you've ever felt—it's a scream of pure horror, the scream of someone who has just come face-to-face with their own mortality and their demise simultaneously. It's the sound of a life ending. The closest comparison would be the sound Westley makes when the six-fingered man hooks him up to the Machine: the sound of Ultimate Suffering.

Calvin's face is ashen by the time we get back to the warehouse. I kick the door open and call out to Mel, who wobbles to life immediately. She stands up, struggling under the weight of her enormous belly. Chaz attentively follows her every move with his eyes, his forehead wrinkled in concern.

"Lay him on the table!" she yells. "What happened?"

"Guy in the woods. We tried to help him, and he cut Cal."

She takes off Calvin's shirt and hands it to me, instructing me to keep pressure on the wound.

"What can I do, honey?" Mae asks.

"Hot water, leave the fire going, a packet of gauze—maybe two—and our cleanest knife."

Mae brings the water she was already boiling as well as the gauze. Then she pulls one of Calvin's Bowie knives—which he keeps immaculately clean—out of its holster. She holds it out to Mel, who is trickling some of the hot water on the wound. When she's done she takes the knife and plunges it into the rest of the water and thrusts it into my hands. I know what comes next.

"Hold that over the fire until it's red, Nana," I say, wiping the knife off and giving it to Mae.

Mae holds the knife over the flame. When the blade glows red, Mel takes off her leather belt and hands it to Calvin.

"Cal, listen to me." She holds his face in her hands. "I need you to bite down on this. Okay?" She kisses him on the forehead. "I love you."

He bites hard on the belt when she presses the flat of the blade to his skin. A vein pops out in his forehead, and beads of sweat form on his upper lip. He groans. The sound of his flesh sizzling is almost as loud. It's not something easily described, the sound and smell of flesh burning. But once you've experienced it, you can't forget it.

Once he's bandaged, he swings his legs over the table's edge and stands.

"Cate, walk with me. I wanna make sure that maniac didn't draw any zombies in."

I think he just doesn't want Mel to see him in this much pain. After all, the guy wasn't close enough to our camp to be a real danger, but I play along. We walk at a snail's pace one lap around the building, and then another. There's no sign of a threat, but we keep walking anyway.

"How's the gut?" I ask. "You ever been cauterized before?"

He places a hand gingerly on the thickly bandaged wound. It reminds me of the way Mel touches her baby bump.

"Nope, this is my first rodeo."

"The first few days will be really awful," I tell him. "After it's healed enough that you can get it wet, take a dip in the stream. It'll feel like you died and went to heaven, I bet."

He looks me up and down. "What do you know about cauterizing, kid?"

"Plenty." I lift my tank top just enough to reveal the gnarly purplish-black scar on my left hip. It's circular, sort of, and the skin is lumpy and uneven where it knitted back together. The veins around it have turned permanently black, but only about an inch around the wound itself.

Calvin sucks in a breath through his teeth. "What the hell happened?"

"Got bit," I mumble, yanking my shirt back down.

He stops walking. "What? No way you got bit, Cate, not there. You couldn't amputate. You'd be dead."

"I should be."

"What happened?" he asks again. It's an obvious question; I knew it was coming.

I haven't ever told anyone out loud what happened, but I've gone over it in my head a million times. I trace the scar through my shirt with my index finger.

"It was the first night Mel and I spent on our own..."

Seventeen: Cauterization hurts like hell.

Our first days alone were tumultuous. Messy. Terrifying. Survival didn't come naturally to me. Not that Mel was a master survivalist either, though she definitely had more of a knack for zombie killing than I did. It's a lot more difficult to destroy a skull or aim for an eye socket in the heat of a fight than you'd think. There's this horrible, putrid creature, sometimes two or more, clawing and gnashing teeth at you, trying to tear you apart. They don't feel anything either, so the best you can hope for when you shove them back a few steps is that your aim will be true when they get close again. Because if it isn't, if your weapon hits but doesn't kill, most of the time it ends up lodged in the body. And then what? You'd better have a backup weapon, that's what.

I took things for granted in the beginning, too. Things like sleeping and washing my face. Keeping my eyes closed for any length of time proved to be hazardous before I learned to use my other senses effectively. Listening is key. Sleep light, and always *always* have a weapon within reach. Be constantly alert. But despite all of the things I had to learn, things which quickly became second nature to both my sister and me, I attribute my still being alive mostly to luck.

Several hours after leaving the church, right after hitting the coast highway, we ran out of fuel. The three stations we passed all had signs hanging in the window that said some variation of "no gas." So just before the sun went down, the truck puttered to a stop in the middle of the highway. We were somewhere in the northernmost part of Oregon, with a pretty impressive view of the ocean. The sunset wasn't the kind you see in magazines with tons of puffy cotton-candy clouds and an orange-and-blue sky that reflects colorfully on the gently rolling waves, but a simple palette of yellow by the horizon that faded gently into jewel blue, then deep midnight blue. The sky did reflect on the water's surface, but on the angry winter waves the chopped-up reflections of light looked more like broken glass floating on the gray water. You know, if glass could float.

Once the sky was deep velvet blue and the water was black, Mel yawned and stretched her arms over her head.

"Let's turn in. I'm exhausted."

We took out the bikes and curled up in the truck bed.

"Wish we had a sleeping bag," I grumbled as I laid my head on my arm.

Mel huffed.

"Stupid Gary."

My old self would have made a "hope he gets eaten by zombies" joke. Instead, I rolled over to face Mel, who was lying on her arm exactly as I was.

"Doesn't matter. If we power through and we have minimal detours or stops or whatever, we could be in San Francisco like next week."

"You really think?" Mel whispered. The look on her face was so hopeful, so damn desperate to cling to any shred of hope, however tenuous, that it made me feel guilty for saying anything.

Because the truth was I had no idea how we would manage that, and my optimism had pretty strict limits. The best I could offer was "I really hope so."

We slept well into the next afternoon. We were exhausted. We slept hard, which was why we didn't hear the lone fresh zombie wandering our way until it was leaning over the side of the truck. It took me a second to register where I was, but Mel was quick with her little knife. She stabbed it right through the temple. Before she killed it, though, it bit me.

We both cried as Mel cleaned the wound and wrapped a bandage around my waist to stop the bleeding. We'd seen what happened after this: the fever, burning for a few hours, and death. Then came the worst part, the part where she'd have to dispatch me quickly or become like me. We'd seen the time frame last anywhere from thirty seconds to five minutes. Marco had once told me that a person could last as long as five hours from initial infection to death, but that reanimation was always within minutes. As far as we'd seen, that was exactly right. Minutes. I told her not to wait.

"When I stop breathing, you put that knife in my skull," I told her. "Don't hesitate, Mel. Just do it, okay?"

She nodded without meeting my gaze. What choice did she have?

We spent the next couple of hours sitting together in the truck bed, sometimes just listening to the ocean, sometimes talking about things like what was left in the pack; a future that no longer included me.

"At least the rations will last you twice as long," I half joked. "Now you get all the trail mix."

"God, Cate." Mel flicked tears away from her eyes and pulled me into a tight hug.

"Ow, hey, watch it. You're hurting my deathblow."

"Sorry."

I didn't know if it was just the way my brain worked or if this was how it felt to know you were dying. I was sort of relieved that there was an end in sight. I wouldn't have to be afraid anymore, wouldn't have to worry about food and water and Mel and Alcatraz. And Mel? She could take care of herself, probably better without me to worry about. I could be done. And maybe if there was some kind of afterlife, everyone was already waiting for me.

I didn't tell Mel any of that, of course.

Halfway into the fourth hour, Mel spoke up.

"How do you feel?"

How did I feel? I took stock of my current state: achy back, woozy, *really* hungry, wound hurt like hell. But all in all...

"Fine," I told her. "I feel fine."

She just stared at me. "You feel fine." She put the inside of her wrist to my forehead, the way my mom used to, and took my pulse. Then she lifted my arm and looked down at my watch. "It's been almost five hours, Cate."

Five hours? It felt like days, or maybe minutes. I glanced at my watch to see if she was right, but I just stared into the moving cogs, not really looking at anything.

"Cate. Did you hear me? It's almost five hours."

I nodded. "Yeah, five..." Suddenly, what she had said finally registered. "Five hours." I looked at Mel. "It probably just takes more time sometimes. I'm young and healthy, right?" As far as we knew at the time, the result of a bite or a scratch from a zombie was invariably the same.

"Cate, you're not even feverish. Your pulse is normal. You're fine." Her tone became brighter, even a little frantic as she started to dig around in my bag. "I think, for whatever reason, you're maybe immune to this...this whatever it is. We have to clean it again, though, before bacterial infec—"

"Mel," I interrupted her. Now it was my turn to be stern. I held her gaze. "I'm done. It might be taking longer with me—who knows why. But a bite always equals death. I'm infected. You need to put me down and keep going."

"Cate, don't be a martyr. I'm not leaving you here." She continued with what she'd been doing. She soaked a cotton ball, one of only ten, and moved to unwrap my bandages.

I pulled away. "Don't waste that on me, Mel!" A flock of seagulls burst out of the tree in a cacophony of caws. We both looked around to make sure I hadn't alerted any nearby zombies. I dropped my voice. "You're limited on medical supplies, and you have a long way to go. Be realistic. I'm done."

Her eyes filled with tears. "Listen to me, Catherine. Quit being a brat. I'm not going anywhere unless you're with me. Now if you want me to stay safe, to move on, you have to at least let me try."

After a second of deliberation, knowing that Mel's stubbornness could and would outlast my own, I agreed. "Fine."

She cleaned the wound, this time more thoroughly, and then clicked her tongue.

"What?"

"It's still bleeding. We should cauterize it now that it's clean."

Images of movie heroes biting down on leather belts while their skin sizzled flashed in my mind. Badass. I touched my belt to make sure it was there.

We found a restaurant less than a block away that had an old gas stove. I took the cigarette lighter out of the inside pocket of Marco's jacket and handed it to Mel cautiously. After she lit the burner, she searched a bit until she landed on a heavy-duty spatula, which she scrubbed to within an inch of its life with hand sanitizer and then some of our precious water. Once she was satisfied, she set it across the flame.

"It's going to hurt like hell," she said. "It's extremely rudimentary, but it's clean enough. Cauterizing doesn't necessarily keep out infection, but it's better than you bleeding out, and if we keep it clean while it heals, you'll be fine." She pulled her hair into a ponytail and smiled reassuringly.

Suppressing an epic eye roll, I took my jacket off, pulled up my shirt, and shimmied my jeans down below my hipbone. "I will probably still die anyway," I told her flatly. "This might be for nothing."

"Shh" was all she said. She was in nurse mode now. She pushed her glasses up the bridge of her nose with her middle finger and used a drop of hand sanitizer to clean her hands. "Hop up here—" She pointed to the counter. "—and whatever you do, don't scream."

"Got that covered," I said, whipping off my belt.

Clutching the belt, I climbed onto the counter with my bitten left hip facing the stove. I put my belt to my lips, not feeling so badass all of a sudden, and steeled myself in preparation for what I assumed would be the most painful experience of my life to date.

And I was right. The second the metal came into contact with my flesh, a rank smell like barbecued death filled the air, as did the sickening sound of sizzling and popping. The sounds and smells of my flesh burning. I bit down on the belt and groaned. Hot tears soaked my face. I was sure that this was it—my threshold for pain had been maxed out. For a blinding second, I thought I might just die from the pain alone. But I didn't. Mel wrapped my wound with a clean bandage—leaving us with only one more gauze packet. We stuffed the few cans of food we had found into our packs and took our bikes out of the truck bed. We split a can of peaches, hopped on our bikes, and rode away from the spot that I had assumed would be my final resting place. I started sleeping with my axe in my hand after that.

I didn't know what made me immune. Still don't. I don't have any real way of figuring it out either. The fear of being dissected in some underground government lab somewhere was and is too great for me to go yapping about it. Because if there's still a government, they'll be looking for a cure. And I'm a hell of a good start.

Eighteen: You don't have to eat the dog.

Going from midnight ice cream runs and surfing Netflix to searching abandoned buildings for a can or two of food was a jarring change. But we slowly grew accustomed to life on the move and, even more slowly, to zombies. After we found the fishing pole in Hood River, Mel's fishing skills proved to be incredibly useful.

"This is a good spot, right?" I asked her as we rolled to a stop for the first time that day. "The ocean looks calm here. That's good, right?"

"Fine," she said irritably. "Good as any. We'll get as many bites here as we did yesterday. None."

Mel had been uncommonly grouchy the last several days, combination PMS and an extended case of the hangries. I'd been trying and failing not to let it bug me.

"Okay, well"—I tried to keep my tone even—"let's try." I dipped a hand into the water. Frigid. "It would be really cool if we found a gas stove soon. I need a hot bath."

She scoffed. "Yeah you do."

I chucked our second-to-last tampon at her, hitting her right on the forehead.

"You're no rose garden yourself."

She made a face and rolled her eyes so far back I thought they'd snap off and just keep spinning. Then, grumbling all the way, she cast out from the shore. We were somewhere north of Newport; the fishing had been thin for days so we discussed what we knew about edible indigenous berries, which we found out was collectively nothing.

While we talked about our options, a high-pitched sound came from somewhere in the wooded area behind us. It was neither zombie nor human.

"What is that?" I asked Mel.

"How should I know?"

It got closer. The bushes rustled behind us; Mel set the pole down and took up her hammer.

"No, stay here," I muttered. "We need to eat or we'll die anyway."

The bushes rustled again. The sound grew louder and more frantic. It had to be an animal.

"Be right back!" I called as I ran toward the sound and the shaking foliage, drawing my knife from my jacket pocket.

Tangled up on the other side of the huge thorny bush was a skinny, dirty white dog. A lab, maybe? The dog's leash had been wound around the bottom of the bush, and he was wailing frantically, struggling against the tangled leash. At first, I wondered what was making the dog so crazy; by the time I got to him, he was whimpering and barking and thrashing madly on the leash like a caught fish. Soon I saw why. Not ten feet away, ambling across the clearing toward us was a lone bearded zombie.

This thing was old, had to have died in the first days of the outbreak. Its lumberjack beard was caked with dried blood and other, less identifiable stuff. I was surprised it was still walking on its rotten legs, the calves of which had been chewed completely away.

"Gross."

I shuddered and gripped my knife like Marco had showed me, with the blade sticking out the pinky-side of my hand. I waited until it was within reach, and then I dispatched it quickly and quietly, shoving my knife into its brain.

The dog was still crying after the zombie's body hit the ground, but the volume had decreased substantially. I yanked my knife out of the festering head and wiped it off on the zombie's shirt. The dog whimpered and lifted his paw, his big brown eyes boring a hole into me. I remember reflecting for just a second on the absolute accuracy of the phrase "puppy eyes" before one of his louder cries jerked me back to the situation at hand. He lifted his paw again and pushed forward with his nose.

"Hi there, big boy," I said soothingly.

Mel came jogging through the trees behind me. "Did you find what—" She stopped when she saw the dog. "Oh!" She clasped her hands together. "Wook at the widdle baby!" Mel was a master of weird baby talk. She turned to me and put her hand on her hip. "Cate, we have to help him."

I held up my knife, keeping my sarcastic "you think?" to myself. I turned my attention back to the dog. He was staring at us with his head tilted.

"All right, buddy," I said quietly. "I'm gonna get you loose, okay? Don't bite me please."

He wrinkled his forehead and gave me those eyes again. I slowly approached him. He didn't growl, but he did lower his head and scoot backward.

"No problem." I sat on the ground a few feet away. I scooted a foot closer, keeping my tone low and soft. "We weren't catching anything anyway. We've got all day."

I heard Mel moving behind me, but I kept my attention on the dog.

He didn't move, just kept staring. He looked from me to Mel, and then back to me.

I scooted a little closer. "That's a nice leash. I guess you had someone once. So you know the word...treat?"

The dog's ears pricked up; the tip of his tail wiggled.

I scooted closer. I was close enough to touch him, but I didn't. I held out my hand for him to smell.

"If you let me cut you loose, you can have a treat."

He sniffed my hand, his tail still wagging timidly. Then he pushed his nose into my palm and licked it.

"That's a good boy," I murmured. A triumphant little smile crept over my face. "Now let's get you loose." I scooted the rest of the way to him, another foot or two, and unhooked the leash from the matching blue-and-brown collar. On the collar hung a blue paw-shaped dog tag. I turned it over in my hand. I looked for Mel, who I found had been scooting right along with me and was practically breathing down my neck.

"His name is Chaz," I told her.

She grinned and put her hand out for his inspection.

"Hi, Chaz. Hi, cutie," she cooed. "Look at you. You're so skinny. And so dirty!"

"You've been on your own a while, haven't you, Chaz?" I guessed.

He wagged his tail at the sound of his name. He licked Mel's hand and pawed my lap. Then all at once, he jumped up and bounded across the little clearing and back. I looked at Mel, who just grinned and shrugged, so I untangled the leash from the bush and hooked it to his collar. Chaz waited patiently while I clipped the leash on, and as soon as it was hooked, he jumped up and pulled me around until he found a pond where he drank half his weight in water.

"Thirsty boy," I said.

"Hungry too, I bet. Now I really need to catch something."

An hour later, Mel finally got a bite. It was a fair-sized fish too, enough to feed the three of us a decent serving. We lit a fire on the beach and cooked the fish when the sun went down. Chaz mowed through his piece with zeal; I guessed by the ribs showing through his muddy fur that he hadn't eaten in a while. I hadn't eaten anything but half a can of beans in the last forty-eight hours, and my stomach felt like it might consume itself soon, but I took several generous mouthfuls and slid the rest of my portion onto the dirt in front of Chaz. I couldn't help smiling as he gulped it down.

Looking at Mel across the fire that night, I could tell she had some misgivings about taking him with us, as did I.

"So?" I asked. She knew what I meant.

"He's emaciated, Cate," Mel replied as she stroked his sticking-out ribs. "And I don't know if you noticed, but he's clearly favoring his left front leg."

"I noticed."

"Plus, based on how we found him, I'd say he's useless for zombie defense."

"Basically, he's a liability."

"And do we really need another liability? Or another stomach to fill?"

"So what, should we just eat him and be done with it? We'd probably be saving him from a worse death in the future."

Mel nodded. "Probably."

But as his eyelids began to droop in exhaustion, an unexpected surge of protective instinct rushed through me. I think Mel felt the same too. We looked at each other for a long moment in the dying light. She kissed his forehead, and he sighed.

"We're not going to do that, are we?" I asked.

"No."

I couldn't deny that that was the answer I'd hoped for. Even though he was another liability, another life to protect and another mouth to feed, even though we were close to starvation ourselves, we decided not to eat him.

Nineteen: If you see something, say something.

"Focus," Calvin whispers from behind me. "Throw on the exhale."

I take a deep breath and aim. The end of his blade is pinched between my thumb and first two fingertips; the handle points directly back past my right ear. When I exhale, I send the knife flying toward my target, a wild turkey (I have to force myself to see the bird as a target, because though I will thoroughly enjoy eating it tonight, should I kill it, I still feel tremendous guilt about the act itself). The knife spins through the air for a second with barely a whisper, and then it cleanly slices off the bird's head. An instant kill. Sort of. The turkey twitches and flaps around, blood spraying out of its neck the whole time. It's horrible.

Calvin retrieves his blade as soon as the bird stops moving, but there's still a little bit of blood dribbling out of the neck. "Excellent shot, Cate."

"Thanks." I feel a little sick.

I don't tell him that or that I was aiming for the bird's body. Instead, I relish the ill-gotten praise.

I'm actually sort of a baby about the killing part of most of our meals. I don't think I would be hunting today if he wasn't still healing from the wild-man-gut-slice incident, but he says I need to practice anyway. Practice aiming or practice killing my food? I'm not entirely sure.

Calvin stuffs the turkey into the garbage bag we brought for precisely this purpose, and we head back toward the warehouse. "Let's get this bird back." He grins.

"How far out are we today?" I ask.

"Four klicks, give or take."

"They'll be giddy over this."

He hums in reply. Then he stops suddenly, drops the turkey, and unsheathes a knife. "Looks like three coming our way," he says quietly. "I got 'em."

"No." I pull him back. "Mel will shoot you if that wound rips open again."

I get it, though. He has a lot of steam to blow off. This baby thing has his nerves frayed and fried to crisps. I finish them off as expediently as I can—two fresh, one barely standing—with two well-aimed blows. I decapitate the oldie and in the same swing, implant my axe into another's eye. I yank my knife out just in time to shove it into the base of Number Three's skull. They're all down in two seconds flat. Learning how to use both my weapons at once has changed everything.

"Jesus, Cate," Calvin says.

"Language!" I whine.

But of course I'm teasing. When we're out here in the wild, we embrace each other's rough edges. I think I didn't give him a fair chance at first, not because of him but because of Mel. She has dated some of the absolute worst guys, tried to save them, change their shitty personalities. She is lottery-lucky to have found a guy like Calvin, especially in a world where there are so few people left.

"Cal?" I say as we walk.

"Yeah?"

"Well..." I want to tell him all of that and that I'm glad we found them. I want to tell him that I've always wanted a big brother. Instead, I hip-bump him and say, "Thanks for carrying the turkey."

A rustling in the nearby foliage alerts us both. Another zombie in the middle of mealtime. But it's the victim that strikes me as odd. He's a cop, uniform and all, and a fresh kill. The zombie stands and turns, and I'm thanking whomever it's just a zombie.

Calvin circles behind it as I draw it in. He sinks his blade into the back of its head, and it drops.

"I think I tore it open." He lifts up his shirt, and sure enough, there's a trickle of blood seeping out of his wound.

"Again? It was nice knowing you. She'll kill you for sure this time."

He pulls his shirt back down. "Only if you tell her." He circles around to the cop, who is covered in bruises. His eye is swollen to nearly the size of a baseball.

"See that gash?" Calvin runs a hand through his bushy hair, and then he's crouching down to examine the ear-to-ear slice in the cop's throat.

"Pretty gnarly," I agree.

"I'll say. No claws can do that. And there's no reason to cut a dead man's throat... And these bites. No bleeding. He was already dead when this one got to him." He gestures vaguely in the fourth zombie's direction.

I shake my head. "Whatever it was, this wasn't an accident."

Calvin hums in agreement.

"So we've got a killer," Calvin says more than asks, rubbing his hands together. I can't tell if he's worried or hungry for a fight. Maybe both. He stares into the trees like he expects the killer to just come running out of the woods.

"We'll do extra patrols for a while. It'll be fine. We're pretty far from camp."

He looks down at me like he almost forgot I was there.

"Patrols, yeah." But he's already looking back into the trees, scanning intently. "Have you seen anything suspicious around camp?"

An image of the watcher with the ball cap comes to mind.

"Nope," I lie. After all, it was probably just a zombie. Why worry him?

Twenty: Hole up if you have to, but don't get soft.

The night after we found Chaz, the temperature plummeted, and a harsh winter storm came through. The wind whipped and howled; cotton-ball-sized snowflakes pelted us unforgivingly. We found an empty car and huddled in the back seat.

"Th-this isn't w-w-working," Mel stammered after what seemed like hours.

Chaz shivered as if in agreement.

"What're we s-s-s'posed to do?" I asked through chattering teeth. Even speaking sapped my energy.

"Has to be a b-building in town."

So we climbed numbly out of the car, Mel and I both wincing as the cold air smacked us. It took me several tries to attach the dog's leash to my handlebars. He limped alongside us while we walked our bikes through the shin-deep snow into Newport.

We stopped at the first house we saw, a little brick house I swore I'd seen in a Kinkade painting once, snow and all. Mel took her knife and a hairpin and began to pick the lock.

Chaz whined and pawed at the door.

"Did Gabriel teach you to do that too?" I asked, slathering on sarcasm.

"No. Paul did."

"Senior Year Paul? Prom Date Paul?"

"Yes."

"Man." I sighed. "He was the one guy Mom liked."

Mel giggled. "I know."

The house was packed to the gills with clutter but seemingly devoid of anyone living or undead. We wandered through each room, finding more and more and more: eclectic furniture, books, newspapers, several huge half-finished puzzles, collector toys in boxes, three computers, a *lot* of pot paraphernalia, and many, many boxes holding yet more crap.

When we got back to the living room, Mel gasped and pointed behind me at the fireplace. "Cate, look!"

"I know," I said. "Didn't you see that when we came in?"

Mel looked at me like I was missing the point (rude), and pointed at the picture above the fireplace, a portrait of a portly bearded man and a dog.

"Um, nice."

"Look at the collar, dude. It's Chaz!"

I looked closer at the picture, and sure enough, the dog in the photo had on a blue-and-brown collar with a little blue paw-shaped tag.

"No way."

"Why not? We only found him a mile or so from here."

I turned to Chaz, who was rolling around on an extremely comfortable-looking dog bed with a stuffed bird in his mouth. "Is this your house, buddy? Is that your bird?"

He kept rolling.

"His owner must have taken him out on a walk and never come home," Mel guessed.

"Well, he's home now, aren't you, Chaz?"

He wagged his tail.

"You know what that means?" I yawned, lying down next to him on his plush bed. "There's probably a stash of dog food somewhere."

"It will take ages to find in this mess." Mel yawned. "Let's check tomorrow."

"We'll go through the whole house. Why not? It's not like we're in a rush."

This little brick house with only tiny slit-windows and miniature skylights and with its solid front door could serve as a safe hideout until the storm passed. There was even a decent pile of halved logs next to the fireplace. We lit a fire that night, deciding that the wind would carry away the smoke and thus any evidence of our presence. The three of us shared the jar of peanut butter we found in the kitchen and slept in the living room, shoes on, in case we needed to make a quick exit.

First thing in the morning, we sifted through the mess. We found a worn tennis ball and six cans of dog food almost immediately. Chaz was elated, gobbling up the half can we gave him with gusto. But I think he was more excited about the ball. He played with it relentlessly, first with us and then by himself while we continued our search. He had a surprising amount of energy. His limp was hardly noticeable as he loped across the room and back.

"How old do you think he is?" I asked Mel as we picked through the kitchen cupboards, coming up with zilch.

Mel sucked her teeth and squinted. "Hm, probably at least eight."

The second he saw that he had our attention, Chaz rolled the ball under a piece of furniture for the hundredth time, this time a floor-to-ceiling hallway bookshelf. I had to wonder if it was on purpose.

"Your turn," Mel said, intentionally turning her head away from the ball.

Believe me, the irony of retrieving something for a Labrador retriever was not lost on us. I got on all fours and reached under the shelf. When I grabbed the ball, however, I felt something else. Something cold.

"Mel, check this out. Grab the flashlight."

She heaved a dramatic sigh and walked over.

"Feel this."

Chaz whined behind us. I sat up and tossed the ball back.

She obligingly put her hand under the shelf. Her eyebrows scrunched as she felt around a little more. Then she clicked on the light and peered underneath with one eye.

"There's nothing under there."

"So why the draft?" I asked.

She shrugged and waved her hand around under the shelf, then did the same thing just in front of the shelf.

"It's not coming from underneath," she finally said.

I hovered my hand above the floor where hers had been. There was a draft, but she was right. It wasn't coming from underneath the shelf. It was coming from...the floor?

I stood, backed up a bit, and motioned for her to do the same. I tried to lift the corner of the rug we had been sitting on and found it to be attached to the hardwood floor. As the rug lifted, so did the floor.

"It's a door!" she practically shouted.

The trapdoor was unlocked, so we told Chaz to stay put and we crept down into the basement. Neither of us had a weapon, but we figured there probably wouldn't be a zombie in a hidden basement. I turned on the flashlight, but as soon as we stepped into the room, a bright overhead light switched on. Mel and I both jumped, and then she tapped me on the shoulder and pointed to the small gray box in the upper right corner of the room.

"Motion sensor lights," she said. "I saw solar panels on the roof when we brought in the bikes this morning. I don't know how I forgot to mention that."

"Wouldn't the snow have covered them?" I asked.

"No, they're raised and really steep, like this." She held her hand at about a sixty-degree angle.

The room was larger than I'd expected, with two sets of bunk beds and a dresser to the right, a full-sized bathroom and two-burner stove to the left, and at the other end of the room were several long shelves stacked totally full with bottled water and all kinds of canned food. There was even a half shelf dedicated to dog food and treats, the same kind as we'd found upstairs.

"Jackpot!" I cheered.

Mel and I did a little happy dance. We ran to the food shelves and began examining the contents.

A familiar sound made us both freeze.

There was a zombie in the bunker.

I turned around slowly, setting down the box of dry pasta I was holding. It was the portly man from the photo, plus a few days of decay. It was too near for us to run away, moving in on the shelves we were standing between. It was almost close enough to touch us, and there we were without our weapons. I grabbed the first thing my hand touched—a can of tomato soup—and heaved it at the zombie's skull. The can hit its target, but didn't kill the thing. Not even almost.

Suddenly, Mel, yelling like she was in a war movie, charged from behind me and shoved the zombie hard in the chest. When it came back, she was ready. She grabbed an industrial-sized can of black beans with both hands and caved the zombie's head in.

When she was finished, she dropped the can, went into the bathroom, and did the last thing I'd ever expected. She turned on the faucet.

I ran into the bathroom. She finished washing her hands and face with the steaming water. "Solar panels," she repeated, grinning.

That was my favorite night. After we disposed of the basement zombie—taking it out back so not to upset Chaz—we brought Chaz and our stuff down to the basement.

While I prepared dinner, Mel charged herself with picking a wine from the ten-bottle stash. She picked one, read the label, turned the bottle upside down a few times, and gave it a little wiggle.

"This is a pretty good wine. Should pair nicely with the food."

I nodded indulgently, though I was fairly sure she didn't have a clue one way or the other.

After dinner, we each showered, which was glorious, and bathed the dog, who sorely needed it. When we were all clean, we changed into some too-big pajamas we'd found in the dresser, brought the wine upstairs, and lit a fire. We sipped, and then gulped, the tart red liquid straight from the bottle.

"You were right about this wine," I said.

Mel took a long pull. "I was guessing. I liked the design on the label."

I'd never liked wine—or drinking in general—but I welcomed the warm, buzzing head high of wine-drunkenness that settled over me as we stayed up late into the night, long after the fire died down to embers, chatting up a storm like we used to before. I even powered on my phone for a quick selfie of the three of us.

When it got too chilly in the darkened room, Mel poured a cup of water over what was left of the glowing ashes and the three of us went down to the bunker. We all slept in beds that night, even Chaz, whose cushy dog bed we dragged downstairs with us.

The second morning, we woke to an unexpectedly different landscape: the snow had fallen all night and snowed us in.

"On the bright side," I said as we stood on the tiny porch, "all the bodies are probably frozen solid."

"Yeah but there is no way we're getting out of here on our bikes," Mel said. "It's gotta be chest-deep. We'll have to clear a path just to let the dog out."

I smirked. "May as well stay until the weather calms down, I *guess*."

"Probably safer that way," Mel agreed, stroking her chin for effect.

But this time, we didn't fool ourselves. We knew this wasn't the end of the line. We spent our weeks in the house organizing and reorganizing our newly stocked packs, reviewing the map, and showering every other day, knowing that when we left that would be it for hot showers. We read and read and read. Books about survival, books about plants, about history, novels, memoirs, even comic books. We tore through them, sometimes not speaking to each other for hours. Because who knew how long it would be before we had time to read again?

Our entire stay in the brick house was zombie-free as well, with Bunker Zombie being our only encounter all winter.

A couple of months later, when the snow had melted away and the sun was starting to warm the frozen ground again, we packed up the rest of the food, showered one more time, and changed back into our travel clothes, which we'd eschewed in favor of the pajamas since the first night. Mel had washed them three days prior in preparation for our leaving, saying it might be the last time we had clean clothes for a long time. We hitched up the dog's new bike trailer, which Mel had found in the house's attached garage hitched to an old one-speed. It even had a rain shield over the top. We connected it to Mel's bike first, agreeing to switch off every few hours. I cut out a large chunk of the dog's bed and placed it into the bottom of the trailer. Chaz hopped in with his tennis ball.

"This is it," Mel said with a pout. "Goodbye, warmth. Goodbye, hygiene."

I stuffed one extra pair of socks into her bag and cinched it closed.

"Oh come on. We'll get to San Francisco before you know it. And if you can hot-wire a boat like you can hot-wire a car, you criminal, we'll be in Alcatraz the same day."

"I'm fairly certain it's not the same thing."

"Never know until you try," I said, mounting my bike. "Hear that?"

"That scratching?"

A half-thawed zombie came wandering around the corner, followed by two, nope, three more.

It took the two of us around seven minutes to kill four zombies, one of which had only one whole leg and no arms at all. That doesn't seem like a long time, but try setting a timer for seven minutes and then tell me that is not a ridiculously long time to only take down four zombies.

Go ahead. I'll wait.

By the end of the seven minutes, we were both dirty and panting and a little sweaty, and I had a nice big bruise already blooming on my thigh. I could tell without looking. The dog had not moved. I did my best to brush the dirt off me, but it was mostly mud so I ended up with it smeared all over my hands and my freshly washed clothes. I climbed back on my bike.

"That was harder than I remember," said Mel.

"We're out of practice. It's been months since we've even seen a zombie."

"Or anyone but each other," Mel muttered.

I hummed in agreement.

"Just promise me something," Mel said as we pedaled away from the little brick house. "Promise me that when we get to the island, we will find a way to make hot showers a thing again."

I chuckled. "We'll do what we can."

Twenty-One: Don't go running off.

The incident with the screaming guy two weeks ago was, surprisingly, the only major disturbance we've had in our entire time at the warehouse, as well as our only contact with another living person. We've had plenty of contact with the dead, always in small numbers, but they're easy. After a while, I muse while I press my fingers into the soil and drop a seed in each hole, splitting a skull takes less and less out of you.

Press, drop. Press, drop.

"Oh!" Mel clutches her belly and doubles over. Not fully, just a little bend.

Mae sits upright, her hands still buried in the soil.

"Melody?"

"I'm good, Nana," Mel answers. "Just a—oh!" She sits down on the ground.

There's a clatter inside, and a shirtless, hammer-wielding Calvin comes running out.

"Melody! Nana? Melody! Cate, what's happening?" His eyes are wide and terrified.

"All good, my love," says Mel.

"Is it time? Is it happening?"

"Not yet," Mel says, wiping the dirt off her hands and leading him by the elbow back toward the house. "But the baby is coming and it will need a bassinet."

Calvin wipes the fresh beads of sweat off his face with the back of his hand and heads back inside, shaking his fluffy head and mumbling about the best damn bassinet you've ever seen.

"I'm not sure Calvin will be much help when the time comes," I whisper.

Press, drop. Press, drop.

Mae chuckles. "Men are useless. When Calvin was born, I stayed with his mama. Charlie didn't step foot in that delivery room until near the end, and when he did, he passed out cold. They're good at a lot of things, but bless their hearts, when it comes to delivering babies, men are about as useless as a screen door on a submarine. We'll be fine, just us." She turns and calls to Chaz, who is rooting around in the dirt nearby: "Except you, baby. You're welcome everywhere!"

He turns and wiggles his tail, and then goes back to his important sniffing duties.

"How did you end up with Calvin?" I ask.

"Desiree and James were both in the Army. That's how they met, in fact. She wrote to me that very day and told me about him. I remember because she called me every week, and that call came three days early. Waters, his name was. James Waters 'with a voice like thunder and the body to back it up,' she said.

"They got married right before James was shipped out to Iraq. Only time I met him. He was a mountain of a man. Desiree got pregnant, I guess, right before the wedding." Mae's face changes, seeming much older. "James died a week before Calvin was born. A bomb went off where he was patrolling. Painless for him, so they told us. But not for my Desiree. I think her poor heart just gave out. She died giving life to Calvin."

I look up at Mel and Calvin on the grass. He's apparently done with the crib, at least for now, and helping her practice throwing a decent punch. She swings a right hook, aiming for his raised hand, and stumbles when she misses. He steadies her and rests a hand delicately on her giant abdomen.

I wish our parents could see her so happy.

"I used to carry around a picture of them," Mae says quietly, almost to herself, obviously still more in her memories than here with me. "Taken the day of the wedding. Only picture of Calvin's daddy we had. He was a beautiful man. Calvin got his build, wiry and lean, and he got my Desiree's face. I left the picture sitting on my nightstand at our hotel in Ashland." She dabs her eyes with the clean part of her sleeve. "Anyway, listen to me goin' on. I've got to start our anniversary supper. Can you believe it's a year today since we first met?"

"No hints as to what we should expect?"

"I told you before, child. I'm a steel trap. Melody! Supper. Come on."

They handle the food most nights. Mel fishes in the creek behind the warehouse, and Mae is a miracle worker with the few spices we've found—pepper, garlic salt, and anise. She saves the anise for Chaz, explaining that it's like catnip for dogs. "And he'll love it, just you watch."

And he does.

Just after eleven in the morning, under a heavily overcast sky, Calvin and I cruise the camp's perimeter. I walk counterclockwise, opposite Calvin, taking my time. We used to do this about three times a day. Now every hour or so, we walk in opposite directions around the perimeter, scanning for threats, disposing of any zombies that might have gotten caught in the fence or made it through. Between the naked Abnormal and the murdered cop, Calvin insisted that we bump up perimeter walks. Can't say I blame him. He says it's better to walk this way, opposite, because if one of us misses something, the other is sure to spot it.

I pass him at the backside of the building and automatically hold up the okay signal, meaning I didn't see anything worth mentioning on my side. But his okay finger is temporarily occupied, knuckle-deep in his nose.

"Catch anything good?" I call, laughing harder than necessary to further embarrass him.

He jumps and hastily withdraws the finger. "Laugh it up, fuzz ball."

"I'm telling Mel."

"Go ahead. I'll tell her about that chocolate bar you're hoarding."

"You wouldn't."

"Try me."

He's probably not bluffing.

"*Touché.*"

He grins and claps me on the shoulder on his way by. "Good man."

"Ass," I mutter as he walks away. "And put a damn shirt on, will you! That wound is gross."

I'm met with a pebble to the back of the head. But when I turn around to retaliate, his boots are already disappearing around the corner.

That is when I hear the softest noise from where he just came, a distant rustling. I look toward the source of the sound, the bushes at the south end of camp. And there he is—the man with the baseball cap. The watcher.

To be clear, I am still not sure if the watcher is human or another Abnormal, but it is the same guy as before: slight build, pasty skin. Red shirt, black ball cap. Just watching, never moving. Suddenly, a surge of anger bubbles up inside me. Who is this guy, and *what* is his deal? It's time to find out. I cup my hands over my mouth and whistle a bird call, the sound Calvin and I use to signal if one of us goes off course for any reason. He whistles back. He heard me. I stomp through the tall grass toward the watcher. At first, he just stares at me, the creep. But then he turns and jogs away.

"Hey!" I shout.

There's no way he's getting away that easily. I'm almost positive that he's been lurking around since we arrived here four months ago, and I intend to find out why. Today, right now. I stop at the perimeter to make sure I have my axe. Then I sprint into the trees after him.

I don't make it ten steps into the woods before I lose him. I stand perfectly still for a moment, using the tracking skills Calvin has taught me. Listening. Looking. Trying to feel the movement of the earth under my feet. I hear a twig crack to my left, and I run toward it. But suddenly, I'm stopped in my tracks and lifted off the ground. I try to reach for my axe, but my arms are pinned to my sides by two large, hairy appendages. The watcher emerges from behind a nearby tree with a sick, oily smile spread across his face. He rubs his hands together.

"I thought you were crazy when you said she'd leave her people to come after you, Alex," grunts the man who grabbed me. He huffs a chuckle, and his breath almost knocks me out. I try to breathe through my clenched teeth, but that turns out to be worse. It almost distracts me from the fact that I'm being held three feet off the ground and that I'm probably in deep shit.

"I knew she'd come after me again," says the watcher. His voice is so high in pitch that it sounds almost prepubescent. He looks me up and down. "This one's the fighter." He comes to stand directly in front of me. "But she ain't that bright, I guess. You ever even *seen* a horror movie? Who the hell goes running off into the woods alone? She was asking to be caught!"

I kick and writhe and open my mouth to scream, but the giant who has me clamps a hand over my mouth before any sound escapes. The hand smells worse than the breath. My eyes burn.

Alex's grin widens.

"Now you can struggle all you like," he squeaks, "but my man Hank here won't give an inch. Will you, Hank? So I can stand here and wait while you tire yourself out, or you can just listen, Cate."

I stop struggling.

"That got your attention, didn't it? I also know that there are only four of you in that little building, not counting the crippled dog." He holds up four fingers. "One is too old to be of much use." He puts his pinky finger down. "One is too pregnant." Ring finger. "So that leaves you and, what's his name, Calvin? Yes, Calvin. And I also know he's been injured pretty severely recently, which couldn't have worked any better if I'd planned it myself..." His grin reminds me of a deranged Dr. Seuss character as he curls another finger, leaving only the index, which he points at me like a gun. "And then there was one." His smile disappears instantly, and he glances at the guy holding me. "Hank's going to let you speak now, but know that if you try to scream, he'll snap your fucking neck before you make a sound. Don't make him do that, okay?"

Hank's hand uncovers my mouth slowly. I gulp the fresh air.

"What do you want?" I ask.

Alex just stands there for a minute, that same creepy smile returning.

"What do I want?" The question seems to amuse him. He comes closer, sliding his hand slowly up my leg, keeping eye contact with me. My stomach twists into infuriated, disgusted knots. His hand stops at my waist, and he takes my axe and my knife. "I want..." He pockets the knife and slips the axe through his own belt loop. "A better existence, free of living corpses. I want to lead this dark, stinking shit pile of a world back into the light. But I'm getting ahead of myself. That's my long-term goal, see. Right now, in this moment, all I want is all you've got." He looks up at Hank, nods, and spreads his arms out to his sides like a corrupted Jesus figure. "Men," he calls out, "arise."

Twenty-Two: Utilize group skills.

The moment Alex gives the command, seven other people emerge from the surrounding forest, snarling and pungent, all heavily armed. They look to Alex for their next order.

But Alex is looking at me.

There's something off-putting about his gaze, like he's not quite human, but some other kind of predator. I wonder for a second if the end of the world made him this way, but when he grins again, I think not. This chaotic new world probably released the worst parts of him. If Calvin were to lump Alex into one of his two categories of people—those who changed to survive and those who became more themselves—I'd say he fits nicely in category two. With me.

"I have eleven more men waiting back at your camp," he murmurs, like he's saying something seductive.

I make my face into a mask of stone. "Why not just kill us in our sleep and take our stuff?"

"Try to listen because I hate repeating myself: I want all you've got. *All.* People are commodities these days. The more people we have, the better our chances."

"And you really expect a quiet surrender?"

At first, no one notices the zombie but me. Then it grabs onto one of them and tears out a chunk of his shoulder.

Before he even screams, both the old man and the zombie are put down, the zombie with a buck knife to the eye and the old man with my axe.

"No, not at all," Alex replies, wiping his flunky's blood off my axe with his bare hand, and his hand on another man's shirt. "That's the very reason I have you now. See?"

I feel my stomach lurch and my mouth go dry. I do see. I'm the bait. There's a way out of this. I know there is. I just need to get closer to him, or get him to come to me. If I can just get hold of my axe…

But as soon as he's finished talking, Alex gives the next order—move out. No one even looks at the old man, who seconds ago was one of their own. Hank sets me down, but the knife he presses into my back keeps me from trying anything right now. But maybe I could, I don't know, stomp on his foot? Grab my axe from Alex and what, make a run for it? Is that the worst idea in the world?

I'm no closer to a plan by the time we arrive at the warehouse. We stop just behind the tree line, and I see Mel and Mae picking tomatoes. Chaz is rolling in the grass nearby. Calvin is nowhere in sight. Alex and his men move in quickly, cutting through our perimeter and surrounding the warehouse in seconds. Mel and Mae look up, their expressions going from placid to terrified. Their fear grows exponentially when they see Hank, that boulder of a man, holding his knife to my throat.

Mel reaches into her waistband and pulls out her knife.

"You won't be needing that, Melody," Alex calls to her in his sickeningly cordial tone. Then he turns to Hank and me and feigns shock. "Hank, let poor Cate go! What are we, animals?" He turns back to Mel and Mae with an embarrassed hand-to-heart gesture.

Hank sets me down with a dumbfounded "Um."

As soon as my feet touch earth, I decide to make a run for it, but I don't even get a step before Alex's hand closes around my braid, yanking me backward. He holds my own knife up to my throat, pressing the cold steel against my skin. His breath is worse than Hank's.

"Drop the knife," he says sweetly.

Mel drops her knife without hesitation.

"Cal!" she shouts, not taking her eyes off me.

"Yes, do call Calvin," Alex mocks. "Save us the trouble of going in and fetching him."

Calvin comes barreling out of the warehouse, knives ready, but a fat guy with a baseball bat is waiting for him just outside the door. He swings hard at Calvin's face, and then his gut, connecting with the wound. Calvin drops, and the guy swings a few more times.

Mel screams.

Chaz barks but, thankfully, stays put.

"I lied about keeping you all alive," Alex whispers in my ear. Then he calls to the bat wielder. "Leave him now, Tony. Leave him for the dead." He turns back to Mel and Mae. "These are what we're here for."

Mel steps in front of Mae, who at this point is probably a more able fighter than Mel.

"What do you want with us?" she asks, her voice cracking in the middle of the question.

"It's like I told Cate. I want all you've got." He turns to his men, who are all chomping at the proverbial bit. To the five on his right, he says, "First, the building. Take it all."

They cheer and run toward the warehouse, brandishing their weapons like movie extras in a Viking-era battle scene.

"Take this." He nods to Hank, who wraps one mammoth arm around my neck. "Come here, ladies," he calls.

Mel, who is quaking and trying her damnedest not to cry, takes Mae's arm and leads her toward us. Alex walks around Mel and Mae. He pauses on Mel's left to lean in and smell her hair.

"Mmmmm," he growls. "Smell that, boys? Smells like honeysuckle. This one'll be prime breeding stock once she's popped." Then he says to Mel, loudly enough for us all to hear, "As for the offspring, well. No meat more tender than that."

I fantasize about putting my axe right into that sick smile, cracking all those cardboard-colored teeth in the process.

Mel looks straight at me, avoiding Alex's piercing gaze on her left and the hungry expressions of the invaders all around us. I try to convey a vibe of *It's okay. We're okay.*

But are we?

"You said you wouldn't hurt them, Alex!"

Mel sees the source of the outburst before I do. Her eyes widen and then narrow very quickly.

"What are you doing with these people?"

Someone walks past me.

No way.

"They found me after you two abandoned me at the church. They took me in." Gary turns to look at me. His face is much thinner than the last time we saw him. It looks like he hasn't slept since that day either. He's sporting a jagged, uneven scar down his right cheek, a fresh purple bruise on his other cheek, and an older, yellowing one on his eye. "It's all about surviving now."

"Are you the reason they've been watching us?" I ask, nausea washing over me, flooding my mouth with sour, pre-vomit saliva. "Did you help them find us?"

"Actually," Alex answers for him, "that was a coincidence." He saunters toward Gary, letting his hand slide across Mel's belly as he steps away. "But once he knew who it was we were following, he made an adorable little plea for your safety. I indulged him, but only to ensure his cooperation... Now fall in line, Gary. You're a predator or you're prey."

Gary stays put. "You promised—"

Alex rounds on him in a split second, delivering a hard, businesslike blow to Gary's face with the butt of his handgun. Without hesitation, he aims the gun at Gary's chest and fires. His expression doesn't even change. Gary falls backward in what seems like slow motion, blood and soft tissue spraying out behind him as the bullet exits through his back. The shot echoes off the warehouse, drowning out our screams at first.

"Apologies for the interruption," says Alex as he picks up his hat, which fell off when he hit Gary. He pushes his greasy yellow hair out of his face and puts the hat back on. "I guess he's prey." He chuckles at his own joke. A throaty, self-indulgent, I'm-so-naughty chuckle, like he just told an offensive joke at a cocktail party.

I vomit, aiming for Alex's shoes.

He glances furiously at Hank, who throws me down next to my dead cousin. My temple smacks a half-buried rock, sending a blinding pain through my whole head. Spots obscure most of my vision. All I can see are a thousand little white pinpricks, and through that, Gary's blood-spattered face. Upturned, eyes open. A permanent look of shock is his final expression. Alex puts his boot on the side of my head to hold me in place.

"Now, Melody," he continues.

But Mel and Mae are wailing now, both for the loss of Calvin and Gary and in sheer terror of what will become of us.

"*Excuse me*!" he screeches, shooting a round into the air. *Bang!*

The crying doesn't stop, but it falls silent. Like someone hit the mute button. Their faces are still contorted, mouths agape in silent sobbing. Mel's stare darts between Gary's ruined corpse and my face. Mae's eyes are squeezed shut.

Alex regains his eerie composure instantly. "Thank you. Now, since you've made it this far, you already know that those gunshots will bring in all manner of unsavory characters, human and otherwise." Dramatic pause for effect. Then, with a sickening faux-gallantry, he adds, "If you want safety, come with us. I promise you'll live."

"Promise like you promised Gary?" I seethe.

He grinds his boot into my head, sending fresh hot pain through my skull. I think at this point everyone wants to imagine that they'd be strong, somehow stoic in the face of such agony and terror. I certainly hoped I would. But I'm not strong. I cry out in a high yelp that makes a few of the men grunt with laughter.

"Go to hell!" I shout at him, at all of them. Warm tears spring traitorously from my eyes.

More weight on my skull.

I cry out again.

"Okay!" Mel shouts. "Will you promise not to hurt us?"

"Well, no." Alex chuckles that cocky piece-of-shit chuckle again. "That was never the offer. Through pain comes strength, Melody. But I'll tell you what. If you both come with me now, no more bullshit, I won't blow your dog's brains out and make you eat him."

"Both?" Mel sputters. "There are three of us."

"The breeding potential is all dried up in old Nana, I'm afraid." He waves his hand dismissively. "She'll be put to better use as live bait. She'll slow them down long enough for us to get out of here. Survival of the fittest, you understand."

I'm fighting back tears and vomit (both of which are winning currently) and the urge to scream until my throat is raw. I guess we were so busy protecting ourselves against the dead that we forgot what monsters the living could be. There has to be a way out of this, something we didn't think of before. This isn't how it's supposed to be!

But before I have even a shadow of an idea, I hear the moans of many approaching zombies. I instinctively try to get up, which catches the attention of our sadistic captor.

"Look at that," he says with what sounds like sincere surprise. "It looks like we have company already. Better make your decision, Melody. Old useless Nana? Or dear, sweet Cate?" He bends down and brushes his thumb along my cheek. The sour taste in my mouth intensifies.

I can't see them, but I can hear them. They're coming fast.

"She can cook!" Mel shouts desperately. "She's useful in the kitchen. She can clean and sew too. If you take us all, we'll go right now."

Alex hums quietly. "Well, I'll have to think about it..."

I can practically feel him smiling. The sicko is stalling.

"All right then!" he says with a little too much enthusiasm. An abrupt, tight pain flares across my scalp as he yanks me up by my hair. "Take the other two!" he barks. "I want us back at camp by dark. Nana, you'd better prove your salt as a cook." Another despicable chuckle. "Pun not intended. Really, though, consider tonight's dinner your chance to prove your worth. Or tomorrow, you'll be dinner for the dead." He looks at Mel like a foodie staring at a filet mignon. "I simply cannot wait until you're unencumbered. But until then—" He squeezes my face with his free hand. "—your sister will do."

A warm sensation rolls down my face. Blood? I gingerly touch the wound inflicted by that jagged rock, just above my left temple, and draw back red fingers.

Mel leashes Chaz. He must understand the gravity of our circumstances because he doesn't make a sound. The three of them walk silently toward where Alex still has me by the hair. Both women look at me as they pass, their eyes conveying shock and desperation.

When the zombie sounds turn to zombie sightings, our captors pack up our stuff, and we leave Calvin and our little warehouse behind. Mel and Mae weep silently behind me as we get farther from Calvin, who is sure to be killed by the approaching zombies if he isn't dead already. I sort of hope he is when I consider the alternative.

We're a hundred paces into the trees when a commotion breaks out. Alex, who heads up the group, turns and looks at each of his men in turn. I quickly realize he's counting, seeing if one of his people got left behind. Then he looks past everyone toward the warehouse, where the sound is coming from.

"Come on," he says after a second. "He'll be dead in a minute."

I keep my eyes to the ground as we move, concentrating on forming an escape plan. We only have until we get to their camp before it's too late. Mae shuffles along, dabbing her eyes every so often. She doesn't know it, but she just gave me an idea. I discreetly tap Mel's back and shuffle my feet as we walk, dragging them exaggeratedly across the hard-packed dirt. She catches on and does the same. We make no extra noise, but the ground is noticeably disturbed.

If Calvin lives, at least he can follow us now.

Twenty-Three: Fly under the radar.

The hours and the miles creep by; as the low-hanging cloud layer burns away, the temperature climbs straight past warm to downright unbearable, despite the fact that the sunlight is blocked out almost completely by the trees. It's the sort of heat that makes every exhale feel like your whole body is melting. I can't remember the last time I had a sip of water. Yesterday? Today? I'm sweating so much that it feels like every drop of water in my body is being wrung out. I quietly shed my jacket and drape it over my arm, trying not to react to the leering gazes of several men as I do. At least no one is looking at my feet.

I steal a glance at my watch, which they somehow have not noticed yet: 2:33 in the afternoon. We left Calvin over two hours ago. If he was going to find us, wouldn't he have done it already? Are we leaving a trail for no one? Mel is dragging her feet, but is it still for Calvin or is it now exhaustion? Probably a bit of both. I keep dragging.

After we're several miles farther east than Calvin and I ever went, we walk into a scene that looks like it was plucked right out of a movie: a passenger jet, the kind that seats hundreds, lying in the middle of the woods under a hole in the canopy. It's missing one whole side, wing and all, like a giant pair of hands tore it right down the middle. Mangled bits of metal lie around in the wreckage as do many, many decomposed bodies.

My gaze darts around, looking for anything we can use to escape. No weapons allowed on planes, so that's a no-go. But what about the shrapnel? Sharp, easy to use, I wonder if I can discreetly reach out and grab a piece. The guy with the bat (Tony?) is eyeing me rather closely. But maybe if we stop for a second...

"There are probably tons of supplies in there," I suggest. "Medical stuff, clothes... Maybe even food." If we can get them to stop, even for a minute, there's a chance we can get away.

"We cleared it on our way through," one of the other guys grunts. He notices me looking intently at the wreckage. He bends down so his sweaty, bearded face is right next to my ear. "Got my eye on you, honey."

As we pass the wreckage by, I curse my cowardice. I should have done something, anything! That was probably our last chance, going, going, gone.

After what feels like an eternity, Mel speaks up.

"I can't keep going in this heat."

"You can if you want the old woman to live," Alex calls back without looking. The guy nearest Mae, a tall, thin man with wiry red hair and many missing teeth, grins down at us and claps his crowbar into his hand repeatedly.

A few steps later, Mel falls back in a dead faint.

The ginger instinctively catches her halfway down but then drops her anyway.

"Alex?" he calls toward the front.

I look down at Mel, who appears to be unconscious. But I've seen her pretending to be asleep enough times to know that she's fine. She's buying time. At least one of us is on top of things.

"She needs water and shade. Help her!" I play it up, feigning panic.

Alex sighs audibly and turns around.

"You're shitting me."

"Mel," I say softly, stroking her cheek. I'm really heaping on the drama, fluttering my eyes as though I'm about to weep with distress, oh my poor poor sister, et cetera.

And it works flawlessly.

"Fine," Alex huffs, leaning on a nearby tree and picking the dirt out from under his nails with my knife. "Give her five minutes, and then we move—" He looks pointedly at me. "—with or without her."

Chaz lies down, his bad leg shaking.

Mae strokes Mel's head with one hand and the dog's with the other, her expression begging me to do something.

My mind races as I try to think of a way to use this time to our advantage. Five minutes. It's not a lot, but it's better than I could get us. We're still surrounded, but that isn't necessarily a deal breaker. We've gotten ourselves out of some pretty bad scrapes before. But those were zombies. Dead, slow, and (mostly) absent of thoughts or logic. People can think; they can reason. That makes people about a hundred times more dangerous. And there are like twenty people here. I nonchalantly look around and do a head count. Seventeen. Seventeen of them and three of us. I've only seen Mae kill one zombie, and it had no legs. And we all know Mel isn't in optimal fighting condition. I look around the forest for a rock, a tree branch, anything I might be able to use as a weapon.

"Still got my eye on you," the sweaty bearded guy says.

"Why? You gonna eat her, Barry?" the ginger asks. He throws his head back and fully enjoys his own joke.

Suddenly, I hear a *hiss*, almost silent, and a slightly louder *thunk*. I look up to see an arrow lodged half-shaft-deep in the ginger's throat. He drops his crowbar and turns to look at me, and then at Alex, who isn't paying attention. He mumbles incoherently, clutching at the arrow, and he drops.

The men standing next to him watch in silent confusion, and then all seventeen—sixteen—of them draw their respective weapons and scan the tree line, snarling. The forest is still, or as still as a forest ever is. But a deep, familiar voice calls out from somewhere on our right.

"Cate, fly under the radar!"

I crouch down, covering Mel and Mae as best I can with my body.

Another voice, female, on our left says, "Fire!"

Not half a second after we're down, arrows are flying from all different directions. The three of us make ourselves as small as we can while the arrows, each accompanied by a quiet *hiss*, find their targets with swift efficiency. A few bodies drop in the first second. The less fortunate are shot two and three times before fatal blows are struck. Some who drop are far from dead.

When there's no one left standing, Alex slowly comes to a vertical position. I can see his knees quaking from here. Good.

"You want the girls for yourselves? Take 'em!" he calls, turning in a paranoid little circle. He drops his gun. "There, see? We don't need a confrontation! But I've got another fifty men at my camp, and if I'm not back soon, they have standing instructions to come looking!" His feet don't seem to be working the way he wants them to; he's stumbling around now, a bit desperately, addressing the forest as a whole.

I get a perverse sense of triumph seeing him squirm.

He rambles on, crossing and uncrossing his arms, pointing at us, and holding his hands out like a man pleading innocence. "Go on, take 'em! You'll have no retribution from me. The pregnant one's nothing but a liability. Was about to kill her anyway!"

I expect (read: hope) to see an arrow come sailing out of the trees and into his eye or something badass like that. But nothing happens at first.

Suddenly, a shirtless figure crashes through the trees. He stops two feet from Alex and delivers a front kick to Alex's chest like he's kicking in a door. And then Calvin is on top of him.

"You think you can just take my family?" he shouts, beating Alex mercilessly.

Crack, crack, crack.

Alex's head is lolling by the third hit, but Calvin hits him a few more times anyway. He only stops when Alex goes completely limp and his limbs begin to twitch, at which time Calvin stands, spits, and puts his knife in Alex's eye. He approaches us slowly, head lowered, as though he knows what we just witnessed probably frightened us.

But Chaz rears up and bounds over to Calvin, wagging his tail so hard his whole butt wiggles. Mel follows, getting to her feet unsteadily and then charging him. He lets out an *oomph* as she smashes into him.

"Hey, my love," he murmurs. But he keeps looking around over her head. "Are you coming out or what?" he calls.

One by one, people in all black come out from the trees around us. While the rest of them remove arrows from the bodies, stabbing each one in the eye or temple, one of them, a pixie of a woman, approaches Mae and me. She unties and reties her white-blond hair into a tight ponytail as she marches toward us. We both stand. I tuck Mae behind me and push my hair out of my eyes, pulling away wet fingers. Jesus, am I still bleeding?

The woman stops right in front of me, lifting her face and smiling. Her left eye is almost as black as the eye patch that covers her right eye. She slings her hunting bow over one shoulder.

"Hello." Her voice is a low alto, which would be in comical discord with her tiny figure had she not just ordered the deaths of, what, sixteen men in thirty seconds? She keeps unsettlingly direct eye contact as she speaks. "You must be Cate."

Twenty-Four: Stay hydrated.

Her face matches her voice more than it does her body, stern and commanding with distinctly Gelfling features—the kind of face that could be sixteen or thirty-three.

"Who are you?" I ask.

"My name is Ana. I've heard a lot about you." She thrusts out her hand. "It's a pleasure to finally meet you."

I shake her hand.

She offers it to Mae, who is only an inch taller than her.

"You're Maebelle?"

"Mae's fine. And thank you all for..." She looks around.

"Good to know you, Mae, and it was our pleasure. Your grandson is a hell of a fighter."

She sure seems to know a lot about us. All I can glean from looking her over is that she's practically a one-woman war machine. There are several knives and one very small pistol strapped to various parts of her all-black-clad body so that even without the bow and arrows, she's still plenty deadly.

I do a quick count—seven knives, that I can see.

"Can you believe this?" says Mel as she and Calvin come over. "I mean, can you *believe* what just happened?!" She watches Ana with big, wet pregnancy-eyes. "You saved us. I mean, thank you." Sure enough, here come the waterworks. "Oh God, ignore me. Hormones." She expels a weird, choked laugh-cry from her throat and dabs her eyes with her knuckles. The right side of her face and most of her shirt are smudged with blood. Is that Calvin's blood or Alex's?

"I woke up surrounded by corpses," Calvin tells us. Mel nods in corroboration, eyes wide, as though she knows the story already. "If Ana and her people had showed up any later, I'd have been zombie chow. I told them what happened, and we followed you. Good thinking with the foot dragging by the way, Cate. That was you, right? Cate?"

"Yeah, thanks." I reply distractedly. My head, which has been throbbing since it hit that rock, begins to pound. Little sparks of pain shoot down my face and neck. I look around while Cal keeps talking, half listening. There are five other people. They all have bows—two crossbows and four compound bows. Ana appears to be the only woman. The others walk slowly around the bodies, picking up anything useful, scanning the forest around us every so often.

Mel and Mae tell Calvin about the last few hours—seeing Gary, losing Gary, almost losing Mae, that plane wreckage, which Calvin and the others naturally saw too. There are a few questions on my mind, questions I'm surprised no one is asking, such as who they are and how exactly they came to find our warehouse and Calvin in just the nick of time. I take a step toward the closest of the men, a person about my age with a face like a *Vogue* model or a Ken doll incarnate, but I stumble.

Ana catches me.

"That's quite a head wound you've got there."

"I'm fine," I snap, wiping away a fresh trickle of blood. "Probably dehydrated." Definitely dehydrated. I can hear my tongue suctioning to the roof of my mouth with every syllable. "Have you even seen Calvin? He's way worse off than I am." If she wants to worry about anyone's wounds, let her worry about his. His eye is swollen to the point that it's barely open, and he's leaning some of his weight on Mel. Plus I'm positive at least half that blood is his.

Ana glances at Calvin.

"Calvin has assured us that he's copacetic for the time being. We should move out if we want to get back before dark."

"Where's back?" I ask.

"To the vans." What an annoyingly vague answer. She eyes me with concern. I think it's concern anyway. She's tough to read. "Can you make it a few miles?"

I nod, though I'm fairly sure I'll be horizontal before long. But really, what's my other option? To be carried? Thanks, no.

She waves in the other five, who surround us immediately.

"All dead?"

A beanpole with close-cropped gray hair answers, "All dead, ma'am."

"Excellent," says Ana. She kisses the beanpole full on the mouth for long enough to make it weird. When she breaks the kiss she's all business again. "The roads should still be clear if we shift it."

Ken Doll nods and waves a hand.

"All right, let's roll out!"

"Never saw us comin', the wankers!" shouts a man with an impressive reddish-brown beard.

"Jesus, Murray, a little decorum please?"

"Yes, ma'am. Sorry, ma'am."

"How do you know they're clear?" Mae asks.

Ana's face betrays the faintest hint of a smile. She arches the brow above her patched eye. "Because we cleared them."

"What about all of these bodies?" Mel pipes up from under Calvin's arm. "Are we just going to leave them?"

Ana shrugs. "There's a whole forest full of animals here," she says without casting so much as a glance at the people she helped kill. "They have to eat too."

If I wasn't busy with blinding pain and distrust, I think I would already like Ana.

We gather our weapons from those picked off Alex and his people, and Mel finally trades in her pathetic pocketknife for a mean-looking buck knife with a real sheath.

But somehow no one has my axe. I find it almost immediately, though, under Alex's body.

"I can get that for you," calls Ken Doll, jogging over to help me flip the body.

"I got it!" I snap. "Thanks."

Ken holds up his hands and backs away. "No problem, jeez."

It takes me a couple of grunting attempts to get my axe out from under Alex, but when I slide it back into my belt loop, I feel good.

"Fuck you," I whisper as I walk away.

We walk for the better part of an hour while Ana explains to us that they have a place in San Francisco, safe as can be. She doesn't explain what I really want to know, however, which is how they happened to come by Calvin in the first place, so far from San Francisco, or why they're so ready to accept us into their group, hardly knowing us, or most importantly, why *we* should trust *them*.

She goes on at length about their place, an apartment building, heavily fortified with medical supplies and food and everything. The thought that it sounds too good to be true crosses my mind a few times. We're on a narrow road now, headed downhill toward two parked vans. The sun is hanging low in the sky and shining right into my eyes, but I can make out the shape of a person standing on the far side of the vehicles. No one in Ana's group seems alarmed to see him, so I assume he's one of theirs. If he's really even there.

It could just be the spots I'm seeing. I stumble on, not really listening anymore. The spots morph into a sort of black haze. I try to blink it away and it gets worse. Through the haze, the whole world tilts.

Calvin is saying something about a perfect setup and a real MD and the guy that brought them all together being some kind of genius. "Ana says he knows you, Cate."

That gets my attention, sort of.

"Me?" I ask absently.

Ana nods, keeping her face forward.

We're only a few paces from the vans now. The sunlight is blinding. Or is it? I stare downward. The blackness lingers around me like smoke. I can feel my body swaying.

"It's them, isn't it?" I hear Ana say. "The sisters." Her voice sounds distant, like I'm hearing it through a closed door. I feel fresh blood trailing down my face, but I can't be bothered to wipe it away.

I hear Mel gasp as a pair of worn brown leather boots come around the van, and a very clean hand reaches into my shrinking field of view. It takes my soiled and bloody hand as a soft voice floats to me through the haze.

"Cate?"

I look up, trying to see through the thickening blackness. When I get my eyes to focus, a tan face, huge green eyes, unruly black hair come into view. Beautiful. He smiles and says my name again. His hand squeezes mine.

The blackness turns to whiteness, burning my eyes.

Somewhere far away, a phone is ringing.

My heart pounds in my chest as I try desperately to blink away the white light, to see his face for real. But I know him, of course I do. I try to say his name, but before I can speak, the white goes black again and finally pulls me under.

Broken percussion beats and rhythmic vocals surrounded me, blasting out of my computer speakers and filling my bedroom with music. It was unseasonably warm for April, so my window was wide open, and every once in a while, the breeze would make the pages of my book quiver. It didn't matter; I'd read it a hundred times. I could practically recite it word for word.

My mom said something from downstairs. Yelled was more like it. I sighed and grudgingly turned down my music.

"What?" I snapped through my closed bedroom door.

The door flew open, and Mel came barging in.

"She said they're here." She wrinkled her nose. "Why do you listen to that stuff? You'd think a fifty-year-old woman lives up here."

"His music is timeless."

After I finished reading the page I was on, I reached out to my bedside table and grabbed whatever was closest—a receipt from the drugstore—to save my place with. "What's the new kid's name again?" I asked Mel as we descended the stairs.

"Marco, I think."

Through the glass panels in the front door, we could see the three of them: Aunt Tess, Uncle Bill, and the new addition, Marco, coming up the sidewalk. He looked sullen, dressed in all black and carrying an overstuffed black backpack despite it being spring break.

"Marco, huh?" I repeated. You know how sometimes when you first say a new name, it tastes funny? I mouthed it again. Mar-co.

"He's your age, Cate," Mom said from behind me. She fluffed her hair busily on her way to the front door.

"That old?" asked Mel.

He didn't look my age. His angular jaw and super-thick eyebrows made him look closer to Mel's age. The three of them stepped onto the front porch, and Aunt Tess waved.

Mel and I watched indifferently. Marco was about the tenth kid Tess and Bill had fostered. They always got adopted pretty quickly, too, so we didn't really get to know any of them. I figured this boy wouldn't be much different, apart from his age.

"Hey, gang," Aunt Tess trilled as Mom opened the door. They all shuffled in, and she held her hands up like Vanna. "This is Marco, our family's newest guest!"

Marco pushed a lock of his nearly ass-length black hair out of his face and held up a hand in a gentle wave.

"Hi."

"It's wonderful to meet you, Marco," my mom said cheerily. She almost reached for his bulbous backpack, but she let her hand fall awkwardly to her side. "Um, you can put your book bag down, honey, if you want to."

Marco looked down at my mom—he was easily a head taller than she was—and smiled timidly at her.

"No thank you, Mrs. Mortensen," he muttered.

"So polite! Please call me Marion. My husband, Andrew, is around here somewhere—Andrew!" she shouted, making both Bill and Marco jump a little.

Andrew came fumbling into the front room, his arms full of various grilling supplies and a ridiculously tall chef's hat precariously perched on his head. He set the stuff on the counter and brushed his hands on his jeans.

"Hi, Tess, Bill." He nodded to them in turn. "And you must be Marco. Good to meet you. Meat or no meat?"

"Sorry?"

Andrew chuckled. "I've got veggie patties for Tess, Cate, and Bill, or franks and burgers if you like. Pick your poison."

"Oh. Um. Whatever's fine," Marco replied. Everything he said seemed to be steeped in uncertainty, like he was surrounded by hostile predators.

"Franks and burgers it is. Cheese?"

Another awkward shrug. "Um. Do you have cheddar?"

"Oh do I have cheddar?" Andrew wiggled his eyebrows and leaned in like he was about to sell stolen goods. "You ever try aged English cheddar?"

Marco looked like he wanted to run away. "No?"

"Well, prepare for an unexpected culinary journey, Master Baggins! Ha! Cheddar, cheddar, more's the better!" he sang as he danced to the backyard, chef's hat still askew.

Mom rolled her eyes. "He's the funniest person he knows."

Aunt Tess patted Marco on the arm.

"Marion and I are going to do the side dishes while Bill and Andrew start up the grill. Bill?" She lifted her eyebrows at Uncle Bill, nodding in Andrew's direction. Bill got the hint and jogged toward the backyard to help Andrew. Tess turned back to Marco. "You can sit in here with the girls if you'd like." She smiled. Then she and my mom scuttled off into the kitchen.

"It's green!" Mom practically shouted, ruffling Tess's spiky hair.

"Yeah, the blue faded like instantly. My hair was silver for almost a month." Tess stuck out her tongue. "So, giving green a go. I think I'll do purple in the fall."

Marco looked at both of us in turn, and then he perched on one of the dining room chairs with his backpack balanced on his lap. He pulled out a spiral-bound sketchbook and a very worn pencil pouch, put a pencil in his mouth, and pulled his hair into a ponytail. Keeping the backpack on his lap, he hunched over his book and started sketching silently.

Mel rolled her eyes and went into the kitchen to help Mom and Tess. When I started to creep back upstairs, Mom caught me and gave me the look. Dejected, I slumped back to the table and pulled up the chair across from Marco. He didn't notice me at first; his pencil moved rapidly in all different directions, seeming to be drawing nothing but a bunch of disjointed lines at first. All at once, the lines took shape: a beautiful, middle-aged woman with dark curly hair and a dazzling smile.

"Who is that?" I asked.

Marco tensed like he'd been shocked and looked up sharply. Man, he really hadn't noticed me.

"Doesn't matter," he said, and smacked the book closed. It was the first thing he'd said yet that didn't sound insanely awkward.

"You've got some real skills," I tried again. "You could make a career of it."

"Too competitive," Marco said, effectively cutting off that avenue of conversation.

Okay then.

Out the window, Andrew and Uncle Bill poured what looked like way too much kerosene on the grill. Andrew dropped a lit match into the kerosene lake, and the whole grill nearly exploded, sending flames up fifteen feet before they calmed down into a normal (-ish) glow. After Andrew and Bill checked themselves for burns, they laughed, slapping one another on the back and then both sneakily peering into the house to make sure Mom and Aunt Tess hadn't noticed, which they pretended not to.

"Those men are going to burn down this house one day," Mom muttered as she stirred what looked like chocolate-chip cookie dough.

"They're worse when they get together," Tess agreed, shaking her head and covering the pasta salad with cellophane.

I looked back and noticed that Marco's giant marble eyes were trained on me, really looking at me for the first time since he'd arrived. When he noticed me noticing, he jerked his gaze away from my face, glancing instead at the red-and-blue lightning bolt on my shirt and sort of cocked his head to the side.

"Was that your music blaring out of the top floor?" he asked.

I nodded and shrugged sheepishly. My mom hated how loudly I listened to my music. She was constantly complaining that the neighbors didn't need or want to hear it.

"He's my favorite artist," I explained. "Or, was. His new album just came out on his birthday, and then—"

"And then he died," Marco finished. "I couldn't believe it." He pulled a portable CD player, the likes of which I hadn't seen in years, out of his backpack and popped it open. Inside was the same CD I'd been listening to. "He was the real deal," Marco said, closing the CD player and stuffing it back into the bag. "What do you think of that sax solo in the title track?"

"Are you guys talking about that old guy Cate's always on about?" Mel asked on her way to the backyard. "How d'you like that, Cate? This kid is just as weird as you are. Are you secretly fifty years old too, Marco?"

Marco just looked at her.

I stuck my tongue out and turned back to Marco. "Mel's not a fan. Sometimes I can't even believe we're related... So you've been with Tess and Bill for what, three weeks now? Have you met Gary?"

"Dude is such a tool."

"Do you want to kill him yet?"

Marco almost chuckled, letting out a huff of air through his teeth.

"Kill? No. He was only home for like two days before he left for spring break. But ask me if I want to shave his head while he sleeps."

I snorted, picturing the absolute freak-out that would ensue. "That's too traceable," I whispered conspiratorially. "Just put some super glue in his hair gel. Does he still use that industrial-sized tub of blue gunk?"

"Yep." Marco nodded. "That was one of the first things he said to me. 'Don't touch my hair gel, freak boy.'" He perfectly imitated Gary's signature posture, combination chest-puff and lower-jaw jut. "As if I'd touch that shit."

"That's an awfully accurate interpretation for having only known Gary two days."

"It was a lasting impression."

"Well, it looks like you two are getting along well," Andrew said, appearing out of nowhere and frankly startling me, smelling strongly of smoke and various meats, his blond eyebrows slightly singed. "Mel told me Marco likes that Star guy too."

"Starman," I reminded him for the hundredth time, "and that isn't his name."

"Terribly sorry," he mocked, poking me in the ribs. "Time to dish up. Come on." He waved us back. "You two have all night to discuss Star Dude. You know how to work a grill, Marco?"

Marco shook his head.

"Well, it's time you learned. Extremely useful skill, grilling. Gets you out of all sorts of awkward social situations." He winked at me.

As we stood up, Andrew put his arm around Marco's narrow shoulders. "Plus, it's a perfectly legitimate excuse to light stuff on fire all day!" He gently steered Marco to the backyard where the rest of the family was already waiting.

Twenty-Five: Catch your breath.

"I think she's waking up."

My eyelids crack open, and that minuscule movement sends a lightning bolt through my head. I'm stretched out across a seat with my head in someone's lap. Mel. Her belly is hard and warm against the uninjured side of my face. My fingers brush something warm and furry on the floor.

"Cate?" Mel's voice is soft and soothing. Her hand strokes my hair. Her belly presses gently against my face.

I smile despite the ice pick in my left eye. The baby kicks again, a little more insistently this time.

"He wants you to wake up too," Mel whispers.

"He?" I hear Calvin say.

Mel hums and I feel a not-unpleasant vibration in my head.

"It feels like a boy."

My eyes close against my will. I feel myself being tugged back down into the darkness.

"Go!"

I wrench my eyes open.

We're not in the van anymore, but outside.

And we are surrounded by the undead.

"Just run!" a woman shouts.

Gunshots.

"We got this. You get them inside!" A man this time.

Calvin's face looms above me, looking ahead. His huge arms support me. The world around us moves fast. We're running.

"Through that door," shouts the same woman, "GO!"

Suddenly, we're in the dark. It's pitch-black, but I can still hear the fight going on outside.

A door slams shut behind us.

I know I'm dreaming, but it's one of those dreams where you know and you don't care because the last thing you want to do is wake up. Sam is smiling into my eyes. Her hand is on my cheek. I touch her hair, her face, her hands. My Sam.

Cate.

She doesn't say it out loud, but I can hear her voice in my head clearly.

Her hand finds the back of my neck. She pulls me gently toward herself and kisses me. She kisses me like she hasn't seen me in over a year. She kisses me like I remember, soft and warm and sweet. I taste her vanilla lip balm, feel her breath on my face.

Sam.

My heart races. Maybe she really is here. Or maybe, maybe if I wish hard enough, I won't have to leave wherever this is. Maybe I can stay here with Sam forever. But the kiss changes, becomes desperate. Sam bites my lip until it hurts, and at that exact moment, I smell the rotten flesh. I yank away from her and cry out in horror and anguish. The beautiful girl I loved has been replaced by a monster, a rotting stinking zombie. It has her features but distorted. Wrong. I know what comes next, what needs to be done, but how can I do it?

Oh, Sam. My beautiful Samantha.

I raise my knife...

I wake up seconds later. Or has it been hours? Days? I open my eyes slowly, gently. The pain in my head has thankfully receded to a dull ache. I'm a little surprised to find myself in a bed. A real bed with real blankets. I close my eyes for a second and relish the long-forgotten luxury of being comfortable. "Comfy, cozy," Andrew would have said, to which my mom would invariably add "snug as a bug in a rug."

Mom. Andrew.

That ache for them has not subsided, not even a little.

Across the room (because I'm in an actual room, with powder-blue painted walls and everything), the window is covered with white gossamer curtains that glow pale gold in the afternoon light. At least, I think it's afternoon. There's a wooden dresser in one corner, and on it are a yellow teapot and matching mug. A basic first aid kit sits open on the bedside table. There are two chairs by the door.

How long was I out? Was I dreaming? Am I still?

The door opens. A familiar face pops in and grins.

"Well, hey, Cate! Welcome back to the world!" Mae shuffles into the room without closing the door. Through the opening, five or six people are visible, only two of whom I recognize—Mel and the woman with the eye patch. Anne? Mae plunks down in one of the chairs and turns toward the opening. "Melody!"

Mel comes running into the room with Chaz in tow. A huge smile brightens her face when she sees me awake.

"Hey, sis," she murmurs, scooting the second chair next to the bed. "How are you feeling?"

"Been better," I croak.

She nods and wrinkles her nose. "You've been in and out for more than a day. You look like hell."

I glare at her. "You've looked better yourself," I retort automatically.

But when I get a good look at Mel, and at Mae for that matter, I see that they both look cleaner and more rested than any of us have in months.

"Did you take a shower?" I ask.

"Better," she says. "A *bath*. Cate, I had a hot bath last night. It was *glorious*." She places a hand on her giant abdomen. "The baby loved it. Kept kicking the whole time." She puts the same hand on my arm. "Ana helped me wash you too," she says tentatively.

Ana. That's her name.

I lift the comforter. I smell good, at least. Clean. Like Dial soap. I'm dressed in an oversized white T-shirt, which is not mine, and a pair of drawstring pants, also not mine. An invisible, ice-cold hand squeezes my heart. I scramble into an upright position (*ouch*). Chaz snags the opportunity and jumps onto the recently vacated end of the bed.

"Where are my clothes, Mel?" I ask, my voice edged with accusation. "Where the hell's my jacket, my watch, where's my goddamned *axe, Mel!*"

"Calm down." Mel puts a restraining hand on my shoulder to keep me from jumping out of the bed. "Ana took the clothes to be cleaned and the weapons for maintenance." She stands, crosses the room, and reaches behind the door.

She pulls something off a hook and brings it to me. "We're safe here," she says as she lays Marco's jacket across my lap. I snatch it up and hold it to my chest like a security blanket, which if I'm being honest, is exactly what it is.

I don't see that Ana has come into the room until she's right in front of me. The woman with the Targaryen hair and the eye patch. "Good to see you awake." she says.

Mel takes my hand. "Do you remember what happened? Do you know where we are?"

I shake my head slowly, eyes closed, trying to reconnect the dots. All at once memories flood back. I recall frustration and suspicion as I ran to confront the watcher in the woods. Alex. The name makes my insides turn to stone. Everything that happened at the warehouse, terror and guilt. Why did I have to run after him? How selfish and stupid. I remember all of us walking through the woods, that boundless, helpless rage. And all of those arrows: uncertainty and a sliver of hope...

"You saved us," I say to Ana. Then that nagging question from before comes floating back up to the surface. "But how did you find us?"

"Calvin led us to you," Ana reminds me.

"Calvin, right..." But no, that's not the right question. "Calvin was unconscious. How did you find him in the first place?" There it is.

Ana shifts her weight.

"We weren't looking for him," she finally says, "not at first. Our scouts spotted your cousin a few days ago on a run. We were planning to extract him. We were keeping tabs on Alex and his men until an opportunity presented itself. We stumbled on your people by complete accident when your two groups crossed paths."

The gruesome image of Gary's last moments swims up into my conscious mind, and I feel sick to my stomach. But I still don't understand. It's frustrating; all of the events from the day Alex attacked are jumbled in my head. So many little pieces scattered in complete disarray. I try to assemble the pieces I recognize first—the watcher, the attack, Calvin down, the forest...

"So you saw what happened and did nothing," I accuse. "You saw them kill Gary, saw them almost kill Calvin, and did nothing to help us?"

Ana straightens up to her full four foot ten or whatever and puts her hands firmly on her hips. "We didn't see that part, Cate." The way she says my name sounds an awful lot like *you ungrateful little shit.* "We were following Gary's part of the group, at an incredibly safe distance. We heard the gunshots and picked up the pace, but we didn't even see your camp until Gary was dead and they had already taken you."

"Oh." I purse my lips, feeling like a scolded child. Whatever they didn't do, they did save our lives. "Okay, so why did you want to get Gary in the first place? I mean him, specifically."

"Sweetie, don't you remember?" Mel asks.

I close my eyes and try again to recall what I can. The missing piece. Watcher, attack, Calvin down, rescue...and vans. There were vans and they took us...somewhere. Mel, Calvin, Mae, and me all in one van. In the other, I guess, Ana and her men. But if we were all in the back, who was driving our van? I attempt to recall the fleeting memory of when I came to in the back of the moving vehicle. My head in Mel's lap, Chaz on the floor, Mae and Calvin behind us...

Who was driving?

My breath catches in my throat.

I look up at Mel, who seems to know exactly where my thoughts have ended up.

"Marco?" I ask. For some reason, I'm afraid that saying his name will somehow jinx it.

But Mel's smile grows so wide it threatens to crack her face in half. She turns to Mae, who is already standing by the door.

"I'll go get him," says Mae. "Had to lock him out last night. He was hovering all night, wouldn't move an inch from you. Calvin finally convinced him to eat something and get some rest, but only after we swore that we'd fetch him as soon as you were up." She smiles and leaves, followed by Ana.

"I think Cal wants to see you too," says Mel as she stands slowly and stretches her back. "I'll be back in a second. Are you all right on your own?"

I roll my eyes. "I'm fine, Mel. We're safe here, right?"

"Yeah, right," she says with a little head shake. A strand of honey-colored hair falls in her face, and I realize how long it has been since I've seen her hair down. God, it's getting long. She kisses my forehead and leaves the room, closing the door behind her with a soft *click*.

How long has it been since I've heard a door close instead of slamming? How long since there was anything on the other side but the sounds of imminent death or silence?

My heart is in my throat the second she leaves. I focus my gaze out the window, trying to will myself calm. Even though I just received verbal confirmation that Marco is not only alive but *here*, in the same place as me, I can't believe it. Not until I see him myself.

I focus on the dust floating in the sunlight, trying to calm my nerves, to steel myself against a probable letdown. I've had so many dreams like this, where our family is back together, and then I wake up alone and the disappointment is crushing.

In four, out eight.

The room smells completely different from any other place we've found shelter in since Connell. It smells clean. No rot, no grime. I can't be sure, but I think I smell lemon oil. And is that *fabric softener*? There are sounds floating in from the other side of the closed door—chatter, laughter, other doors opening and closing. How many people are here?

Where *is* here?

Suddenly restless, I push the covers off myself and swing my legs over the side of the bed. The hardwood floor is cold beneath my bare feet. I press down with each aimless step I take, trying to capture the solidity, and look up to find myself in front of the window. I pull the curtains aside, slide the window open, and lean out.

In four.

I smell the sea, salty and heavy, and the distinct odor of hot asphalt.

Out eight.

The sun beats down on my head. A seagull glides directly across my line of sight, its beady little carnivore eyes staring into mine as it forces out a piercing *Caw!* We must be high up; I can see the rooftops of a few buildings below me. We're in the city. We must be. There are buildings and abandoned cars everywhere and nothing is unpaved. Hills roll and undulate under the pavement. Homes and buildings are built right onto the steep inclines, taller than they are wide, squished together on every inch of available space. It's a city made of hills.

There are at least thirty zombies on this block alone. I'm grateful to be so high up; I don't think I would be all that useful in a fight just now. I lean out and whistle for the hell of it. Only one looks up, and its attention is quickly diverted back to something scurrying below, a squirrel or a cat or something. Then a stiff ocean wind picks up, blowing the curtains all around me, sort of enclosing me in a gossamer cocoon. I bring my upper half back inside and start to untangle myself.

The door clicks open behind me. I turn to see Mae's little silhouette shuffling in, followed by a second, much taller figure that hovers in the doorway. I reach out to move the curtains, close my fingers around the edge of the fabric, and hesitate. If this is a dream, I'll wake up any second, alone again.

I slowly pull the curtains open.

His hair is cut to his jaw, and he has a mustache. He isn't dressed all in black anymore either. But it's him. He doesn't move at first, but eventually he takes a tentative step in my direction. Another. I stay put, thinking the same thought on repeat: *Please don't wake up. Please don't wake up.*

Not this time.

With a few large steps, he is standing right in front of me. He reaches a hand out tentatively, and I hold my breath.

Please don't wake up.

He smiles a little and tucks a wayward strand of hair behind his ear.

"Cate," he whispers. His voice sounds exactly like I remember.

"Marco?" I finally say, and in that instant my arms are around him like a vise.

"Hey," he says. "You made it."

"Where did we make it to, though?" I ask, letting go. "Are we really in San Francisco?"

"See the ocean?" he says, pointing out the window. "Far out that way, past the three brick buildings?"

I nod.

"If we were to sail straight out from that point, we'd reach Alcatraz in an hour."

"We're that close?"

"Yup. We got here about six months ago, me and a few others. Brought in new people here and there. Did have to kick one guy out. That was a whole thing."

"And Lucy and Bill?" I ask.

Marco shakes his head sadly. "I was really hoping when my scouts told me they'd found Gary, that maybe we'd find Bill too. That day at the church, I saw him, surrounded by all those zombies. I ran to him. I tried, Cate, but by the time I got to where he'd been, he wasn't even there anymore. He was just gone. No body, no blood. Nothing. I thought that if he'd lived, he must be with you or Gary, but..." He runs a hand over his face. "And Lucy, I don't think she even made it out of the church."

After a soft knock at the door, Calvin pops his bandaged head in.

"You're up," he says with a wide grin. "About time, kid."

I wrinkle my nose at the obnoxious nickname. "Not that easy to kill me," I retort. "What about you? You took quite a beating at the warehouse."

"Eh." Calvin shrugs and taps the thin bandage that's wrapped around his head. "This is all that's left. This and a few bruises. Nothing compared to yours."

I bring a hand up to the wound and find my whole head is wrapped in a thick layer of gauze. Jesus, it's basically a helmet.

"So this is Marco, huh?" He walks over to us and stops a few feet away, crossing his arms over his chest. "This is the guy you've been pining for since we met."

I cross my arms too. "Shut up, it's not like that."

"Then why are you blushing?" Calvin doesn't wait for an answer. Instead, he sizes Marco up and narrows his eyes. "I sure do hope he's as good as you and Melody said, Cate. Hate to have to kick his skinny ass."

"Wait, haven't you already met?" I ask.

Calvin immediately breaks the tough guy routine and chuckles, uncrossing his arms. "Yeah we've met. I just wanted to see what you'd do if I went all macho-protector on you. He's all right. I've been talking with some of his people. They really respect him. He runs a hell of an organization."

"His people? Runs?" I repeat, turning around to face Marco.

"Well, I told you I started with a few people. For a while, it was just me, then I found Duchess. I just called her Dog. When we met Tanya and Amy in Oregon, she sort of became their dog. We met Henry and Sylvia's family in Eureka, and Ana and Joaquin right after. That was when Nick's brother Nate died. It was really rough. We found this place by accident, or, it sort of found us, and we've been improving ever since."

"And everyone is here because of you."

He shrugs and studies the floor, a glimmer of the old, painfully awkward Marco peeking through. "I guess."

"So now that we're all up to speed," Mel interjects from behind Calvin, "where are we sleeping tonight? I don't think I can do one more night in that chair." She looks disdainfully at the chair by the bed.

"You and Calvin can take the one-bedroom he's been staying in if you want," Marco answers. "Four-C. It's big enough for two—" He glances at her belly, and adds, "Or three. Congratulations, by the way."

"Thank you," Mel and Calvin say in unison.

Good God.

"We try to reserve the big apartments for common areas and families. Since you'll be a family in a week or so, you definitely qualify for more than a studio. You'll have to double-check with David in Six-E to be sure about available places, but I think Mae can have the place directly to the left of you, Four-B. If not, Four-D is probably vacant. Unless you want to live together, then ask David about which two-bedrooms are available. Should be one or two."

Mel, Calvin, and Mae thank Marco and leave to find their new dwellings. Chaz stays behind for a second until he realizes Mae is leaving too, at which point he scrambles off the bed and bounds down the hall after her.

"What about me?" I ask when they're all gone. "Is this my room?"

"This is the infirmary," says Marco. "The doctor lives here. Well, Doc; her wife, Tanya; and their dog, Duchess."

"So where will I be staying?"

"Whichever place Mae doesn't choose will be up for grabs. We'll talk to David."

A minute later, Mae, Mel, and Calvin come back with their new addresses. Mae has opted for her own place, with Chaz of course, so that Mel and Calvin can have their privacy.

"But it's right next door, so I can make myself useful. And David, oh he's a sweet man—he said you can have the room just to the other side. Number Four-D. Ain't it perfect? Anyway," she continues, "we're off to look around. You comin', Cate?"

I shake my head. "I think I need to lie down for a bit," I lie. Apparently, Marco understands because he stays behind when the others go. I climb onto the bed, and he sits next to me.

"You still have my jacket," he says when we're alone again.

"Pretty sure it's mine now."

An hour later, we leave the only room I've seen so far to find my apartment. We get to the stairs, descend three levels, and walk down a short hall to an apartment marked *4D*.

"It isn't a very big place," says Marco as he opens the door. The walls are the same blue as the infirmary. "It's a studio, like Mae's and like mine. But there's enough room to live comfortably."

"Are you kidding?" I say as I walk past him into the apartment. "I've spent the last several months holed up in a place this size with three other people and a dog. This is great."

"Kitchen is there," he says, pointing to a tiny kitchenette with a two-burner stove, "and the bathroom is through there. We have solar power, so there is electricity, though it's pretty limited. There's running water too, hot and cold, but we try to stick to one shower a week each."

I nod mutely. One shower *a week*? I'm not about to tell him that I've been bathing in streams for most of the last year. One hot shower a week is more than I ever thought I'd have again.

Somebody comes to the door for Marco. He promises to be back before dinner, and then I'm alone in the apartment. My apartment. I walk around, opening and closing empty drawers and cupboards, turning the bathroom light on and off. I steer clear of the mirror.

Outside, the sun is setting and the sky is bright orange. I walk halfway to the window, but a dizzy heat washes over me so I redirect to the twin bed in the corner. I lie down and close my eyes. Just for a minute.

Twenty-Six: Take a walk.

I jerk up in a sweaty panic, awakened by my own mumbling. My heart feels as though it might pound right through my chest bone. The nightmare was not remarkable, same stuff I've been dreaming about since Halloween before last—zombies, death, more zombies. Maybe it was more frightening since I haven't seen a zombie for days (how many, exactly? Two? Three?). I sit back on the twin bed—*my* bed—and steady my breathing.

In four, out eight.

My head is pounding; this gauze is too tight. I claw at it until I make a small tear, and then I shred the stuff until it's a pile of scraps on my lap. I bring my fingers gingerly to the wound. There's still a little dressing left, should be fine. Satisfied, I stand up and creep toward the door. I put my boots on as soon as they gave them back to me, but for the first time since I was bit, I left my knife and my axe on a little table by the door while I slept. Now if I can just locate my weapons in this pitch-black apartment...

Crash!

I bump right into the table, knocking both weapons to the floor. Cringing at my own lack of stealth, I pick them up, slip the knife into my pocket, and put the axe back on the table.

Then I exit apartment 4D, checking and double-checking that the door isn't locked before I close it.

It's still and dark in the hall, with only one window at the end letting in the tiniest rays of starlight. Someone in one of the nearby apartments is sawing some serious logs. It's so loud it almost sounds intentional. I walk slowly, aimlessly up and down the corridor. When I pass my door for the third time, I hear a noise at the opposite end of the hall. I instinctively pull out my knife and walk toward it. It's coming from inside the stairwell. It sounds like human footsteps, with their distinct non-dragging rhythm, so I fold my knife closed and tentatively slide it back into the pocket of my borrowed, too-big sweatpants.

The door to the stairwell opens before I am halfway down the hall, and someone emerges. It's too dark to even try to make out a face. I flatten myself against the nearest door and wait silently for whomever it is to pass. But they don't. Instead they walk closer and stop halfway between the stairs and where I'm hiding. They take a couple more steps toward me and stop again.

"Cate?"

I come out of the doorway and turn toward the voice. "Marco?" I whisper.

My eyes finally begin to adjust. He's standing in the middle of the hallway in nothing but a pair of gray sweatpants that are as baggy as mine.

"I heard a crash up here," he says.

Oops.

"Sorry, that was me."

"Are you all right?"

"I'm fine." I wave a hand dismissively, though I'm sure he can't see it. "I walked into a table on my way out of the apartment. I'm surprised you heard it from another floor."

He tiredly ties his hair back into a ponytail. "I'm right below you," he says. "Three-D"

"I'm sorry I woke you."

"I was up anyway," he says, taking the last few steps and closing the gap between us. "What about you? Still an insomniac, huh?"

"Nightmares," I say with a shrug.

"Well, since we're both up, you want to walk?"

"I'd like that."

As we walk, he tells me a little about what's behind some of the doors. For the most part, my floor seems to house the weaker, dependent people. Children, elderly, that sort of thing. I don't let on that I'm disappointed to be lumped into that group, but I make a mental goal to get off of floor four.

"Where are you?" I ask. "You said you're below me, right? Are there a lot of people on the third floor?"

"Not many," he answers. "Third floor is for the fighters; the first line of defense, I guess you'd say. It's me, Ana and her husband, and the rest of Ana's men."

Floor three is where I want to be.

Just then my stomach grumbles audibly. How long since I've eaten? "Is there a pantry around here?" I ask.

"Pantry is on the seventh floor," says Marco. "Locked most of the time except for ration day. But if you're hungry, we can eat at my place. I have plenty of food."

"Sure, okay."

He leads me down one level to his apartment, 3D, a studio just like mine but with more furnishings. He clicks on the one standing lamp in the corner by the door, which casts a dim white glow over the whole apartment. There's a papasan in the far corner by the bathroom and a small, neatly made bed in the other corner with a bedside table next to it. On the table is a familiar sight—his little brown leather-bound notebook sitting on top of his sketchbook. The pencil next to the books is barely two inches long. I run my fingers across the spiral binding.

"You're still drawing?" I ask.

"Sometimes," he says, closing the door but not bothering to lock it. Hm.

"Any chance you have a hairbrush here?" I ask half jokingly, reaching up to unbraid my hair. "I haven't brushed my hair with anything but my fingers in literally months." Awkward chuckle.

But when I look up, he's staring mutely at my abdomen. I look down and realize that my shirt has come up, revealing my scar. *Shit*. I yank my shirt back into place, my face growing hot.

"Cate, what happened?"

"I, ah...got bit."

"You *what*?" he practically shouts. His thick brows knit together over saucer eyes. "How is that possible?"

"I don't know," I confess, sounding quite a lot more defensive than I mean to. *Tone it down, Cate.* I take a slow breath. "It happened when we got separated. Or, that night. Or, well, the next morning. It bit me while I slept. But nothing happened. I mean, nothing but a whole lot of pain. After five hours, Mel cauterized it, which hurt a hell of a lot more than the bite itself if you're wondering. I don't know what happened. I just...I just didn't die." I avert my eyes because I can't stand that concerned, pitying expression. "I know it's ugly," I mumble, wishing he'd look anywhere else.

"Don't be an idiot," says Marco. "I mean, you basically have a superpower. Who even cares about a scar these days?"

I laugh despite myself. "You sound like a comic book."

"Maybe." He chuckles. Then his face gets serious again. "But you're the only person I've ever heard of who hasn't died from a bite." He bends down, unlaces his boots, and sets them neatly by the door.

"You take your shoes off now?" I ask.

He shrugs and grins. "Only in my apartment. But yeah. We're safe here."

"Huh." I bend down to take off my own and toss them to the door. The carpet is not the crappy berber you usually find in industrial inner-city apartments such as this one, but thick and plushy, softer than the bedroll I've been using for the past however long. I flex and wiggle my sock-clad toes deeper into the fibers, thanking whomever that they gave me new socks while I slept.

We eat sitting cross-legged at his little coffee table. I'm full after six saltines and half a can of peaches. We regale each other with stories from our time apart, him on his bed and me curled up in a blanket nest in the papasan. I tell him about how we found Chaz and Mae and Calvin; he tells me about how they found the apartment building thanks to a man named David and his wife, Eunice, and how long it took them to fortify. I nod at appropriate times, trying to focus on the story, trying not to fall asleep. But the blanket nest is beyond comfortable and I feel myself slipping further down. I blink. When I open my eyes, I'm in a bed. Marco is sitting on the papasan reading a comic book by the light of one candle. When he sees me sit up, he sets it down.

"Oh hey. Welcome back."

"How long was I out?" I ask hoarsely, stretching my arms over my head.

"Couple of hours."

"What about you?" I ask. "Aren't you tired?"

"Not really," he says. "I was on duty an hour ago. Always gets my blood moving."

"On duty?"

"Security," he answers. "I'll show you in the morning. So tell me more about your trip down. How was your first winter?"

"That was rough."

"Tell me about it." He chuckles. "I nearly died twice. Neither time from a zombie, mind you."

The sky outside lightens, first to a dark gunmetal gray and then to bright jewel blue in the time we spend talking. We spend the morning totally undisturbed. As the day wears on, he tells me the particularly strange story of how he found a little boy named Francis all alone living in a dumpster downtown.

"I'll introduce you two tomorrow."

Around one in the afternoon, a guy who looks like a heavily tattooed Santa Claus knocks on Marco's door and pulls him into the hall. An hour goes by, and then two. I consider leaving the apartment, but the thought is banished as quickly as it comes. The last thing I want is to deal with people. I especially don't want to meet any new people, which requires infinitely more energy than dealing with familiar people. I feel my eyelids getting heavy, and although I fight it at first, I eventually curl up and succumb to exhaustion.

Twenty-Seven: Know your surroundings.

I wake up I don't know how many hours later to a faint scratching sound. I couldn't put my finger on what felt off about this place until now, but there it is. The absence of sound. In my old life, the world was assaulted by constant sounds. The buzz of TV, phones going off in ten different ways, cars, planes, sirens, people, dogs... After the end of life as we knew it, there were still sounds, different ones, but still constant. Here it's quiet. Three floors up, in a secure building, the silence is almost stifling. The world is on mute except for that *scratch-scratch*ing.

The room is dark when I open my eyes except for the one lamp, which has been moved right next to the papasan, where Marco is sitting with his sketchbook in his lap.

"What time is it?" I ask, automatically checking my wrist only to find it annoyingly still naked.

"A little after four in the morning," Marco says, glancing up.

I sit up and stretch. Then I get out of bed, keeping his thin flannel blanket wrapped around my shoulders like a cape, and shuffle toward where he's sitting.

"What are you drawing?" I ask.

He makes no effort to conceal his sketch as he did the only other time I looked. Instead, he lays it flat on his lap. A reclaimed city stretches across two pages. Buildings torn apart by explosion or disaster, trees and vines growing in the ruins. A lone zombie wandering down the root-warped sidewalk. In the middle of one page, a doe is drinking from a long-forgotten fountain.

"Where is that?" I ask.

"Here," he replies. "I'll show you if you want." He closes the book and sets it on the bedside table. "But not right now. You hungry?"

By the time we've finished eating breakfast—fresh fruit which Marco tells me came from the roof garden—the sky is already a pale gray-blue and growing lighter by the second. I peer out the window, forgetting how much closer I am to the ground than the last time I looked. With nothing to arouse them, the zombies below mill around aimlessly in the fog. A small part of me, the part that's always itching for some kind of confrontation and deathly bored when there's none to be had, wants to tap on the glass to see what they'll do. Probably, they'll look up. That many could bring on a full-scale attack.

I put my fingertips to the windowpane.

"Come on," says Marco, drawing my attention back inside. "I want to give you the tour."

He leads me out the door and upstairs to the fourth floor. We wake Mel and Calvin to take them along. Mae and Chaz are sleeping so soundly in Mae's place that we decide to let them be.

"The building is really old," Marco tells us as we ascend the remaining flights of stairs to level seven. "It was built in 1926 according to David."

He points out places of interest as we go: the infirmary, which we've seen too much of, the laundry room, with several huge wash tubs and a hose coiled neatly in the corner. Clothing, towels, and bedsheets hang on lines strung across the room. We pass a few early risers in the hall. Some watch as we go by, but most of them look too tired to want to start up a conversation. Which is fine by me.

Mel stops the tour with a dramatic little gasp. "Marco, do I smell coffee?"

"That pregnancy nose is no joke, huh?" says Marco as he leads us to the other end of the hall. The door to apartment 7J is closed, but now that we're closer, I can smell coffee too. "We found some a few weeks ago," he explains. "A whole stash of coffee beans. I mean *pounds*. We had to go back with a car just to get it all back here. David grinds it by hand every other day."

Mel inhales deeply. "I miss coffee more than anything."

Marco smiles. "Then this will probably be your favorite room." He opens the door, Wonka granting access to his factory. "J for java," he says. I can practically hear the Oompa Loompas.

The smell of fresh coffee wafts out of the room. Mel and I both inhale several times as we creep closer. The apartment is set up like a staff room, three couches and several chairs in a circle with a coffee table in the middle. There are two three-gallon metal pots steaming on the stove.

"Are we, I mean, is it...?" Mel nods her head toward the pots.

"Of course," Marco answers. "Just keep it to one cup per day per person. There's no cream but we have sugar. The pot on the left is decaf."

Mel hugs him, I mean really, properly hugs him for maybe the first time ever, and then she grabs Calvin's hand

and dashes inside, filling an *I Hate Mondays* mug with decaf and a pinch of sugar and sipping it like it's the elixir of life. She rests a hand on her belly.

"You like that, don't you?" she coos, and she takes Calvin's hand and places it in the same spot. "He likes hot coffee too." Then her face brightens even more, if that's possible. "Cal," she says, grabbing another mug, "how about we give Nana the best wake up ever? Does she like decaf or caffeinated?"

Calvin grins, kisses Mel's cheek. "Caffeinated, I think."

I swear the farther along she gets, the more unbearably saccharine their interactions are. Pretty soon, they'll probably meld into one person.

They fill a mug for Mae and leave Marco and me to do the rest of the tour ourselves. When we step back into the hall, there are people all over. I watch them working, chatting, drinking coffee from mismatched mugs.

"How many people live here?" I ask Marco.

"We had nineteen people in total, now twenty-three with you guys. The kids, Francis, Adrienne and Nick, are five, seven, and four years old, respectively. Everyone has a job and everyone is in charge of security in some way."

"Even the kids?"

"Not them. Their main job is just to try to be kids. That's hard enough."

"Marco!" A little boy with red hair comes careening down the hall. He slams full-speed into Marco and hugs him tightly around the legs.

"Hey, Francis." Marco hugs the boy back. "How you doing, buddy?"

Instead of answering, Francis looks expectantly up at me, his little face dead-serious.

"Hi." I grin. "I'm Cate. It's nice to meet you." I hold out my hand to shake.

Francis seems unconvinced that that's even my real name. He draws his own hands under his arms and studies me with open distrust.

I've never been great with kids; they make me nervous. I just stand there smiling awkwardly for a minute until Marco speaks up.

"Francis," he says, crouching down to be on the boy's level, "remember when I told you I was looking for my friends?"

"Uh-huh." Francis nods his little head, totally enthralled the second Marco starts talking.

"This is my friend. We found her and her sister and their new friends too."

Francis nods some more, glancing at me only briefly before his full attention is back on Marco.

"Are they staying with us now?" he asks as if he doesn't really care one way or the other, and only wants to know for the sake of knowing.

"Yup," says Marco, "the more the merrier, right?"

"Right," Francis mutters, still unconvinced. When a woman down the hall calls his name, he gives Marco one last quick hug—and me one more sour face—and then bolts off in her direction.

Marco stands up. "I think he likes you," he says.

"You're kidding, right?"

"Marco," calls a big man with a beard. He grabs another guy, and they jog over to meet us. "The outer perimeter is in some dire disrepair, my man."

The skinny guy picks up right where the big man left off. "Hole on the west corner is almost big enough for them things to just waltz right in."

"Surprised they ain't," the big man chimes in. He stops and turns to me as if I just appeared out of thin air. "Who's this?"

"This is Cate," says Marco. "From the group we found up north."

The skinny guy holds out a hand. "Jax."

"I'm Toby," big man says, stepping slightly in front of Jax, "but the ladies call me Big Daddy." He arches an eyebrow and grins.

"Nobody calls you that," says Jax.

"Come on, brother!" Toby whines. "Quit shitting on my game!"

"You got no game, Tobias."

"So," Marco pipes up, "the wall?"

"Wall. Right." Toby clears his throat. "Jax and I could have it done in less than an hour, but we ain't got the supplies."

"We've been unlucky on runs lately, I know," Marco says. "What do you need to get the job done?"

Toby lifts his gaze to the ceiling for a moment, stroking his epic blond beard. The word *mama* adorns his knuckles in thick, faded black script.

"We've got the tools," Jax answers for him.

"Just need something to patch up the hole," Toby continues.

"We could manage with maybe a couple o' two-by-fours for now..."

"Just enough to keep them at bay."

"Won't be pretty."

"We're not aiming for curbside appeal here, Jax."

"I was just sa—"

"Okay," Marco interjects, "take what you need from the spare units. Use furniture, doors, whatever you need. David can tell you which ones to raid. Stick to the upper floors so the noise doesn't bring them in."

"But that won't hold forever, y'know," says Toby.

"It doesn't need to," Marco assures them. "We'll be ready by week's end."

"You mean, *ready*?" says Jax, his yellow eyebrows shooting up into his hairline.

"Should we get the captain?" Toby asks excitedly.

"I spoke to him this morning," Marco says, putting a hand on each of their shoulders. "I'm making the official announcement tonight at dinner. Seven days from tomorrow."

Toby and Jax high-five. "All *riiiight*!"

"Buh-bye, Frisco!"

"Guys." Marco stops them as they turn to leave. "Perimeter is priority."

Nods all around.

"There's a hole in the perimeter?" I ask when they're gone, careful to keep my voice low. "Do people know?"

"They know if they're working their assigned shifts." He points back to the closed door of 7J. On the outside hangs a whiteboard, which upon closer inspection displays a weekly schedule with names and times listed in twenty-four hours.

"Every adult has a shift on the outer perimeter," Marco explains. "Four at a time, one-hour rotations, twenty-four hours a day. Mel will be the only exception for now." He points to his name next to the number twenty-three. "I've got my next shift at 2300. Since you need training anyway, you should come out with me. Or if you'd rather train in daylight, you can go with Ana at..." He scales the list with his finger. "Oh-nine-hundred." He looks at me expectantly.

I try to remember what I know about military time. Do you add twelve hours, or subtract? No, that makes no sense. "I'll go with you."

He jots down my initial next to his shift.

"So just to clarify, there's a zombie-sized hole in your wall, every adult knows about it, and no one is panicking?"

"*Our* wall," Marco corrects me, "and no. Why would they?"

"Self-preservation, maybe?"

His mouth turns up at one side. "No," he says. "Come on."

On the second floor, there are two armed men in black standing just outside the stairwell door. They're Ana's people—the kissing guy and the Ken doll. My God, he's even more beautiful close-up. I'd like to be his Barbie.

"Joaquin, Rob." Marco nods. "This is Cate. Cate, you probably recognize these two from the woods."

The kissing guy steps forward and thrusts out a hand.

"Good to meet you, Cate. Rob." He says it with a curt nod and no smile, as if even the time it took to shake my hand was time improperly allocated.

"Rob is Ana's husband," Marco offers.

That explains the makeout sesh in the woods.

"I'm Joaquin," says the Ken doll, taking my hand and (no joke) kissing it. "I'm nobody's husband." He gives me a slick wink, ignoring Rob's not-so-subtle glare, and flashes a devastatingly perfect smile. How do his teeth stay so white?

I take back my hand and try not to stare. My stomach is suddenly full of pterodactyls, and I'm wishing I was wearing anything but these baggy sweats.

"Nice to meet both of you," I say to Joaquin.

"I'm taking Cate down to see the perimeter," Marco explains, eyeing Joaquin. "Won't be long."

He hustles me through a heavily reinforced door. The stairs to the ground level have been destroyed and replaced with a fifteen-foot ladder that isn't permanently attached to anything, which I'm guessing is for easy removal should the need arise. Marco climbs down first.

"Careful," he says as I mount the first rung. "It's wobbly as hell."

And he isn't kidding. Even with Marco at the bottom holding the ladder steady, my descent is reminiscent of a Charlie Chaplin routine.

Floor one is completely dark. Every door is permanently fixed shut. Even the windows have two layers of boards cross-hatched over them. Only one door has a tiny slit cut out, a couple of inches across and about a foot tall. Just enough to see out of.

"I can see why one hole won't be the end of things," I whisper. "You use this whole floor as a buffer?"

"Exactly. It took us months to complete the outer wall, but since then, we've had only two breaches, only one of which counts."

"How's that?"

"Because the other time Sylvia left the door open. She's the kids' mom. She teaches them too. She's scary smart, worked for NASA or something before, but she's got like zero common sense. You'll meet her at dinner."

"Who else will be at dinner?"

"Everybody." He peeks outside for a second and waves me over. "Want to go outside?"

I peer through the slit. The outer wall is a mass of bricks, wood, and other less-identifiable materials. I crouch down and try to see the top. It has to be about fifteen feet high.

"Can we?"

Grinning, Marco displaces the handmade latch. The door swings open, and warm, humid air rushes in.

Twenty-Eight: Listen to people who know better.

There are ladders at each corner of the wall that lead to small, crow's-nest-type platforms at the top. Between the platforms, there are loops of some mean-looking razor wire. Or barbed wire? Something wire.

I whistle. "There's no getting over that."

Well, unless any Abnormal zombies come to the party. I shudder.

I stop and turn around to face him. He's surprisingly close; my nose is almost touching his collarbone.

He takes an awkward half step back.

"Hey, have you..."

"Hm?"

"Have you seen any—" How do I phrase this? "—weird zombies?"

I expect him to look at me like I just grew another head. Instead he nods. "Yeah. Tons, actually."

"They do weird things? Running and stuff?"

"Yeah." Then he addresses a sentry who sits atop the wall, a middle-aged woman with a thick gray ponytail and a rifle in her lap. "Hey, Eunice, back soon. Just showing Cate around."

"No problem, kiddo!" Eunice croaks. Marco doesn't seem to mind the nickname the way I do.

He lifts the door, which is built like a skinny garage door.

I draw my knife and simultaneously curse myself for leaving my axe on that stupid little table in my apartment.

"We call them Variants," he continues. "The weird zombies."

"*Variants*?"

"Yeah. Why? What d'you call them?"

"Abnormals."

Marco wrinkles his nose. "What kind of name is that?"

"Better than Variants."

"Abnormal is clunky. Variant rolls off the tongue. Plus it sounds scientific."

"Okay, Professor," I scoff. "So anyway."

"Anyway." Marco picks up where he left off. "Ana thinks the Variants—"

"Abnormals."

He rolls his eyes. "She thinks they originate from somewhere in the city."

"Why does she think that?"

"There seem to be way more here than there were on the way down."

"Speaking of," I say, sliding my knife back into its home, "there don't seem to be many zombies out here at all."

Marco glances over his shoulder at me.

"I mean—" I trip over some kind of rubble, right myself, and jog to catch up to him. "—I just thought, you know, in a bigger city there would be, like, a higher concentration of them. Or something."

He stops to let me catch up fully, picking his fingernails with his knife while he waits. "I have a theory about that. I think it's just another distorted fact. See"—we traverse a graveyard of broken-down cars and other junk—"basically, a zombie is only as good as its brain, right? The center of the disease."

"Sure."

"Well, I did this summer science project when I was like ten. I left ground beef out to rot. One in the sun, one in the shade, one in the fridge. Fridge meat lasted well over a month before it got really putrid. But the two outdoors were rotten in about two weeks flat. I mean *rotten*. Festering and shrinking."

"That's disgusting, Marco."

"But that's the thing. If a zombie is only as good as its brain, then on any given day where the temperature exceeds, say, forty degrees, the zombie is for all intents and purposes just a hunk of exposed meat. It only takes about two weeks for meat to rot in warm air." He holds up two fingers to reiterate. "So I figure the shelf life of your average zombie is only about two weeks, from heart stoppage to brain soup."

"What about the skull?" I ask. "Doesn't that hinder some of the process? And what about conditions? Humidity and stuff?"

"Like I said, it's just a theory. But even with the skull, a zombie probably gets no more than a month of unlife."

"So this might actually have an end?"

As if on cue, a half-rotten zombie comes ambling around the corner toward us. I have my knife out in a millisecond, but I barely have a chance to grip it properly before Marco is cleaning its brain juice off his knife.

"Jesus," I mumble, putting away my knife. Marco was fast before, but if anything, this last year and a half have made him near invincible.

"They seem to slow down the more they decompose too," Marco comments as we continue on.

"I've noticed that too. Hey, another thing I meant to ask you. How do you know so much about all this? I mean, how did you know before?"

"Cindy told me once that the best way to succeed in life is to become an expert in anything that interests you. And I guess zombie lore has always sort of fascinated me. That and survival stuff, and general science and biology, which are all sort of in the same vein."

"So basically you did a bunch of research?" I ask.

"Basically."

I'm not sure why I feel a twinge of disappointment. What else was I expecting? I let my attention drift outward to the buildings and sidewalks around us. Everything is being overtaken by indigenous plants: singular blooms and delicate saplings patiently forcing their way through hairline cracks in the pavement, grasses and vines crawling up building facades undeterred. It's unexpectedly picturesque. Even the unmaintained power line poles, rotting from the inside out, are giving life to various fungi and housing a hundred birds each. Their songs fill the air around us.

A frighteningly fresh zombie comes off an adjacent street. I'm trying to decide if its flesh has the pinkish hue of the living or if it's a trick of the light. While it stumbles across the pretty little scene, not noticing me, Marco turns a quick left into a narrow alley so that I'm left strolling along by myself for a second before I notice he's gone. I turn around to see the heel of his boot disappearing around a corner. I walk back to the alley, but when I get there, it's deserted. It's just me and several fully rotten corpses. The stink is unbearable. I step around and over them slowly, trying not to breathe, listening for Marco or zombies and hearing neither.

I'm abruptly yanked into a pitch-black doorway. I yelp in surprise, for which I'm rewarded with a soft chuckle.

"It's me," says the darkness.

I smack what I now know to be Marco and am met with another chuckle. "Shut up," I whisper.

"Sorry." He takes my hand again. "Come on. I want to show you something."

My eyes slowly adjust as he leads me farther into the darkness. We're in a kitchen of some sort, restaurant-size, with huge sinks for the dishes and long rows of stovetops and walk-in refrigerators. As we walk by one, a soft knocking sound comes from inside.

"Don't worry about it," Marco says when I go to open the door. "I put it in there, a new Variant to show Ana. Last week. You do not want to smell that."

"A new one?" I ask.

"Not really new, we've seen a few like it. Just has a new thing."

Through the abandoned kitchen is a small café where a few of the tables are still littered with evidence of previous use—half-full coffee cups, a few jackets hanging on chair backs, fancy cloth napkins folded like fans. It must have happened so quickly here. A snap of the fingers.

I touch the lipstick-stained rim of a coffee cup as we walk by, wondering what it was like to live through (or not live through) such a terminal event in such a populated city. I can almost hear the screams of the patrons as they probably trampled each other trying to flee to safety. How many made it? Where did they go?

Now we're standing in front of a set of sheer-curtained french doors. Marco opens them gently. The room beyond is grand in both size and appearance. Many large windows send shafts of light across the whole space. It looks like the lobby of a fancy hotel, the kind I'd always seen on TV but never had the chance to see in person.

"God," I breathe, "it's otherworldly."

Marco leans on what was probably the reception desk. "I know, right? Someone like me would never have had a reason to even walk into a place like this before." He grins and crosses his arms. "Now I come here all the time."

There are chandeliers of varying sizes hanging all over, now tarnished and full of cobwebs, lending to them a ghostly sort of beauty, like those images you see from the submarine cameras that dive down to the Titanic. Long-forgotten elegance and luxury, frozen in time.

I run my fingers along the reception desk, making a trail in the dust. Then the fountain in the center of the room catches my eye.

"That fountain! It's the one from your drawing."

"Yeah, the deer is somewhere around here too. It took a while, but she trusts me now. Sometimes, I bring her vegetables from the garden."

There's a squishing sound somewhere behind us, in the shadowed corners of the lobby. I draw my knife, tiptoe toward the sound. It only sounds like one or two, thankfully.

"Oh man," I whisper when I get closer. The two zombies spring up and charge me at full speed. "Shit!" I yelp. I stumble back, but muscle memory takes over and I quickly slide into Calvin's form. I duck and knife one in the temple. Roll away from the second, come into a loose crouch, take it out at the knees, and put my blade in its eye as soon as it hits the ground. The eyes have color. Go figure.

"Wow," Marco says when I stand up. "Look at you."

"Yeah, Calvin's a great teacher. Oh, and I, uh…I found the deer."

"Bummer." Marco bows his head. After a minute, he perks up again. "Come on. The best part is through here."

I follow him to an elevator with open doors. There's a ladder inside that goes through the escape hatch.

"How high does this go?" I ask, letting Marco climb up before me.

"To the roof."

I ascend after him, and about thirty feet up, I'm already puffing and a little sweaty. No wonder he's so fit these days. His life is a series of ladders and staircases. I have to take several embarrassingly long breaks on the way up. Marco indulges me but doesn't pass up the opportunity to give me shit.

"What did you do all year, sleep?" He chuckles. "You're in worse shape than last time I saw you. How is that possible?"

"Shut *up*," I huff.

About a week later, we emerge onto an exquisite rooftop garden. Even after more than a year of neglect, it's breathtaking. A gravel path winds its way through a maze of unkempt hedges and wooden archways dripping with roses and jasmine and several little fountains modeled after the big one in the lobby. There are even a few little stone benches along the way that are almost totally overgrown with ivy. I inhale deeply several times, trying to commit the scents of each flower to memory. No clue when I'll ever smell jasmine again.

"What made you come up here?" I ask between sniffs. "Was the ladder your doing, or did you find it that way?"

Marco is interrupted by a shuffling sound from across the garden. Another noise accompanies it. In the corner farthest from where we are, there is the unmistakable sound of a child crying.

"Hello?" I call.

A little voice cries out. "Please."

I start to walk over to where the child is hiding, hoping against hope that they're not bitten or something. I know I cannot kill a kid (hell, even that little Abnormal tugged at my heart strings and it was full zombie), which means that either Marco would have to do it, or we'd have to just watch the little one die and kill them as soon as they turn. Neither prospect seems preferable. My head goes to all the dark places as I inch closer to the kid. I utter a silent chant in my brain: *Please don't be bit. Please don't be bit.*

Marco grabs my forearm. "Wait," he whispers.

"What are you talking about?" I ask, not bothering to whisper. "That kid needs help."

He doesn't let go of my arm, instead walking with me toward the child, whose cries are becoming more adamant the closer we get. He pulls out his axe when we're close enough to see the child. It's a little girl, maybe three or four years old, sitting tucked into a more overgrown corner of the maze. Her knees are drawn up to her chest, and her head is on her crossed arms. She raises just her eyes when we approach but keeps the rest of her face hidden and continues to sob.

"Hi there," I say in my sweetest voice, taking one step closer. "Do you need help? Are your parents here?"

"Mommy," she whines.

"Cate." Marco tightens his grip, trying to keep me from going any farther forward.

I wrench away and walk up to the kid, who is looking at me but still bawling her eyes out.

"It's okay," I say, squatting down a few feet from her in an effort not to startle her. She's pale and skinny, probably been hiding for days, and her chestnut-brown hair is matted and dirty. Poor little thing.

"Come on," I murmur, standing her up.

She clings to my arms and whimpers. Her hands are cold and clammy.

"*Cate.*"

I snap my head around and glare daggers at him. "*What?*" This kid clearly needs our help, so what is his problem?

The sudden stinging pain of my flesh being torn away makes me cry out. I turn back to the kid, who I hadn't noticed until this second is no longer crying, but giggling. She looks up at me with her big brown eyes, hand still holding mine, and she draws one little razor nail slowly down my arm, grinning.

"Cate!" Marco says again. "MOVE!"

Before either of us can react, the child drops my arm and sprints toward the fire escape. She—it—leaps over the ledge and disappears.

"What the shit!" I stumble backward, try to stand, trip on myself, and fall back on my ass. "What did you—you just—and she, you... What the hell was that?" I sputter as I finally manage to pull myself up on a nearby tree and begin to uncontrollably sob. *Oh, perfect.*

"I thought you said you've seen these things before?" Marco asks incredulously.

"Seen *what* things? Are you telling me that little girl was a *zombie*? A zombie who cries and climbs ladders and, and *talks*?"

"Yeah, she's a goddamned Variant!" Marco shouts, grabbing my arm where the girl did indeed leave five nasty gashes. I pull away instinctively, but his grip is iron. "Let me look," he snaps. He turns my arm over to see the extent of the damage. He clicks his tongue. "These are deep."

"I'm fine." I pout, yanking my arm back. "I'm immune, remember? The Incredible Zombie-Proof Girl." I wiggle my fingers in self-mockery, eliciting a hot tearing sensation in my forearm.

"You're not immune to infections, though, are you?" Marco shoots back.

Why am I being so venomous when he clearly just saved my ignorant ass?

"No, I guess not." I hold my arm up to examine the scratches. "So what now? You didn't happen to bring a first aid kit, did you?" I chuckle nervously, trying to break the tension I created.

"I did, actually." He pats his pocket. "I bring one every time I go outside the wall, just in case." While he talks, he removes the kit and pours a stinging clear liquid over the wounds, and then wraps them with gauze. "But this is just a patch-up kit," he says when he's finished. "It's already bleeding through. I can't fix this on my own. We need the doctor."

Twenty-Nine: Get that wound checked out.

After switching shirts with me, donning my tank top, and giving me his long-sleeved tee to hide my wounds, Marco leads me hurriedly back to the apartment. Joaquin is alone when we get back, and since his attention is occupied by my ass, or maybe Marco's ass, he doesn't notice that there's blood leaking through my sleeve.

He does, however, do that beautiful smiling thing again as we pass, though again, I can't discern the intended recipient. But it distracts me blissfully from the sting in my arm. Just in case, I hazard a breezy, attractive smile back. Carefree, hint of sexy. *More teeth, like you mean it. Jesus, no. This isn't a dental exam!*

"Switched shirts, eh? Suits you."

He winks at Marco.

Oh. Marco. Damn.

Marco doesn't even pretend to play along.

"Seen Amy around?" he asks.

Joaquin's smile disappears as his gaze finally lands on my bloody arm. "Cate, what happened to you?"

Marco answers for me, delivering the lie like it's nothing.

"We got into a jam. Cut herself on a broken window."

Without another word, we ascend the stairwell and don't stop until we reach the seventh floor. I keep my arms crossed as we pass a few others to avoid unwelcome questions.

When we step out on floor seven, we speed-walk toward the infirmary. Almost immediately after Marco knocks, the door swings open. The woman on the other side smiles warmly as she steps aside to let us in. Her jet-black hair is cut in a steep A-line.

"Hey, Doc."

"Marco, Cate, what can I do for you?" Her voice is like the Christmas bell from *The Polar Express*.

I hold out my right arm and she lets out a little "oh," and she gingerly lifts up my sleeve and asks, "What have we got here?"

"I got scratched."

She starts to unwind the bloody bandages. "By what?"

Marco answers for me again. "A Variant."

Doctor Li's face pales. "Oh my," she says as she clips back her hair. "Cate, please lie on the table." She points to a sheet-covered table. "This won't be nice for you. In fact, it's going to hurt quite a lot. I think we have some liquor left over from the last amputation…"

"No, you misunderstood." Marco puts a hand on her shoulder to slow her down. When she jerks like she just stuck a fork in a toaster, he yanks his hand back. "Um. Sorry. Cate's circumstances are sort of special. She just needs stitches."

"I don't think I follow, Marco."

"I'm immune, Doctor," I say, bypassing further discussion and/or lies. "The infection doesn't, you know, infect me."

Her expression denotes more professional interest than legitimate surprise. It's almost as if she expected that someone, somewhere, would eventually be immune and that now she'd met that person. Box checked.

"I see," she says after a second. "Okay then, stitches it is." She pats the table and I hop up. "And please, call me Amy."

While she's stitching the fifth and final wound, she asks, "So who else knows about your...circumstances?"

"Just my people," I say, wincing for the thousandth time, "and Marco."

"Try to hold still."

"Sorry."

"No need." She ties off the last stitch. "And your secret is safe with me."

"Thank you. Your discretion means a lot."

"Of course, Cate. Part of the job. Speaking of which, may I check your head wound?"

I nod, and she lifts the thin square of gauze I left behind, saying nothing about the absence of the rest.

"Looks good. No pain?"

I shake my head, shrug. "A little."

"Totally normal."

"Thank you, for, um...fixing me up. Twice."

"It was my pleasure," she says, opening the front door. "Aside from one incident after we first arrived, my work normally consists of minor scrapes and the occasional sniffle. It was good to have a change in pace. Marco, do you have a minute?"

"You okay for a second, Cate?" he asks.

I crunch up my face like *whatever*.

"I'm not six years old, Marco."

"Okay. Stay here, back in a flash."

"And Cate," says Amy, "ask Calvin to swing by soon. I want to check up on his leg, make sure everything's working properly."

"No problem."

With a nod, she shuts the infirmary door, leaving me standing in the seventh-floor hallway with a bunch of people I still haven't met. I'm actually paralyzingly uncomfortable, but I'm not about to admit it. Hopefully, my presence will go unnoticed until he gets back. I scoot into the corner.

Marco and Amy stay gone forever, though, which in real time is probably about three minutes. Weird how slowly time seems to pass when you're not constantly waiting for danger or looking for food. I turn around and watch the others going about their duties. Some carry laundry; some carry tools. One woman who looks like she could be a direct relation to Marilyn Monroe is writing something on a clipboard, looking sultry and serious.

Behind her and down the hall a bit, a small, portly, sweater-clad man stands staring at me. He's in his late fifties, I'd guess, with poofy gray hair and wire-rimmed spectacles that sit halfway down his nose. He pushes them up, not bothering to pretend he's not watching me.

Okay, buddy. There's polite curiosity and then there's blatant creepery.

After a minute, he shuffles over, looking oddly timid for a guy who spends his time staring people down. He adjusts his sweater and smiles. I'm not at all surprised that argyle has survived the apocalypse. Much like cockroaches, it apparently cannot be killed.

"We've all been waiting a long time for you," he whispers.

"Me?" I ask. "You sure about that?"

"Marco told me all about you, Cate." He clasps his hands over his belly. "You're what we've been waiting for. You're the missing piece." He raises his eyebrows as if inviting me to ask what he means. He seems to have a flair for the dramatic.

Okay, I'll bite. "How so?"

"Well—" He pushes up his glasses and gestures grandly at the rest of the hallway. "—everyone here is waiting to go to Alcatraz. We've had a plan since March. Not to brag, but it's a hell of a plan. But every time we're close to being ready"—he emphasizes "every" and "time" with a little backhanded clap—"our Marco pulls the plug. Always with an excuse. Part of the plan is missing, or something needs repairing, on and on. Meanwhile, we're all standing here with our schlongs in our hands—pardon the obscenity— waiting for the green light. But the thing is, now that I've seen you, I'm fairly certain you're the missing piece."

I'm skeptical, but the presence of an actual plan is news to me. I press further, making my skepticism as obvious as humanly possible. "In that?"

"In that the plan's been perfect since day one, dolly. The things that needed repairing—" He shakes his head. "— didn't really need repairing. The parts of the plan that we revised, I've never seen such minor alterations. It's you he was waiting for." He cups my face, unsolicited. "His family."

I back away enough that his hands fall to his side. He seems not to even notice.

"I've seen him drawing when he thinks no one's looking," he continues. "Sometimes, it's a landscape or a monster, nothing." Dismissive wave. "But more often than not, he's drawing faces."

I don't take the bait this time.

He forges on, sans encouragement. "One is your face. I just knew that the day the people from his sketchbook appeared would be the day we started really preparing to leave. And now here you are. My name is David." He offers a hand. "It is beyond words to finally meet you."

"Cate." I shake his hand. "But I guess you knew that."

"Indeed I did."

He shuffles off just as the infirmary door opens behind me.

"Sorry about that," Marco says, rejoining me. "Talking shop."

"No biggie. I was just talking to, um, David?"

"Oh, yeah?" Marco says. He must notice my face, because he continues with "David comes off a little, um, familiar? But he's harmless. One of my closest friends."

"He's great," I say immediately, though I'm not sure I mean it. "We were just talking about the place. You know, security, food. And stuff."

Why am I lying?

"He's lived here since before. He's been the building's caretaker for twenty-seven years or something."

Marco leads me into the stairwell, and we start to ascend.

"Really?"

"Mm-hm. He saved us from a horde the size of Texas. I'm serious, at least a hundred zombies, and it was just a small group of us. David and Eunice let us in here just in time. The horde came around the corner right as I shut the door, and they just kept on walking right past the building."

"That's pretty amazing," I reply. "So what you're saying is, I have him to thank for you still being alive." I'm sort of joking, but Marco is dead serious.

"Yeah, absolutely. Not that you'd ever hear it from him."

We reach the last staircase, and not a moment too soon. I would have thought my legs must be pretty toned after more than a year of bike riding. But after a few days off the bike, despite climbing about ten thousand stairs in the interim, my muscles feel like useless meat. I huff as I mount the final step. Marco tries not to laugh at me, and I shoot him a withering glare.

Then he opens the door to the roof. It's nearly sunset; the temperature is cooling rapidly. The breeze kisses my skin and raises goose bumps on my arms.

"This is the garden," Marco says, "everyone's favorite spot. It took all of us, including the kids, to make it what it is. The soil and planter boxes alone took a month to gather and build."

There are twelve giant rectangular planter boxes lining the roof in rows of four, each with a fruit or vegetable or herb. A boy and a girl are playing tag, running through the spaces between the crops.

"Those are the other kids, Nick and Adrienne," Marco whispers.

They stop short when they see us. The girl approaches first. The boy stays behind, peeking around her timidly.

"Hello," she says with a voice more like an adult than a seven-year-old. She has blonde hair and a zillion freckles. "I'm Adrienne. Who are you?"

"I'm Cate," I tell her, offering my hand.

She grips it firmly in her little fingers and shakes it horizontally. "That's how I shake hands," she says proudly. "My daddy said it's not the right way, but Mom says it's unique. That was a Word of the Day. Mommy gives us a new word to learn each day, and that was yesterday's. I like being unique. Can you spell unique? I can."

"Let's hear it," I say.

She stands up a little taller.

"U-N-I-Q-U-E. I like words with Qs in them. I think they're unique. You're from the new group, aren't you?"

"I am."

"Are you Marco's girlfriend?"

I shake my head. "Nope, just friends."

"And what about that other lady? She's your sister, isn't she? That's what my mommy said. Is she going to have her baby soon? Her belly is huge!"

I can't help but grin at the undaunted little extrovert and her cut-and-dry line of questioning. "Yes, she'll probably have it soon. Her name is Melody."

"Like a song?" Adrienne asks.

"Exactly."

"Melody was our word of the day—" She counts on her little fingers. "—a lot of days ago. M-E-L-O-D-Y."

The little boy hasn't said a word. He's a male doppelganger of Adrienne, with the same inquisitive blue eyes and round, freckled face.

"Is that your brother?" I whisper to Adrienne.

She turns. "Come on, Nick. Come meet Cate."

He takes a tentative step around his big sister.

"Hi, Nick," I say, squatting to his level. "My name is Cate."

Nick just stares at me for a minute, biting his lip.

"Nick doesn't talk a lot," Adrienne explains. "We had another brother, Nate, but he died. And now Nick is really quiet."

"I'm sorry," I murmur. Then I smile sweetly and whisper to Nick, "It's okay not to talk. I don't like to talk much either. It's overrated."

"What's that?" Adrienne asks.

"Overrated? It means, um..." I've never had to explain that before. "It's when people think something is better than it really is."

"Oh. Can you spell it?"

"Sure. O-V-E-R-R-A-T-E-D."

Adrienne repeats the word and the spelling. "Thanks!"

"You're welcome. Now you have two Daily Words."

She rolls her eyes. "Word of the Day. See, Nick? She's nice."

Nick's little face glows red from all of the attention and he runs off. Adrienne follows, resuming their game like they'd never stopped.

"I bet you can see everything from up here," I say as Marco and I gravitate toward the western edge of the roof. "Which way's Alcatraz?"

Marco looks around. "There." He points in the general direction of the water.

I scrutinize the road below, trying to see a route to the water. Zombies wander all over. It's weird how unnatural I feel about not having killed many since we arrived here. I guess after a while anything can become routine. I'm suddenly very aware of the presence of my knife in my left back pocket. *Use it or lose it.*

"There are so many of them down there," I say. "How will we ever get past them with such a big group?"

"We have a plan," Marco answers simply.

When I turn around, he's smiling. Sort of.

"You going to tell me the plan?"

"Of course."

"When?"

"Soon."

"You're infuriating sometimes, you know that?"

We walk through the garden long after the kids have gone back inside, until the sun dips below the ocean and the chill of nighttime settles in. Marco picks a few blackberries from one of the bushes, and we munch. The tangy sweetness makes me thirsty.

"It's about dinnertime," Marco says, glancing at his watch. "Everyone eats together. David calls it the gathering of the five families."

"Great. I could eat a whale. What's for dinner?"

"Whatever the Captain catches, probably not whale, and veggies from the garden. I think we just harvested potatoes yesterday too, so it'll be a big meal."

"Who is this Captain I keep hearing about?" I ask.

Marco holds open the door for me, and we descend the stairs.

"Captain Jacob Roth. He's our fisherman, and when the time is right, he'll drive the boat to Alcatraz."

"Is that what's happening in seven days?" I ask.

Marco sighs. "I really hope so. We'll know after dinner. That'll be tonight's main topic of discussion. I told Jax and Toby to keep it on the hush-hush, but knowing Toby, everyone already knows."

On our way back onto floor seven, the Marilyn lookalike stops us.

"Cate?"

I don't know why it surprises me anymore that everyone knows me before I've met them. "Um, hi."

She grins and gives me a big, squishy, unexpected hug.

"Wonderful to meet you. I'm Sylvia. You met my kids."

"Oh! Yes. They're beautiful."

"Thank you," she says, "but wait till you hear one of Adrienne's famous shit-fits. They had nothing but good things to say about you. Adrienne loves the new word you taught her. She just finished explaining to me that vegetables are overrated and, from now on, she'll be having berries with dinner. So thanks for that."

I squinch up my face in contrition. "Sorry about that. I'm no good with kids."

"No, no. No sorry necessary. Teaching them is all we can do. It's not our fault when they turn it against us." She winks. "So, Marco—" She sidles up next to him in an almost seductive way. Yowza. Those curves! "Did I hear something about seven days to Alcatraz?"

Marco smiles politely and shrugs, taking a decent-sized step away. "Guess you'll find out at dinner."

Dinner, which consists of ocean fish, green beans, and a lot of mashed potatoes, runs exactly an hour. Marco introduces the four of us to everyone; it's a warm and welcoming reception with the general consensus being "the more, the merrier." He also discusses the idea of leaving for Alcatraz in seven days, to which every single person is in full and exuberant agreement. Based on the way they are all chomping at the bit to get out of here, and the way David smiles silently over his glasses at me from the other end of the long table, I'm guessing that what he told me this afternoon was spot-on. These people have been waiting for Marco to give the word for a long time.

And though he's only about my age and there are a lot of older people here, Marco seems to hold everyone's absolute respect as leader. When he speaks, they listen. It's strange and kind of amazing, the confidence with which he now holds himself. I wonder if any part of my personality has discernibly changed. I sort of hope so.

When he concludes the dinner hour by saying "All right, it's settled. We leave for Alcatraz in seven days," everyone cheers. They even bring out two bottles of wine, which Joaquin leans over and whispers to me (swoon) they've been saving specifically for this occasion.

When everyone but Mel and the kids has wine, Joaquin holds up his mug. "To new beginnings!" he says, clinking my mug.

All around the table, mugs clink and people shout, "New beginnings!"

Thirty: Whatever you do, don't open the window.

The next three days there is a shift in pace. There's less sleep, more coffee. Less laughter, more hushed conversation. Even the kids have roles in executing the plan. Nobody has bothered to tell us newcomers the plan in its entirety yet, instead opting to dole out singular tasks at a time.

So we ask Tanya after dinner.

"It's everything we need to do before we leave and some other shit we threw in that seemed like a brilliant idea at the time," she explains between sips of wine. Since the announcement of our imminent departure, there has been a bottle or two at every dinner. A few people have given in to their inner lush, even getting ballsy enough to go out just to hunt for more wine. "Today was Day Four. So tomorrow, Day Three, and every day this week, we each have a cute little checklist." Eye roll. Sip, sip. "It doesn't get real until around Day Three. That's when we block off the route, which will take all day. I mean—" Sip. "—not *we*, obviously. Maybe you, Cate. But this body wasn't made for manual labor." She slides a hand up her thick thigh and strikes a marble-statue pose, chuckling to herself before finishing off her wine.

"Anyway, every family has a copy of the plan. Just go borrow one tomorrow. Or better yet, come by my place. I'll show you mine, and you can let me do something with that hair." She scrunches up her freckled, amber face in pity, slams her mug on the table and scooches her chair.

"Good night, good night," she sings as she weaves out of the room, steadying herself on the doorway in another *Top Model* pose. "My place at six."

"A.m. or p.m.?" Mel calls.

"What the fuck do you think, Melody?" Tanya mutters over her shoulder. "Do I strike you as the type to be conscious at six in the morning? I'll see you at six."

And then she's gone, singing and stumbling down the hallway toward her and Amy's place, which, luckily for her, is two doors down.

Amy is on watch from six to seven the next evening, so it's Tanya who answers the door. Since her work is home-based, she has the luxury of wearing whatever she wants, which she takes full advantage of. Tonight, she's chosen a pair of hot pink micro-shorts and a paisley button-down.

"You're late."

"It's like two minutes past," Mel says.

"Like I said. I could've had you cloaked and combed by now, Cate. In—" Head jerk. "—now."

Tanya ushers us inside where Duchess greets us with enthusiasm.

"Hey, girl," I murmur, scratching the shepherd's ears. "Surprised you're not out with your boyfriend." Duchess and Chaz have become near inseparable since we arrived.

"Where do you get your clothes, Tanya?" Mel asks in her squeaky, people-pleaser voice.

"I have a deal with Joaquin. I tailor his uniform and he brings me goodies. Meanwhile, Cate—" Tanya gives me a slow up-down. "—you're still in baggy borrowed threads. I may have something for you. Even though you wasted two long minutes of my time..."

"Speaking of time, Mel, where's my watch?"

"It's at my place. I've brought it out with me a few times to give back. It's like I only see you at dinner the last few days. It feels wrong."

I don't tell her that Marco and I have been venturing outside the wall any time we don't have a chore to attend to. I also leave out the two Abnormals I've encountered and three injuries I've sustained since we got here. They're all minor, basically, so what's the use of worrying her?

Instead, I just say, "I know what you mean."

"Well, this is all very moving," Tanya says, practically shoving me into the kitchen, "but this mess needs tending to. Cate, kindly sit the fuck down."

I sit on the stool in front of the full-length mirror that's leaning on the fridge. I've had no reason to look at myself this last year, so I'm a little startled by the face looking back now. I look older. Meaner. My eyebrows are caterpillars and my hair is a snarled thicket.

"Jesus, Cate," Tanya mumbles, "your hair's too thick to leave to its own devices. You need a comb. Here." She shoves a wide-tooth comb under the old sheet that serves as my cloak. "Keep this. Make friends with it. You have more hair than half the people in here put together."

Tell me about it.

While Tanya cloaks-and-combs me, Mel wanders around the infirmary-slash-apartment, touching everything, the snoop. Duchess follows, bumping her hand every once in a while for pets.

"Where's your copy of the plan?" she calls from the other room.

"It's in here," Tanya shouts while she works the many rat's nests out of my hair. "Most people keep it on their fridge," she scoffs. "No shortage of fuckin' magnets at the end of the world. Try to get some two-ply toilet paper, though." She makes a sound with her teeth and intensifies her efforts on a stubborn tangle. "This half-ply shit, it's like wiping your ass with sandpaper."

I resist the urge to blink away the tears forming at the corners of my eyes. My mom always used to say that with hair as thick as mine, I'd need to develop a tough scalp. "You're going to have your hair pulled your whole life, Cate," she would say while yanking at my follicles. "Better get used to it."

I never did.

Mom... I hate that she's not here, that she didn't see her girls surviving the end of everything.

"So. Cate," Tanya says, either missing or ignoring my sadness. "You and Marco."

"Me and...what? Oh, no. No." I chuckle. "No."

"Stay still."

"Sorry. I don't know why people go there, but we're friends. He's basically my cousin."

"Yeah, he told me. Basically ain't blood, sweetie. And Marco is one hell of a guy."

"Yeah. I know. What about Joaquin? What's his story?"

Bang-crash!

Mel breezes in. "Nothing to worry about." She giggles, stroking her belly. "I didn't break it."

Tanya spins me to face her and yanks a little harder on my hair, saying nothing. Good lord, could this be more painful than a zombie bite?

Mel steps up to the plan, which is taped to Tanya's full-length mirror, and peers over her glasses.

"Tanya's right about tomorrow being the day where it gets real," she says. "They're blocking off the roads and all kinds of other junk. But I don't see anything about fueling the boat."

"Captain has it under control," says Tanya. "That boat was his before. It's where we found him. He keeps it up."

"Looks like the last day is a big one too. Want to look, Cate?" She reaches for the paper, but Tanya slaps her hand away.

"She can look when I'm through. Now wobble along, Melody. Your sister and I need to concentrate on controlling this mayhem." After Mel and Duchess leave, Tanya bends down in front of me, and her multicolored eyes dart this way and that. "Hm," she says.

"So why isn't yours on the fridge?" I ask after she stands up.

"One, magnets are très passé. Two, I'm in front of the mirror every day, if not for myself or my beautiful wife, then to keep this raggedy bunch looking halfway decent, which is a hellish chore in itself. Speaking of. We have some work to do, darling. When's your shift?"

"Nine to ten."

Tanya sighs. "I've done more with less."

Tanya is nothing if not flawlessly stylish. When I first met her three nights ago, I hoped we'd be friends. "I'm the style ambassador for the new world," she proclaimed over the table to me. "Somebody's got to do it, and let's be honest, the panache cup here doesn't exactly runneth over, you know? I doubt half these people could even spell panache. So, benevolent goddess that I am, I've nominated myself."

"So how exactly did Ana and them find you?" she asks as she struggles with the last of my knots.

"We were kidnapped—" I wince. "—by a group of guys." *Ow!* "Leader gave me the head gash. He was a piece of work."

"I know what you mean. The men Marco found Amy and me with? Same shit. The world is in literal ruins, and somehow there are still predatory pricks aplenty."

"Tell me about it."

She drops her comb hand with a sigh and lets my hair fall around my shoulders. It hangs, somehow both heavy and wildly frizzy, almost to my belly button.

"Any requests?" she asks.

"I don't know." I shrug. "Surprise me."

Tanya grins like the Cheshire cat.

"Turn around, face away from the mirror. I like a big reveal."

An hour and thirty minutes later, I'm standing in front of the mirror in Tanya's kitchen with less than half the hair I came in with. It's not even long enough to braid. I don't like it. I am also in a dress. Black, cotton, long-sleeved. That I do like.

I crouch down, kick, swing a couple of punches.

"That dress is apocalypse-chic," Tanya says, clicking her tongue. "And it doesn't sacrifice function for style either." She darts out of the room and returns with a brown leather belt. "Here, for your weapons."

"Thank you." I put it on, spin around quick, land in a crouch. "But there does seem to be an issue with, you know, down under."

Tanya gives me a look that falls somewhere between disapproval and entertainment and walks out of the room again.

"You know, we're all adults here," she shouts from the back room.

"Not all of us."

"Right, those. Anyway..." She comes back out with the raggy sweats and shirt I came in with. "People won't die if they see your undies. But if you're that worried about it, I'll fix it. Come back after your shift. I cannot bear to see you in those oversized rags."

I've barely flopped into bed that night when there's a soft knock at the door. I open my eyes slowly and will myself up. I take my time trudging across the room.

The second knock is more insistent. I open the door to find Mae and Chaz standing in the hall. Chaz can barely keep his eyes open. He sways a little on his feet. Mae is wide awake.

"Cate," she says. "It's time."

I rub my eyes. "Time?"

A pitiful moan comes from inside Mel's apartment.

"Cate?" Marco whispers as he comes stumbling out of the stairwell. "What's up? Somebody crying up here?"

Another moan, louder and more emphatic, answers the question.

Marco's eyes bug out a little. "Right, I'll get Amy."

"Thank you, Marco," Mae says, already shuffling away. When I don't immediately follow, she stops. "Come on now, Cate."

I grab my knife from the table by the door—you know, just in case—and jog down the hall after Mae. Jesus, I've never seen her move like this before.

"Now listen, I haven't told her yet, but this won't be an easy delivery. She's a nurse, so she knows the basics. But nothing can prepare you for delivering a child, and she's skinny as a rail." She stops me outside Mel and Calvin's apartment door, taking my hand and a deep breath. "She's gonna need her sister."

Inside, one small lamp with the shade discarded does its best to light the living room. Mel is sitting on the floor in an oversized T-shirt, propped up by what I'm guessing is every pillow in the apartment and then some. Calvin hasn't even bothered to dress; he's crouched in his briefs by her side, stroking her forehead and looking absolutely petrified when her next contraction hits. Mae puts a hand on his shoulder, and only then does he notice that they're not alone anymore.

"You did good, sweetheart," Mae murmurs. "Now go wait in the hall. Marco will be along shortly with the doctor." When Calvin doesn't move, Mae takes his face in her hands, forcing him to look her in the eye. "Calvin, everything is fine. But you're no use to anyone this way."

"Okay, Nana," he says, and after a quick peck on Mel's forehead, he's on his way out.

"Calvin." She stops him just as he opens the door. "Put on some damn pants."

"Yes, Nana."

Mel takes a break from crying to laugh. But two seconds later, she's at full volume again. It's a damn good thing we are where we are. For a lot of reasons. I don't think we could have done this in the warehouse.

"Hey, sis," I say softly, trying to distract her and maybe bring the hysterics down a notch. "You ready to be a mom?"

The contraction ends, and Mel is back, at least for the moment. She touches my face, and then my hair.

"Your hair," she whispers. "I love it... Are you wearing a dress?"

"Yeah, sort of." I stand up and twirl. Distractions are good, right? "Tanya sewed the middle together and added pockets."

Mel smiles, but when another contraction hits she's back in hell. Her face is slicked with sweat and tears.

Amy walks in unannounced, washes her hands, and drops unceremoniously to her knees between Mel's feet.

"Good to see you again, Melody."

More moaning.

"How far apart are contractions?" she asks no one in particular while she checks Mel out.

Before anyone can answer, Mel stiffens and clutches her abdomen.

"No time like the present." Amy pulls up the sleeve of her pajamas and curses at the pale stripe on her wrist. "Who's got a watch?"

"Oh! I've got Cate's," Mae says, handing me the watch.

I put my watch back on, relishing the feeling of the cold metal being back where it should be, and check the time.

"Eleven-oh-two."

"Okay," Amy says as soon as Mel goes limp, "while we wait for the next one, I need you, Cate, to get a big pot of water boiling. Biggest you can find. Mae, find me every clean towel you can. Marco!"

Marco pokes his head in, keeping his eyes on his shoes.

"What's up, Doc?"

"Get Tanya. She'll be expecting you. Tell her I need gauze, a set of clamps, my stethoscope, and the big apron."

"Gauze, clamps, stethoscope, big apron. Got it."

"Thank you. How we doing, Melody?"

"Okay, Doctor," Mel whispers. "Dying for some water."

I rush over with a glass; she gulps it down and asks for another. Suddenly, midgulp, she shoves the glass into my hands and cringes.

"God!" she says through gritted teeth.

"Cate, time?" Amy asks me.

I check my watch. "Four minutes apart."

Mel's eyes bug out. She looks frantically at Amy, who puts a hand on Mel's hand and shakes her head to derail the emotional train wreck.

"Four minutes sounds close," she says, "but we have time. Just do me a favor and breathe." Amy strokes Mel's hand. "With me, Melody. Can I call you Mel?"

"Uh-huh." She sighs as the contraction ends.

"Okay, Mel. Close your eyes and breathe. In and out. In. And out."

Mel hyperventilates.

"Mel, if you can't calm down, this is going to be a difficult labor for you and the baby." Even when she's chastising someone, Amy still manages to sound like a cheerleader.

"I need air," Mel sobs. "Open the window, Cate."

"I'm not sure that's a good idea, sis—"

"GODDAMMIT, CATE, JUST OPEN THE FUCKING WINDOW!"

"I'll open it," Mae says, laying a stack of towels next to us.

I pour some water from the glass onto a smaller towel and put it on Mel's head. "Mel," I murmur, taking her hand, "let's breathe together, okay? Yoga breathing. Just like that old video of Mom's, remember? The bearded guy in the purple sweats?"

Mel expels a choked laugh-cry.

"In four, out eight. There you go."

"I wish—my dad—was here," she says between sobs.

"I know. But wherever he is now, he's watching. Mom too. So how about we do them both proud and have this baby like a champ, okay?"

She nods.

I sigh in relief. "Okay. In four, out eight."

Not a minute later, the door opens and Tanya glides in with a black canvas bag.

"Hey, got your stuff," she says with a quick kiss on Amy's cheek. She gathers up her green silk robe and settles herself next to me. "What's the status?"

Thirty-One: Always have a plan B.

It's almost 3:30 in the morning when Amy finally says the words. "Mel, it's time. On three, push. One, two, three..."

I don't think anyone expects the scream that erupts out of my sister's mouth, or any of the subsequent screams that accompany each of the doctor's commands to push. The delivery goes really quickly after that. I think. How would I know? The last birth I attended was my own.

"Somebody get a sock," Tanya mumbles while she hands Amy another towel. "Bitch is gonna bring in every zombie within a hundred miles."

"Shut it, Tanya," I snap. I take hold of Mel's hand and rattle off a few (hopefully) encouraging things that I've mostly picked up from birth scenes in movies. "Okay, sweetie, you're doing great... You're going to be a mom soon!"

Even as the words are tumbling out of my mouth, they taste strongly of bullshit. I'm trying to sound encouraging, but I'm out of my mind with panic. I glance at the open window for the tenth time. I too am convinced that Mel's screaming is going to attract every zombie in the city, and even if it doesn't, there's so much blood. Amy assures us that this is normal. I only believe her because Mae, bless her heart, is cool as a cucumber. She's busily tending to Mel per Amy's instructions, and then all of a sudden Amy is holding the slimiest, most beautiful baby boy I've ever seen in my life.

"Cate, time?" Amy says as soon as he starts crying.

"Three forty-seven."

"Three forty-seven," she repeats. "Tanya?"

Tanya removes a small notebook from her bathrobe pocket and begins to write.

"Born at three forty-seven. Do we have a name?"

Mel's mouth hangs open. "I mean, we discussed a few, but we thought we had another week or two."

"Baby Waters for now," says Tanya.

"Doc, can I...?" I nod toward the door.

"Yes!" she cries.

I suspect she may have forgotten there was a horrendously anxious father waiting for news outside. I spring up and run into the hall where everyone (yes, everyone) stops murmuring and looks at me expectantly. They're all here, even the kids. Even the Captain, who has yet to say one word to any of us newcomers, stands near the back of the group just watching. Calvin's face is drawn, exhausted, but oh so hopeful. And clean-shaven for the first time in months, though he kept the hair up top.

"A boy!" I cry, slamming into Calvin for a bear hug. "They're both doing great."

The whole hall erupts into quiet cheers. Many people clap Calvin on the back with a word of congratulations; someone passes a bottle of wine around.

"Why is everyone here?" I ask Marco amid the cheers.

He shrugs.

"This is the first new-world baby. This means something to everybody. There's been so much death this year, I guess we're just ready for some life... Are you wearing a dress?"

"Yeah, sort of. Cute, right? Way better than those sweats."

"Try impractical, you're totally exposed. Tomorrow is clearing day. You'll want to change."

"Um, no. I have your jacket up top and leather up to my knees. I'm as exposed as you are. And way cuter. *And* I bet I have better range of motion. So suck on that."

Marco opens his mouth, but then there's a tap on my shoulder. Calvin is looking from me to the door in anticipation.

I peer into the apartment to ask if he can come in—

"Cate! Come back! We need you!"

I'm fairly sure Calvin's face mirrors my own.

"Just...stay here, Cal." I dash inside and slam the door behind me.

Amy hands me Mel's son, who is now clean (-ish) and wrapped in a white hand towel.

"She's ready to push again," says Amy.

Wait a minute. "Again?"

"It's twins?" Mae cries. "Sweet miracle, you're gonna be a mother of two babies, Melody!"

Mel's face crumples in on itself like tissue paper. "I can't. I can't do that again! Please!"

Mae takes hold of Mel's face. "I know it hurts, baby, but you have another life to give. You're a survivor, and you will survive this. Are you ready?"

Mel takes a deep breath and nods, blinking away tears.

The second scream has a few decibels on the first. If I wasn't sitting here watching, I'd think someone was being ripped apart by zombies. But this time is shorter than the first; a minute later, my nephew has a twin sister. Amy hands her to Mel. Then she wipes her brow on her forearm and takes her gloves off.

"Three fifty-three," I say before Tanya asks.

Tanya makes note.

"They're beautiful," Mae says, carefully putting Mel's glasses on for her.

"Hell of a thing you did, Melody," Tanya whispers. "Nothing I'd ever do, but they are pretty babies."

"You did it," I murmur, pushing her hair away from her face with my free hand.

I make for the door again, but it slams open and in storms Calvin, who charges past me and whips his head around frantically.

"Mel?" he cries. "What the hell's going on in here?" He stops when he sees her. She smiles weakly, and Mae stands to make room as he crouches next to her. "Look at him," he whispers.

"Look at her," Mel corrects him.

"Her?"

I sit on Mel's other side, across from Calvin, and hold their son out to him. "This is him," I say quietly.

Calvin takes the baby in his hands and cradles him gently. "Two?" he asks Mel.

"Two."

Calvin just grins and kisses Mel's forehead, and then both of them fall into silence while they stare at the tiny people they made.

I sneak back to my apartment and grab my phone. This moment needs to be remembered. First babies of the new world. I turn it on—45 percent—and snap a picture of the four of them.

Crack!

A noise so loud that I can almost feel it shatters the silence. Sixty seconds later, Marco bursts into the room.

"Doc. Cate."

The doctor and I follow him into the hall. Everyone is buzzing around except us.

"The breach in the wall," Marco explains, "we figured our patch would suffice with only a week to spare. But there's a higher concentration in the area for some reason, and the screaming brought them right to us. It had to happen simultaneously, which I mean the chances alone... There are never more than three or four zombie kills a night around here, literally, and right now, according to the four who were on duty, there are at least fifty out there. And they broke through."

"How bad?" Amy asks.

"Not good. We have the first-floor buffer, but this'll make getting out incredibly tough. Plus, it's only a matter of time before they get up here."

Two delicate creases form in Amy's brow.

"Get up here? How?"

"They'll eventually get too packed into the first floor, right?" I guess. "And then they'll start trampling each other. Piling up."

"Okay. So how long do we have?"

"Depends on a few things." Marco shrugs. "We'll know more when Joaquin and Eunice get back from the roof. Best case, we only have to worry about getting out when the time comes. Worst case, we're out tonight."

When Joaquin and Eunice come running down the hall a few minutes later, our fears are confirmed. There's not only a high concentration of zombies around the building—as many as ten deep on all sides—but there are too many already inside the wall for us to even consider leaving through the front door.

"Okay"—Marco begins to brainstorm out loud—"can't leave through the door, so west is a no. North, no. East, definitely no. Fire escape and the south alley could work. We have food, weapons. Doc, are your supplies packed?"

"They can be in fifteen minutes."

"Is the road clear at the other end of the alley?" he asks Joaquin and Eunice.

"Can't tell," Eunice answers, letting loose a wet smoker's cough. "Too much fog down there to see much of anything."

He retreats into himself for a minute, calculating, and then he heaves a six-hundred-pound sigh. "Damn it. It's like ten to one we all die tonight, but it sounds like it's our only shot anyway. Here's the plan..."

Thirty-Two: Improvise.

Since we're still three days out, our route has been neither cleared nor blocked off, and we've loaded almost nothing into the vehicles. On the bright side, Amy has had most of her medical stuff packed for days, and Tanya coolly announces that she, too, has the tools of her trade safely packed for the journey. We'll be out of ammo in a month or less; out of food in half that time, but we'll have proper medical attention and perfect hair. So I guess there's that.

I volunteer to break the news to Mel, who takes it as well as any brand-new mom would take the news that her only safe haven is no longer safe. Calvin's jaw tightens, but he's practically made for this high-intensity stuff. Mel's goody bag of preggo hormones rips open in a mess of tears (both hers and the twins'), words I didn't think she even knew, and eventually a pseudo-catatonic shock. Mae and Amy give Mel and the babies their first and possibly last sponge bath while the rest of us prep.

Thirty minutes later, with about half the supplies we'd intended to bring, we silently descend the fire escape one by one. It's still dark, basically, but it's foggy as hell. Marco, Ana, and the rest of her team go down first. When we get the all-clear (three quick flashlight flashes), we begin to send down the most vulnerable people—the kids and their dad, Henry; Mae; Calvin carries Mel down; then Sylvia and I climb down, each of us holding a baby.

"Mommy," Adrienne says as we all load into our respective vehicles, "when will we get to the new place?"

"Shh." Sylvia kneels in front of her daughter. "Soon, baby. But right now, we have to stay very quiet."

"Like a game?" Francis whispers.

"No, not a game. It's much more important, understand? Now, Adrienne, hold Nick's hand, and, Nick, you hold on to Francis. Don't let go. No matter how scared you are, don't let go of each other."

"Cate." Ana waves me over. "You okay to take point with Marco?"

"Sure." Why would I mind being responsible for everyone? My gut twists into iron knots.

"Great." She shoves a key into my hand. "Marco will ride shotgun and navigate. Everyone! Keep all lights off. Load up, we roll in sixty seconds."

Before we even turn out of the alley, it's obvious that the street is not as deserted as we'd hoped. There aren't enough zombies that we have to stop or get out and fight, but enough that I have to swerve around them, meaning more often than not I have to drive over a half-decomposed carcass instead. Thank God for good suspension.

"Is this going to be okay?" I ask Marco. I veer around a zombie that used to be a preteen wandering down the middle of the street, and *ba-bump!* over the top half of another.

"We didn't have time to follow through with the most crucial parts of the plan," Marco replies, consulting the map. "Turn right up here. But as long as everyone stays in line and no one does anything reckless, we should get to the docks no problem... Turn left in two blocks, then straight on. We're almost there."

Around the final corner, we come to a fire truck flipped onto its side that barricades the whole street.

"Did you know this was here?" I ask Marco.

"No. We used a map to plan out the route. None of us have been this way yet. Captain doesn't even take this route to fish."

"And tomorrow was clearing day."

"Yup." He clenches his jaw a few times, and then flings open his door and hangs out to address the convoy. "We can go the rest of the way on foot," he says to Eunice, who thankfully pulled her van up close enough that he hardly has to speak above a whisper. "Boat is less than a hundred feet past this truck."

Eunice spits out her window. "Fantastic."

"Two minutes, we grab what we can carry and we run. Pass it along," Marco instructs.

There are whispers and a few curses as the message is handed back, barely audible over the din of growls and groans. My God, there have to be over a hundred zombies out there. How have they not noticed us?

After two minutes, Marco nods and zips up his jacket.

"This is it," I say.

"This is it." He turns to our people in the back seat. "Ready?"

Everyone nods stiffly. Mel and Calvin zip their newborns into their jackets, each holding a baby in one arm and a weapon in the other hand. Mae zips up the leather jacket that David insisted she borrow for the journey.

"Okay," Marco says, and we all step into the fog.

Once we're out, everyone else exits in a surprisingly orderly fashion, considering the absurd danger we're all in. Thankfully, there seem to be a lot fewer zombies than I thought I heard. Almost none, really. We form into sort of a teardrop formation with Marco at the lead, Ana and me at front left and right, and her team filling in sides and flank. The group instinctively shuffles the new parents into the center with Mae and the kids. Duchess and Chaz trail not far behind, probably the safest of all of us.

"Stay together!" Marco calls as we run. I guess he doesn't see a point in keeping his voice down since there are like four zombies around.

Shick! He slices the spinal cord of one nearby zombie and then plants his knife in the temple of another, without breaking stride.

I shove a third away from the group; we're moving too fast for me to attempt to kill it, but by the time it gets back up, we are well past it and filing around the fire truck. But upon reaching the other side, we come to an abrupt halt.

"No," I breathe.

"Fuck," Marco says.

"You gotta be shitting me," Ana replies.

People behind us collide like bumper cars, trying to adjust to the sudden change in pace. There's some "What's happening?" and "Why'd we stop?" before they all see what we see, which is the source of the noise. The horde on this side is much thicker, a bona fide zombie mosh pit. And one by one, they're all starting to notice us.

Thirty-Three: Run.

The dock is right there, also overrun with undead. They're just milling around, their attentions occupied by the lapping water and sea birds. But before we start moving again, someone from the back—one of Ana's guys, what's his name?—immediately breaks formation to make a run for the lone gigantic ferry that's tied up at the end of the dock. Rob goes after him, throwing him unceremoniously back into the group. Just as he pulls his comrade out of harm's way, though, Rob is bitten on the hand. Without missing a beat, he swings his machete hard, chopping off the bitten fingers with a grating yell. Then he gets his payback in zombie flesh. If zombies could bleed, it would be a bloodbath. He takes out so many, some two at a time, swinging his machete in a blur of heroic destruction. But he's bitten again, this time on the meat between shoulder and neck. He turns and nods to Ana, one last goodbye, and then he keeps swinging, killing at least six or seven more zombies before he's overtaken.

Ana allows herself a millisecond to mourn for her husband, whose sacrifice has temporarily cleared a large chunk of the path for us. But by the time we reach the dock, they're coming out of the fog from all sides, grabbing and lunging and snapping at every one of us. The kids are screaming, but thankfully, they have the good sense not to stop moving. We're taking them out as fast as they're coming, but at this rate, we're making almost no headway up the dock. We're still at least thirty feet from the boat.

The man who tried to run before is taken just as the group finally makes it onto the dock. His screams draw the attention of every last zombie around us. Once we're all on the dock, it's impossible to keep formation. The group is no more. People are everywhere, some fighting off zombies, some just trying to stay alive long enough to get on the boat, and some, well, some not staying alive.

I yank one away from my face by its ponytail, throw it down, and kick it into the water without even using my weapon. Then I swing and chop and stab my way through the horde, and I have to admit, it feels sort of good to be back in the fray. The time spent in the apartments probably should have felt like a relief, but days without a fight felt more like a pressure inside me that I couldn't release. If I'm being honest, the field trips I took out into the city with Marco this week were more of a relief than the safety of the apartments could ever be.

To my right, Tanya shoves three zombies off the dock at once to save Amy, narrowly missing a bite to the arm. Amy stabs the biter in the eye with her stiletto knife. Duchess barks ferociously at another as it approaches. It reaches down to grab her and she bites its hand, shaking her head back and forth, throwing the zombie into the water.

On my left, Jax and Toby are standing back-to-back, fending off zombies, Jax with a hammer and Toby with a mammoth wrench, trying to help Henry keep them off Sylvia and the kids. But when Eunice screams for help, Toby thunders across the dock, knocking zombies over the edge like bowling pins. David and Eunice are being accosted by only three zombies, but apparently neither of them is any good with hand-to-hand fighting. While David uses his bag to knock one of them down, Toby whacks another in the temple and throws the third into the water.

"Stay calm!" Marco calls while he fights off two at once. "We can do this!"

Before he's finished his sentence, an Abnormal zombie—I think it is, anyway—crashes out of the dark water and grabs Toby, its claws mangling the flesh of his arm as it tries to pull itself up. Is it smiling? Toby shouts wordlessly as the Abnormal leaves deep marks in his hand, which opens out of reflex, sending his giant wrench splashing into the water.

"Toby!" Jax shouts from across the dock. "Someone help him!"

Before I fully know what I'm doing, I'm at Toby's side, raising my axe to strike. I bring it down, but not on the zombie's head. My axe hacks into Toby's forearm, severing his wounded hand and wrist. The corpse, still clutching the ruined hand, falls back into the depths.

"Fuck you!" Toby shouts at the zombie as it tries to get back out. When it splashes out of the water again, Jax smashes its skull with his sledge hammer. But there's no time for Toby to lament the loss of his hand. Not with a zillion more zombies and a bunch of terrified people around.

Marco whips off his belt and throws it at Toby, yelling, "Tourniquet!"

Jax tightens the leather around his brother's arm and rushes him toward the boat, striking any zombie that comes within reach along the way.

Suddenly, Calvin is handing his baby to me and running back up the dock toward the worst part of the fight.

"Get to the boat!" he shouts.

Jesus. I reposition the baby under my jacket. *What a way to come into the world.*

Behind me, there's a commotion followed directly by a loud body-hitting-water splash.

"Henry!" Sylvia shrieks as her husband is tackled off the dock by a zombie.

Four more follow him into the water. Sylvia screams and tries to run after him, but Joaquin grabs her roughly by the arm. "Whatthefuck're you doing?!" He pulls her back. All three of her terrified kids attach themselves to her legs. Joaquin leads them as swiftly as possible toward the boat. Their faces are empty shock as they pass me.

I move to hand the baby to Sylvia.

Then Mel starts screaming.

"Calvin!" she calls. "Cate! Somebody, please!"

She's brandishing a knife in one hand, clutching a wailing baby to her chest with the other, and two zombies are gnawing at the sleeve of her leather jacket. They can't bite through, not right away, but in her weakened state all Mel can do is stab pitifully at them and back away, slowly and with shaking knees, right toward the edge of the dock.

"Mel, come here!" I shout, knowing she can't even as the words are leaving my mouth.

Calvin bum-rushes five zombies at once with outstretched arms, launching them and his pack off the dock. When no others immediately take their place, Calvin and Mel run for it. They make it about ten feet before several more block their way.

"Cate! We could use! Some help!" Calvin booms between stabs.

But I'm separated from them by about ten zombies and four frightened, flailing people with little idea how to use their knives. Plus, I'm currently one arm short.

Out of nowhere, a white flash flies through the tumult, up the dock, right at Mel. With a thunderous bark, Chaz leaps into the air, knocking the two most threatening assailants off Mel and into the black water.

"Chaz!" Mel and I shout together.

The water roils, but Chaz doesn't resurface.

"Cate! Catherine!"

Marco snaps me back to the present just as a pair of rotting jowls are closing in to rip out my throat. I duck and swipe, knocking the thing down, and finish it with an axe to the head. Then I stand and look around. People are losing this battle. But we're over halfway down the dock; if we all run right now, we might make it with whoever is left.

We might not have to lose anyone else.

"Marco!" I call, thrusting my knife into a milky bloodshot eye. "We can make it if we run!"

He finishes two simultaneously, and then does a quick assessment followed by one decisive dip of his head.

"Run to the boat!" he calls. "Everyone! Run!"

At first, no one does.

"GO!" I shout.

Joaquin ignores the order, continuing to keep the path clear while everyone else makes for the ferry. Mel-plus-one are the first to board. Mel slumps down next to Sylvia and the kids. Tanya practically drags Amy aboard the ferry, throwing elbows and kicking the feet out from under every zombie they cross.

Mae hobbles down the dock after us with Ana in front of her clearing the way. How did she fall so far behind?

"Come on, Nana," Calvin shouts. "You got this!"

I stay on the dock with Marco and Calvin, ushering people to safety and keeping the horde at bay with my free hand.

"Cate, get your ass on the boat!" Calvin barks.

"Okay, load 'em up!" Joaquin shouts. He and the others pile onto the boat, the last ones to board, and Calvin, Marco, and I are nearly overcome by the rest of the zombies. There are at least twenty left, all concentrated to this one corner of the dock, snapping and clawing and clamoring to get onto the boat, which the Captain is still fumbling to untie. The three of us shove and stab for all we're worth. We can't board until it's impossible for them to follow.

"Any time now, Cap!" Marco growls.

Stab, stab. Shove. Stab.

The most fucked-up thing about zombies, probably my least favorite thing, is their relentlessness. And while our strength reserves deplete at breakneck speed, these walking meat bags just keep on keeping on. I can feel my breath getting more labored; my vision is going dark around the edges. Next to me, Calvin is fading fast. Sleep deprivation doesn't look good on him. It probably looks worse on me.

But the horde never pauses. Never tires. Never stops.

A zombie who was apparently very pregnant when it turned grabs at my baby-holding arm like it's trying to pry the child from my grip. The fetal corpse within its swollen belly writhes and pushes, trying to tear its way out of the putrefying host. For a full second, it's Mel's face on the zombie. How easily she could have ended up this way. Still can.

"Cate!"

I snap out of it to see the pregnant zombie tearing a hole in my jacket with its nails. It either breaks skin or doesn't; the sudden burst of adrenaline coursing through me is doing a nice job of numbing any pain I'm supposed to be feeling. Either way, one half second later, Preggo is sliding off my knife and tumbling into the ocean. If only she were the last one. We're being herded farther away from the boat, farther from safety.

"Hey!" I hear from behind me, toward the boat. It's Mae, speed-walking toward Calvin and me and stepping back onto the dock. Miraculously, the horde is so preoccupied with us that they don't even notice her slip behind them.

"Mae!" shouts Marco.

"Nana, get back on the boat!" Calvin calls to her. "You can't fight 'em off, Nana, go back!"

"I ain't fixin' to fight 'em, baby," she calls as she goes farther down the dock, and it's gut-wrenchingly obvious what she means to do. "Hey, I said, HEY!" Much to our horror, all of them but a few turn away from us and toward Mae. She stands at the edge on the other side of the dock and waves her arms. "Come on, ugly!" she shouts.

"Nana, please run!" Calvin calls as he runs toward her.

But he must know she can't. They're already closing in.

"I won't do that, Calvin," Mae calls. "Tell those babies their Nana loved them... Come on now! Come and get it!"

"*Nana!*"

Marco and I kill the three around us like lightning and break into a dead run toward Mae. But it's too late. The horde swarms her in seconds, like I've seen them do so many times before, knocking her off the dock and into the black water. The remaining few zombies follow the commotion and fall in as well. A few float for a minute, their throaty moans turning to bubbles as they bob up and down and eventually sink into the depths.

It takes all of my effort to keep my feet under me. How many people have we lost today, and for what? What if Gary, callous, stubborn Gary, was right all along? What are we really gaining by going to Alcatraz if we lose half our people getting there?

Suddenly, it's silent but for the lapping of the waves on the side of the ferry. One of Mel's babies, still not even a day old, lets out a shaky little whimper. The Captain is still messing with the ropes as Marco, Calvin, and I walk slowly back up the dock. There are still zombies on the street, but they won't get to us in time. On his way by, wearily, Marco cuts the rope with his axe and sits alone at the bow, jacket in his lap, letting his damp hair hang in his face. As the group's leader, I think he feels the most responsible for the way things turned out. I want to sit next to him, to tell him that this isn't his fault. But it's all I can do to just plunk down in the closest available space.

"Toby," Amy says gently, "let me take a look at that arm."

The boat's engine coughs and barks to life, cracking the silence down the middle. It's the sound we've all been longing to hear, the sound that means freedom and a new life. But no one rejoices; there's little reason to. We finally made it, but it cost more than anyone expected. As we're pulling out into the bay, there's a sound that's out of place. Splashing?

There's something in the water behind us.

"Stop!" I shout. "Stop the boat!"

The engine dies immediately, and everyone glances up at me, probably startled by my outburst. But soon they all hear it, and a second later, they see it too. Just a few yards behind us, panting and swimming for all he's worth, Chaz comes paddling toward the boat. Toby and Jax pull him aboard, and he shakes himself dry, spraying all of us in the process. After a brief reunion with Duchess, he begins to pace the deck. He wags his tail and looks around at the people on the ferry. He scans every face. The wagging slows and then stops. He looks at Mel, me, Calvin. He whines and his forehead wrinkles.

"She's gone, Chaz," Calvin murmurs, stroking the dog's ears the way Mae used to. "Nana's gone." He doesn't try to hide the tears streaming down his cheeks. Instead, he lifts his face upward and just lets go. I stand shakily and squeeze in beside him. There's nothing to be said. He just lost the last person from his old life, the most important person he had. So I hold his hand instead.

The engine roars to life again.

The baby Mel is holding begins to cry. Mel strokes the baby's head and hums a song. I recognize it as an old Ray Charles song Mae used to sing while we worked in the garden at the warehouse. Mel is probably thinking about it too, all those peaceful mornings in the sun. How good we had it and how much we took for granted. The baby's eyes flutter and close.

"I think I have a name for her," Mel whispers to Calvin.

He kisses Mel's forehead. "What's her name?"

"Maebelle."

"Perfect," Calvin whispers. "And what about him?"

I open my jacket and hand Maebelle's brother to Calvin.

"Andrew," Mel answers, glancing up at me.

My eyes cloud over with tears again, and I blink them away.

"Hey, Andrew," Calvin coos at his son. The baby stirs but doesn't wake. Mel falls asleep with her head on Calvin's other shoulder.

By the time she wakes up, the island is in full view.

"Land, ho!" Captain Roth calls from his cozy wheelhouse.

Chaz jumps up, putting his front feet on the boat's starboard rail. He barks, sniffs the air, and barks again at the many birds circling overhead.

"Okay, buddy." I leash him as we reach the dock, though he doesn't pull or jump around as I thought he would. He just sits between Mel and me, seeming not to want to get too far away.

"Looks like we've got company," Marco whispers to me, pointing at the movement on the other side of the island.

"People or zombies, you think?" I whisper back.

He watches them for a minute longer.

"Impossible to tell. Hopefully zombies."

Whatever they are, there are a bunch of them.

We disembark slowly, one by one, and stand on the dock while Joaquin and Captain Jacob tie up the boat. But even after they're done, no one moves. We just stand there, watching the distant moving figures as the sun comes up over the prison, each processing in our own way that we are indeed here, on Alcatraz Island. No matter what we left behind or what lies ahead, we made it.

Acknowledgements

Even as I'm writing this, I cannot believe it's happening, that this is a real book and that you're taking the time to read it. So many people put their effort and care into helping me tell this story, and I am beyond grateful to every single one.

To my family, I give my undying gratitude for the encouragement, the love, and the support. Stephen, thank you so much for my beautiful chapter sketches and for all of the long, long walks to talk away the writer's block.

To the people at NineStar, Raevyn and Jason, who gave me a shot and who continue to guide me through my first publishing experience. I have learned so much from you already, and cannot wait to continue to work with you. Kristin, thank you for your feedback and for helping me curb my habit of adding the word "then" where it doesn't belong, and Tonna, thank you for the final clean-up. Natasha, your cover artwork is breathtaking. Thank you for capturing the essence of my story.

To my friends, Tana, Antoinette, and Bethany, thank you for answering my questions at the eleventh hour.

To every instructor who has made me a better writer, a huge, magnificent thank you. Mr. O'Ryan, you gave me the confidence to start writing in the first place. Mr. Owens, you helped me develop my knowledge of character representation and literature in general. Dr. Kruper, you have deepened my understanding of people.

To everyone who read any part of this piece and provided feedback, thank you.

And to you, my gorgeous reader. Thank you for picking up my book. You don't know what it means to me that you did.

About the Author

M. Rose Flores has enjoyed writing since she learned how to string letters together. She grew up in the vast green Pacific Northwest of the United States, which with its dense forests, four seasons, and proximity to the ocean made a perfect setting for *The End*. When she isn't writing on her computer or in a notebook (though scraps of paper and the palm of her hand will do in a pinch), she works as a professional dog trainer and loves every part of it, even the copious amounts of drool. She believes everyone should be represented in literature and all other media. *The End* is her first novel.

Email: writemod7@gmail.com

Facebook: www.facebook.com/writemod

Twitter: @writemod

Also Available from NineStar Press

Connect with NineStar Press

www.ninestarpress.com

www.facebook.com/ninestarpress

www.facebook.com/groups/NineStarNiche

www.twitter.com/ninestarpress

www.tumblr.com/blog/ninestarpress